OUTCAST ORIGINS

A WORLD OF ZENTOS STORY

OUTCAST ORIGINS

Book 1
Tarrenfall Chronicles

AJ Ashton

First published through Amazon 22 December 2022

My Awesome Editor: Yvonne Davis, whysewordswork@gmail.com

Formatting and cover design by AJ Formatting

Outcast Origins

Second Edition 2025

AJ Ashton

ISBN - 978-1-916969-04-9

DEDICATION

To my mum and dad for believing in me. Reading all the different drafts and putting up with all the conversations with me explaining my world and characters.

To my fantastic son, thank you for helping me develop my world with ideas and for giving me inspiration.

WORLD OF ZENTOS BOOKS
IN TIMELINE ORDER

Outcast Origins Book 1 Tarrenfall Chronicles

Outcast New Beginnings Book 2 Tarrenfall Chronicles

Quest of the Stone Book 1 Ranger Chronicles

Quest of the Broken Stone Book 2 Ranger Chronicles

Outcast The Return Book 3 Tarrenfall Chronicles

MOONSTAR

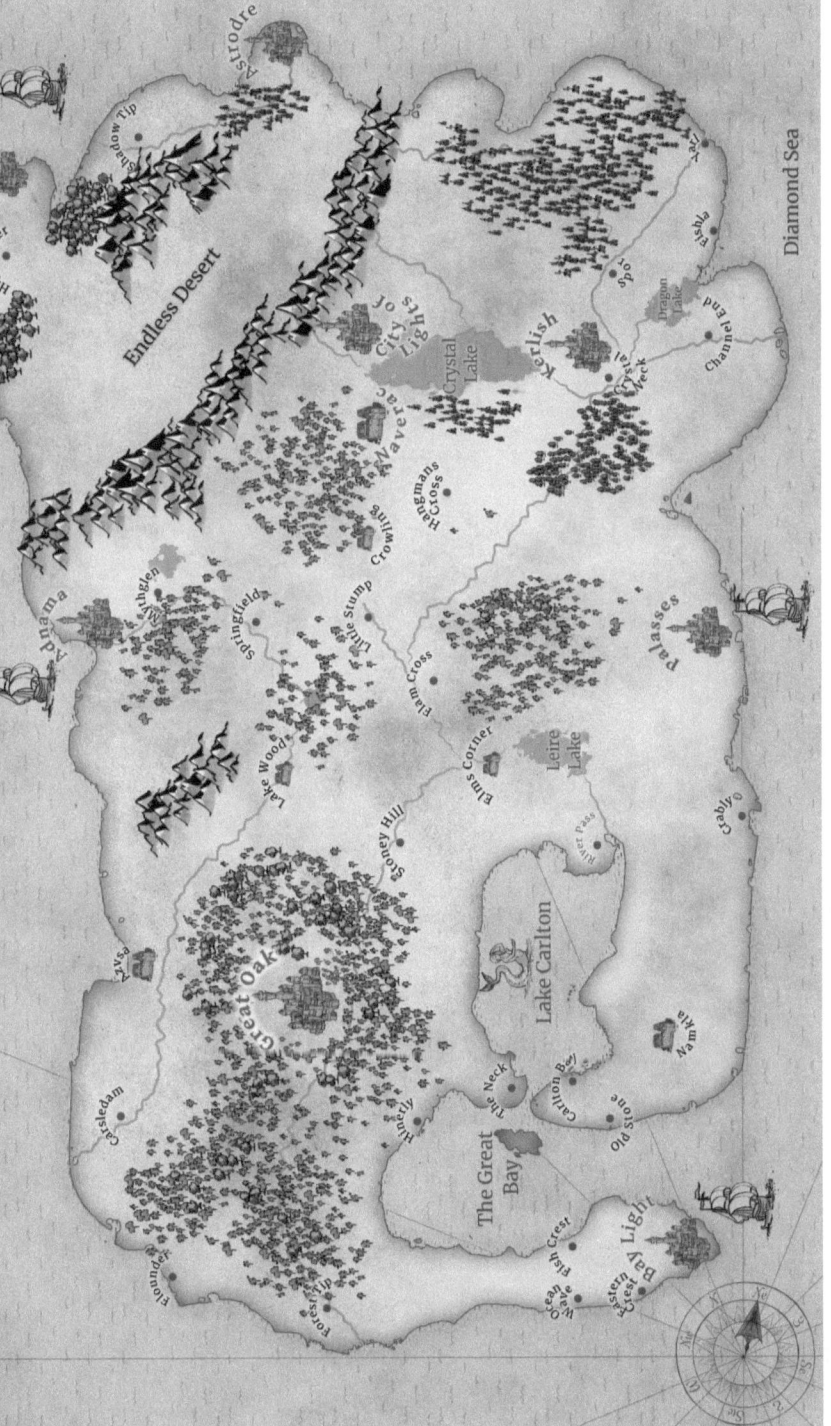

Worlds End Ocean

Diamond Sea

Endless Desert

Astrodre

Meadow Tip

Lanerna

Highwater

Appnama

Heathglen

Lake Woods

Springfield

Little Stump

Waverlac

City of Lights

Crystal Lake

Hangmans Cross

Crosslings

Eltam Cross

Kerlish

Spo

Fishla

Dragon Lake

Creck

Channel

Palasses

Leire Lake

Elsmus Corner

Grablyo

Stoney Hill

Great Oak

Higher Pass

Lake Carlton

Namkla

Crsledam

Flounder Tip

Hunely

Carlton Bay

Old Stone

The Neck

Weeash Crest

Fish Lake

Eastern Light

Great Light

The Great Bay

PROLOGUE

THE alleyway seemed so quiet in the night. Levana savoured the warm blood as it ran down her throat, her full lips suckling on the man's broad neck. There was always something gratifying when drinking from a human who had had way too much alcohol. It gave their blood an edge. A tingle ran through her body. She felt the man go limp, his blood almost gone. She paused when she heard a clatter behind her. It seemed another victim awaited. Dropping the man like a rag doll, she slowly turned to survey the alleyway.

"I know someone is watching me. Don't be shy."

Not far down, from behind a lone cart, a young girl in brown trousers and a white shirt slowly stood. Apparently, the human had been spying on her. Levana stepped forward, brushing down the wrinkles in her red dress from the drunkard who had been pressed against her as she fed. Her features slowly returned to human from vampire, then her eyes changed from red to brown. She focused on the girl; her brow furrowed. She regarded the girl's pretty features; those green eyes were hard to forget. Levana gave a sly smile. She was from the lycan house where Von had died. The girl she had bit, had somehow survived. That was impossible, no lycan could survive the change, the two types of blood would have torn her apart.

Levana strolled towards the girl, wondering how the thing could still be alive. "Well, well, well. So, you managed to survive. What an *abomination* you are."

The girl's features wrinkled in disgust. Levana pursed her lips, cocking her head to one side. As she watched the half-breed plant her feet firmly apart ready for anything. Levana wiped the fresh blood from the corner of her mouth and licked it off her finger before saying, "I will have to make sure I finish you off this time."

The girl took a deep breath, clenching her fists. Levana studied her, remembering the night well. The father had been a good fighter, but Von knew how to deal with lycans, and once dead, he had been such a feast. When they had entered the house, both herself and Von had picked up the heartbeats of the girl and a young boy. They would have drunk well that night, especially with such young blood. Not to mention lycan blood with its magical properties would have sustained them for weeks. Yet, a lycan bite could kill a vampire within days. It was so ironic.

Her mind wandered thinking of her lover. Von had always been clever in knowing where to find victims. How he knew of a lycan family she was not sure and had not cared. Then there was his penchant for devouring a child occasionally. She had never questioned that either, the blood was just so pure.

But that night, they had underestimated the lycan girl and in the fight, she had bitten Von. Levana glared at the brunette, remembering the agony her lover had experienced over the last two days of his life. She remembered looking at the girl's lifeless features before leaving the house, but she was standing right in front of her.

The young girl smiled without emotion. "We'll see about that."

Levana watched as the half-breed's hand transformed into wolf claws. She was not going to let that little bitch get away this time. The vampire lunged at the girl, as her claw-like nails instantly elongated from her fingers. Levana ripped the half-breed's white shirt, as she dodged the vampire. The girl then lunged forward, her wolf claws finding their mark. Levana hissed as they slashed across her chest, ripping the bodice of her favourite dress, and nicking the skin beneath. The half-breed was fast, but no match for her. Levana plunged her hand into the girl's mid-section. Feeling her blood and guts oozing around her hand, she pushed it further in. The girl gasped in surprise as Levana's nails sliced through the human's innards, she slowly moved her hand up towards the girl's heart. Levana grinned, focused on the half-breed's features as she grimaced and coughed up blood. The vampire felt her victim's hands weakly grip her arms as pain burned through her.

Levana smiled with glee and snarled, "You *think* I would let you get away with Von's death? This time, you will be nothing but *dust*."

The human girl coughed up more blood, as Levana's hand moved up, the claw-like nails slicing their way up inside her chest, getting closer and closer to the heart. The half-breed was in so much pain that she was unable to do anything. Levana's arm in her torso was the only thing keeping the girl standing.

This is it. After all these years, Levana was finally getting her revenge. Her fingers were so close to the girl's heart that she could feel the beating of it resonating in her fingertips. She focused on the girl's astonished green eyes. Levana would enjoy seeing her turn to dust and then devour the half-breed's heart.

CHAPTER I

THE early evening air was bitter, the ground covered by a thin layer of old snow, which was crisp underfoot. The group of four stopped cautiously on the outskirts of the small village, their faces hidden by their hoods. They moved carefully towards the stable, staying hidden, the horses within grew restless, sensing the presence of the four. The crescent moon was just creeping over the horizon, stars already in the clear, darkening sky. In the shelter of the stable, the four pulled down their hoods, surveying the village.

The group looked like an odd bunch. The woman, who appeared to be the youngest of the group, had a haunting beauty with long blonde hair and striking blue eyes. Two of the men, who were about ten years apart in age, had dark, short hair and were tall, athletic, and handsome. The fourth companion was a large, muscular, bald brute with a jagged scar across his cheek. He was a little rough around the edges compared to the others, and yet, even with his size, he could match the other three for speed and agility.

They melted into the shadows, watching. The hunger became overpowering, and since it was the first village they had come to; the urge to feed was too much to ignore. No one was moving on the street below, the bitter evening air had discouraged many villagers from leaving their homes. But the inn located in the centre was lit and they could hear laughter within. The leader, the youngest of the men, studied the building, his dark hazel eyes had seen several more years compared to the others.

He turned to his companions. "We will go to the inn; it seems some are still out this eve."

They conversed for a few moments and then the others agreed. They made their way around the village buildings to arrive at the inn, keeping to the shadows. The leader walked down a side alley towards the deserted main street. The striking man paused when a young pretty, brown-haired girl came into view. She walked down the main street alone, her green dress peeking out from beneath her black cloak that she wrapped tightly around herself, to keep the cold at bay. He smiled. Easy pickings. Keeping to the shadows he waited till she passed.

He asked, as he stepped out into the moonlight. "Now aren't you a pleasure on the eyes."

She turned towards him, a little shocked to meet someone at this hour, but on seeing his handsome features, she could not help but smile. "Can I help ya, sir?"

He stepped forward and gazed at her, his eyes lingering on her ample bosom. "Do you live far from here?"

She pointed up the road, her eyes lingering on his. "Nay, not far. Are ya lost, sir?"

He walked closer, stopping in front of her, his eyes focusing on her full lips. "Nay, I'm right where I want to be."

He smiled and focused his hazel eyes on hers, which slowly turned red around the edges and spread inward. At the same time, red veins spread, like spider webs from his eyes across his face. His features contorted, showing his full vampire side. Hers filled with fear. After centuries of practice, he could keep his victims frozen to the spot and they could not struggle when he fed.

He focused on her slender neck. Then glanced at her and smiled as his canines grew into long fangs, his mouth contorting to accommodate them. He placed his lips on hers. His hands slipped under her cloak to caress her breasts. His lips moved onto her neck, and she moaned softly. Her skin was so young and soft. Then he impaled his fangs into the main artery. Her warm, young blood flowed down his throat as he fed, draining the girl of her life. He heard the laughter in the inn turn to screams.

The vampire let go of the drained girl, her pale body falling to the snow-covered floor like a neglected marionette. Her blood made his body zing with renewed energy. He looked at the sky and took a deep breath, letting the euphoria of the life force flow through his body. He then focused on his surroundings, turning to the inn to see a body torn apart outside. He sighed, wishing his companions would be more subtle at killing their victims. They still had so much to learn. He walked over to the inn, his features returning to normal, avoiding the patches of ground stained in blood. He glanced down at the farmhand that had been torn apart, his guts staining the white snow. He turned his attention to his large male companion and the blonde woman.

"Did you have to tear him apart?"

The large man grunted as he sucked his blood-stained fingers, his face also covered in blood.

The vampire leader sighed again, his companion was not too bright and a bit of a liability, but he remained to be useful if they were in any trouble. Being so large, he was almost unstoppable, which was impressive for a vampire. There was rarely an issue against most humans, but if they came across werewolves or cleansers - the vampires who hunt rogue vampires like themselves - they needed a big brute, like him, who could just tear them apart on command.

He tutted under his breath when he noticed even though he tried to avoid it, blood had got onto his expensive boots. He wiped them on the grass poking up through the snow near the entrance. Looking back at his companions, he then turned to the inn and smiled.

When they entered, their other companion already had two drained bodies at his feet. One of which, the leader noted, looked like he had put up a fight. In the corner cowering and whimpering there were two young barmaids and an elderly gentleman, the only ones in the inn still alive. The handsome male leader smiled as the vampires walked slowly towards the victims, their features changing to feed. The villagers cowered in fear, knowing it would be a brutal end as the vampires fed off them.

The following night, miles to the south, there was an unrelenting storm. The wind and rain battered against the wooden shutters, the rafters in the house howled and creaked with the gale. Samuel woke and rubbed his rugged features, the black stubble rough against his hand, but it was not the storm that had woken him. His brown eyes focused on the dark, unlit room as he wondered if something had happened. Then he heard thudding, which seemed to be coming from the front door.

Who's waking us at this hour and in this weather?

Miriel stirred and sighed as she rolled over to face him, saying sleepily, "Whoever that is, they could wake the children."

Samuel reluctantly climbed from the warmth of the furs on the bed. Brushing his shortish black hair out of his eyes with his fingers, his bare feet tensed as they touched the cold wooden floor. Even with it being dark, he could see with ease and did not need to go to the trouble of lighting a candle. "It must be urgent to wake us at this hour. Don't worry. Derwyn and Lara are at the other end of the house. Their hearing won't be as sensitive as ours."

Miriel raised a perfect eyebrow, her green eyes piercing. Stifling a yawn, as she leaned on her elbow. "True, but a teething babe can hear more than you think."

Samuel smiled. They had had many sleepless nights with Derwyn over the months, and he was only just a year old. Their first, Lara, had been so much easier as a babe. He gazed back at his wife, even with her long brown hair ruffled from sleep, she was radiant. "Don't worry he'll be sleeping. I'll see what they want. And will check on Derwyn before I come back to bed."

Miriel sat up, pulling back the furs, exposing her toned, naked body. Climbing out, her long hair cascaded down her back. She pulled on her nightdress that was nearby on the floor. "Don't. I'm awake now, so I'll go check. I just hope whoever it is has something pressing to tell us."

He nodded, pulling on his shorts, which lay on the floor, near Miriel's nightdress. They had stripped so quickly that evening wanting to make love once the children were asleep, that their clothes were strewn all over the floor, the nightclothes thrown from the bed.

Walking barefoot down the stairs to the front door, and hearing the wind and rain, it would not just be something fleeting to be out in the foul weather. As he reached the door, someone thudded on it again. Samuel pulled it open, the icy rain hitting his bare chest.

"What is it?"

In the doorway, in his winter furs, his wet brown hair plastered to his slim face was Jermer. Samuel intuitively knew whatever it was would be urgent, and with his wife Alana behind him, her elegant features just visible under her hood, it was something that could not wait till the morning. Samuel beckoned them in.

Jermer features were a little guilty but also anxious. "Sorry, Samuel, but we have vampires just north of the village."

He responded, "Have you called your men?"

Jermer answered, "Aye. They are waiting by the road. One of them is saddling your horses."

Miriel strolled up behind Samuel. "We best prepare." She gestured a greeting to Jermer's wife. As the stunning blonde entered and pulled down her hood, Miriel added, "Good eve Alana. Both children are sleeping, but Derwyn is teething again so he may wake. Do you need a candle lit for you?"

Alana smiled softly, her clear blue eyes seemed to glow for an instant and then with a wave of her hand a small globe of light appeared before her and moved to float just above her head. "This will suffice and don't worry about Derwyn, I have herbs that will help." She studied the three. "Be careful, all of you, I sense danger, so be on your guard."

They all acknowledged the warning, then Samuel and Miriel ran back upstairs to get dressed. Once in their riding leathers, Miriel asked as they came back down, braiding her hair quickly. "Do you know how many?"

Jermer responded, "We are unsure. From what Alana sensed, there were several deaths to the north the night before, and they are now heading this way. I have already sent one of my men to find out more information, but we will need your keen noses to confirm how many we may be facing."

Both Miriel and Samuel agreed, knowing that Alana's visions were never wrong. He passed his wife her silver sword after she put on her cloak and furs. He pulled on his cloak and carried his sword, ready to strap it to his saddle while they rode. They seldomly used them, but always took them just in case. Leaving the warm house for the bitterly cold, northern wind and rain, they mounted their horses and followed Jermer and his men away from the village. With the bad weather, it would be a little harder to pick up a scent, but they had tracked in storms before and had only been unsuccessful a few times. With rogue vampires on the prowl, it was wise to proceed with caution and ensure they tracked them down.

CHAPTER 2

JERMER sniffed, his nose running from the cold. Even though they were all wearing cloaks and winter furs, they all had hunched shoulders as the cold penetrated to their bones. They stopped at the edge of the line of trees, having chased the four vampires to a forest. The group dismounted, standing in the icy rain as they secured the horses to the trees nearby. Despite the many outer layers to protect them from the elements, their clothes were soaked through from the ride.

Samuel and Miriel appeared from behind the horses having transformed into their wolf forms, one grey and one black with a patch of silver fur on his back left foot. One of the men had taken their clothes and secured them to their horses. The two wolves were over twice the size of normal ones, more muscular and with large retractable claws. When they stopped next to Jermer, they reached his chest. Most who came across lycans would run in fear, yet to Jermer and his men, they were valued companions after years of working together.

Samuel regarded the trees before them, a mix of oak and sycamore still holding onto their golden leaves as winter took hold. Yet Samuel could see even further with his wolf eyes, seeing the path clearly into the trees ahead.

He turned towards his wife Miriel, even with her grey fur soaked she was magnificent, as well as an invaluable hunting companion. She caught his eyes, her green focusing on his brown. Miriel turned back to the woods, sniffing the air, catching the scent of lavender through the winter woodland, the decaying leaves and the damp soil enriched by the rain.

Samuel watched his friend Jermer and the other men with them, all had drawn their swords, and prepared to go. Before he had transformed into his wolf form, he gave everyone strict instructions on how to deal with the rogues. Samuel turned back to the trees. The brutal killers had hoped to lose them in the woods. Yet, he could still smell their lavender scent in the air, they would not get far. Jermers' men, he and Miriel would have to work as a team against the larger one. From what they had been told by a scout Jermer had sent before coming to get them, the large vampire had taken out three men at Springfield, a small village to the north of theirs. It seemed they had bypassed Lake Wood having had their fill, but Samuel was aware they needed to be dealt with before they reached the city of Great Oak where they would be able to vanish or cause even more fatalities. It would be easy to take out the other three one on one but for the larger one, they would have to take him, all at once.

He made a low growl and Miriel and himself trotted into the woods, their human companions following carefully behind. Even with the heavy rain, he could still pick up the vampires' scent, the lavender with a hint of decay, was so distinctive that it was hard to miss. He grunted and the lycans ran towards the scent, the humans close behind.

They were a good way into the woods when he slowed, one of the vampires was just ahead of them. Luckily it was not the big one, and so it should be an easy kill. Another scent was to the east, and the final two to the south. They had split up to evade the hunters. Samuel wondered why they had made such a careless blunder. Yet they would be unaware that he and Miriel would be hunting them too. A mistake the vampires would soon regret. His group also divided, but if they came across the large one, they were to signal for help.

Samuel ran after one vampire; they were fast but so were lycans. He took a different direction cutting the vampire off. Samuel trotted up to the blonde woman growling at her. The vampire sneered and jumped at him. He moved fast, twisting around and bit down hard on her leg. The vampire yelled out, cursing, both knew a lycan bite was deadly to a vampire. Samuel could have left it at that, letting her suffer for several

11

days before finally dying from the toxin in the bite. But even with the atrocities they had caused at the northern village, he could not let her suffer. She tried to limp away. Samuel jumped, his powerful jaw clamping around her neck snapping it and ripping the neck open. Decapitating her. He turned from the lifeless body, as it disintegrated into dust. Sniffing, he started the hunt for his next kill.

He paused in his tracks. He picked up the scent of the larger one, they would need to corner him. He was about to call everyone when he heard a yelp. He sniffed the air and picked up Miriel's scent in the same direction. His heart dropped. Miriel was an accomplished fighter, but that sound. That sound filled him with dread. He ran towards it, weaving between the trees, his legs were fast but not fast enough. As he reached a small clearing, he slowed a little, where was she? Then he saw his wife at the base of a tree. Slowly transforming back to human form. His heart stuck in his throat. She was going to be alright. His heart could not take it if she was not. He ran towards her. He would get her home, and everything would be alright. He skidded to a stop; she was not moving. He whimpered when he saw how her body was bent back too far. She was almost wrapped around the trunk, her mid-section torn open by brutal vampire nails. Both knew how dangerous it would be hunting demons, but he had never needed to protect her. Yet, as he took in the brutal scene, realisation was setting in that his life was changed forever.

She watched him; pain etched across her features. Her slender hand slowly reached up, her fingers combing into his black fur, her breathing laboured and shuddering with pain. She whispered, "I'm sorry my love. He surprised me."

He nudged her naked body with his nose. She cried out in pain. He then nudged her legs, with no response. His eyes focused on her lower back, twisted at an unnatural angle. Then they moved to her wounded torso and her exposed guts. Her blood seeped into the rain-soaked ground. He observed the trees for a moment and sniffed the air. The vampire was not far away, he turned back to his wife. He wanted to find the vampire and tear him limb from limb, but he felt her fingers grabbing his fur.

She whispered, her lungs rattling, "*Nay*. He's too strong to fight. Let him go." She coughed, and blood trickled down her chin. "He knows he can defeat us when alone."

Samuel turned back to Miriel; she was right. She needed him now. He took a breath and turned back to human form. Tears welling in his eyes, he knelt before her, and carefully inspected her injuries. He turned to her when she whispered, "It's bad isn't it."

He bowed his head. His face etched with sadness, unable to hide the inevitable. He kissed her softly. "It will be alright. I will get you home. Everything will be alright."

Samuel went to move her, and Miriel cried out in pain. She grabbed his arm, focusing on his eyes. They could never hide anything from her. "You were never a good liar."

He gazed at her, unable to trust his voice.

She wheezed, "My mid-section is torn open, and I heard my spine snap as soon as he threw me against the tree trunk. I won't make it."

He gazed at her, trying to keep a brave face for her. She would not be able to heal from those injuries. In the rain, their tears were hidden. Samuel stroked her cheek. She smiled softly at him trying to pull herself up despite the pain. "Tell Lara and Derwyn, I love them."

Samuel gently pulled her torso onto his knees, his fingers gently pushed a strand of hair from her cheek and smiled sadly. He needed all his willpower to keep his voice and responded, "You can tell them, my love. You will tuck them in this eve and hum that lullaby to Derwyn as you always do."

Blinking against the rain, she drank in the sight of him. She forced a smile as she struggled to breathe. How she wished to Laycain that his words rang true.

She swallowed. "It's too far, we both know I won't make it."

Against the immense pain, she pulled herself up to his lips. Kissed him passionately and then whispered, "Be strong my love."

Samuel's last resolve to keep his emotions under control, broke. Tears flowed down his cheeks. She studied him intensely, then slowly, her eyes closed. Her hand slipped from his arm. Samuel brushed her cheek, unable to stop the sobs and buried his head in her hair. His whole body shook from his grief, as the world he once knew shattered into a thousand pieces.

Samuel walked slowly out of the woods in the rain. His naked body was covered in mud and blood. He held the body of his wife gently in his arms. Ahead, he could see his friend Jermer and his companions all mounted on their horses, with his and Miriel's beside them. He had heard them signalling to regroup moments after Miriel had died and then Jermer, his closest friend, shouted that the vampires, except the large one, had been dealt with. Samuel was not about to face the large one, so whistled to them all to regroup at the forest edge. He had then gently picked up his wife's lifeless body. He took a deep breath keeping a firm hold of his emotions. When he got closer Jermer gasped, jumping from his horse he ran over and regarded Miriel for a few moments.

He then focused back on his friend. "I'm so sorry."

Samuel responded with bitterness in his voice, still a little uneven from his emotions. "The large fecking one did this."

Jermer glared at him directly in the eyes, determination on his face. "Then we will find him, now."

He shook his head. "Nay, let him go. If he heads this way again, we will deal with him *together*."

Walking to the horses with Jermer's help, they gently placed Miriel's body on hers and covered her with a blanket.

Jermer turned to his friend. "What are you going to tell Lara?"

Samuel snapped as he pulled his clothes from his horse. "It was a riding *accident*." He scrutinised the others. "*Nay* one is to tell her what happened."

"She's nearly at an age to understand what we do. She has a right to know."

Samuel glared at him through the rain, which made it hard to see the tears in his eyes. His clothes almost forgotten in his hands. "Nay. I don't want her or Derwyn to have any part of this."

"You're in pain, Samuel."

Samuel pulled on his black trousers in anger. "Aye, but I am *clear* on this. Miriel and I agreed to let both Lara and Derwyn choose, and not force them to do what we do. And if Lara knew what happened, she would join for revenge and that is the last thing I want her to do."

Jermer responded, glancing at his men, who all silently listened, their faces mirroring the sadness they all felt. "I understand Samuel. You have our word that your children will never know."

Samuel pulled on his shirt, which stuck to his wet skin, then his boots, ignoring that his feet were covered in leaves and mud. He gazed back at the woods; the large vampire was probably on his way to Great Oak. At some point their paths will cross, and he would make the vampire pay dearly for his wife's death. He pulled on his sodden cloak and mounted his horse in anger. Taking the reins of Miriel's horse, he turned away from the woods, his vision blurry from fresh tears.

The group rode quietly back towards Lake Wood as the rain began to subside. On reaching the village at dusk, most split off and headed to their homes, only Jermer followed Samuel to his. The large house was set halfway up the hill overlooking the village with a forest behind it, and open land spreading out around the rest with views of the village, the lake, and the wood where they had been chasing the vampires.

When they reached the stables, Jermer helped Samuel lift Miriel down and he asked his friend. "Do you want Alana and me there when you tell Lara?"

Samuel stared at nothing in particular, seeming lost for a moment, wondering what to do since he would be raising their children alone. He contemplated the house and then the body of his wife in his arms. Could he do it on his own? His heart sank.

He focused on Jermer realising he had asked a question. "Erm, aye. Could you watch Derwyn and . . ." He paused, trying to think.

He would need help. Miriel used to do everything when it came to the children. He had helped, but she would have known what was best. He looked at Jermer and added. "I will need help, could you find me, someone, to help take care of him? With Miriel gone, I...."

Jermer patted him on the shoulder, seeing him struggling with the recent events. "Anything for you, old friend. Alana will know what to do, and we will make sure you and the children are alright. Again, I'm sorry for Miriel's death. When the time is right, we'll find that vampire."

Samuel nodded, taking a deep breath to steady his emotions. "He will pay. But now we need to grieve."

CHAPTER 3

SAMUEL could see the village of Stoney Hill in the distance, the sun already sneaking down towards the horizon. The heartless wind blew across the open plains, he was pleased his thick cloak kept the cold at bay. It had been fifteen years since he had seen Miriel's family. The Greenforges and Tarrenfalls had not been close for many years, not since Miriel's grandfather had been killed by a pack of werewolves. The Greenforge family had blamed Samuel's grandfather, as he had been the leader of the group who had gone hunting for the rogue pack. Yet, it had not been anyone's fault. Just bad luck. But they would not listen to reason and after that, the link between the two families had been strained. Samuel's family had tried to keep in contact, but soon they drifted apart. Years later, due to her choice to be with Samuel, the Greenforges disowned Miriel and they parted fully on bitter terms. He sighed. He had been unsure whether to tell them since her death the month before, but they had a right to know, whatever they thought of him and his family.

Reaching the small village, a similar size to Lake Wood, he rode slowly along the quiet main road through the centre. The road was lined on either side by houses but further in there were shops and a blacksmith. Off the road to the right, a small street opened into a market square, where there were more establishments and a medium-sized inn.

Samuel gazed towards the north where Miriel's family home was located, wondering what their welcome would be. The village seemed quiet in the late afternoon, but he realised that it was not market day and, like Lake Wood, smaller towns and villages were always so much quieter. He was too lost in thought to notice a couple of people watching him closely. He had his eyes on the horizon, remembering his grandfather telling him how the families had once been so close, even before they split from the main northern pack when his grandfather was a young boy. At first, they all believed that it was their duty to protect the pack and the land from evil. But after that fateful accident, things had changed.

Samuel was nineteen when there had been a chance meeting with Miriel. She had been travelling through Lake Wood with her father, and unknown to him, she was aware that Samuel's family lived in the village. She and her father spent the night at the inn in town, when Miriel had snuck away and ventured up to the house. Samuel smiled softly, remembering when he opened the door to her. Her beauty had taken his breath away and there was an instant connection. From then on, Miriel and he would meet whenever they could, mainly to hunt together, loving the freedom it gave them. Over time, they grew closer. When Samuel asked her to be his wife, they had hoped the marriage would bring the families back together. He sighed again. Miriel had been forced to choose, not by him, but by her family; loyalty or love. She never regretted her decision, but Samuel always wondered what would have happened if it had been more amicable. His features frowned slightly, Lara and Derwyn would have met children like themselves instead of being exposed to only human ones.

What was done was done. He just hoped that when Lara came of age to marry, they could find a family with the same values as their own. He would not stop Lara from making her own choice, the same with Derwyn, but to marry out of the lycan line was not wise. Samuel pulled his horse to a stop, shaking his head.

Why did I start thinking of that? Lara is still far too young.

He focused on his surroundings and saw a man similar in age to himself walking down the centre of the road towards him. Samuel picked up the scent. Lycan. He realised how quiet the village was and it would have been quite obvious that a stranger had arrived, so he was not surprised they were alerted. He slowly dismounted as the tall man came up to him.

The man glared at him and snapped as he stopped. "We don't want you here."

Samuel sighed, it seemed the resentment was still there. He focused on the man's rough features. "I've come to talk to Jarl and Yralissa Greenforge."

The man continued to glare at him. He had similar features as Miriel, and Samuel realised he had to be her older brother. "Lashur, I have some news about your sister. News that your family *needs* to know."

Lashur glared at him, with a hint of distaste in his voice. "I don't have a sister." He gestured his head towards the way Samuel had come. "Get back on your horse and go back to where you came from."

Samuel sighed and shook his head. "Nay. You all need to know."

Lashur crossed his arms and glared at him. "Well then, tell me."

He glanced down at his feet and then back up at Miriel's brother. "Miriel died in a riding accident some weeks ago."

Lashur paled slightly and glanced away from Samuel before he said softly, "Oh."

Samuel added. "I'm sorry. But even though we haven't got on, I thought you needed to know."

Lashur looked back at Samuel and replied, "Thank you for coming to tell us." He glanced back up the road where he had come from. "I will tell my parents, but . . . " he paused, studying Samuel. "They will not welcome you."

Samuel responded, "I understand."

Lashur sighed, his features still cold but less strained. "Again, thank you for telling me. But do not come to Stoney Hill again."

Samuel's horse nudged his shoulder. He patted the neck of the mare and asked, "May I at least stay the night at an inn before I return home. It's a good four-day ride."

Lashur pointed back up the road where Samuel had come from. "Aye. There's an inn off the main road back that way. They'll have rooms."

Samuel smiled softly and remounted his horse, recalling that he had seen the inn on the way in. "Thank you. And you will not hear from us again."

He could feel Lashur's eyes on his back as he watched Samuel turn his mare and head back the way he had come.

The medium-sized inn was next to the small market square. The village was almost deserted in the early evening. The winter cold encouraged the villagers to return to their homes. Samuel wondered how many in the village worked for Miriel's family and if they protected the village as did his. The Greenforges had vowed long ago never to endanger their family as they felt the Tarrenfalls had. It did seem that there was some measure in place within the village, as someone had managed to alert them quickly of his arrival.

Samuel tied his horse outside the inn. He would have food and shelter for the night and be on his way back by dawn. He observed the cloudy sky and thought of Miriel, she would be glad he had tried. Lara and Derwyn will never be able to meet her side of the family, yet he would let the children know of them when they asked. But till then, they would never venture to Stoney Hill.

Samuel found a table near the back wall, giving him a full view of the quiet inn, and took a sip of his ale while he waited for his food. The fire was keeping the cold evening chill at bay, and an old man sat next to it warming his hands. Samuel glanced around, the old, but clean, inn did not have many customers. One at the bar, from his dishevelled appearance, had probably been there for most of the day, and a couple of farmers in the corner talking about their pigs and cattle. He surmised that it would be busier on market days. Lake Wood had more trade on the busier days and knew Stoney Hill would be similar. He smiled at the barmaid when she put down his steaming hot bowl of stew and dumplings. Carefully, he ate some of the hot stew, blowing on the full spoon so as not to burn his mouth, even though the aroma made him ravenous. He paused when someone stopped at his table. He froze. He had forgotten how much Miriel took after her mother till the older woman, her greying brown hair pulled up in a neat bun, was standing before him. A black shawl wrapped about her shoulders, her blue dress showed off her still lean figure. She seemed to have only stepped outside for a few moments. Samuel wondered if the encounter was a last-minute decision.

"Good eve, Samuel."

He quickly swallowed the hot stew. "Good eve."

Yralissa took the seat opposite him and considered his features for a moment, then asked, her green eyes steady on his, "How did my daughter die?"

Samuel swallowed nervously. "As I told Lashur, in a riding accident."

She focused on his eyes. "Hmm." Samuel was positive she did not believe him. She added, quietly almost to herself, "I heard there had been some trouble with vampires recently."

He studied the older woman's sad features, and from her eyes, he knew she did not want her informed guess confirmed. She suddenly smiled, her features warming. "So how are the children?"

Samuel was taken aback by the question and stammered, "You know of them?"

Yralissa's eyes focused on his. "Aye, of course. I have always liked to know what is going on. And unlike Jarl, I always thought of Miriel and hoped she was happy."

Samuel smiled and responded, "She was. As for the children; Derwyn, being a babe, just takes longer to settle, but Lara is taking it hard and will need time."

"As any child would." She took a breath and stood, her eyes on his. "Do not return here Samuel. Jarl isn't as understanding as Lashur and I."

He replied, "I intend to leave at dawn."

She said, "Good." She paused glancing back at Samuel. "Lara looks just like Miriel at that age." Then she turned and left.

Samuel watched Yralissa go, wondering how she had managed to see Lara. If she came to Lake Wood, he would not stop her from seeing her grandchildren. But he would not break his word to never return again as he understood completely; they would not be as welcoming next time. When he returned home, he would leave the trip out of the family journal, and even though he had written about what happened with Miriel, he was thinking of removing it. He would put the information elsewhere till he felt it was time to tell Lara and Derwyn everything. He wanted them to be prepared for a hostile welcome if they ever did find out, and he would sooner tell them himself than for them to find the information second-hand in the family book. He had promised his father he would write down everything, but some things he felt needed to be told to his children in person, not for them to find out years later without a full explanation. Once he had finished his stew, Samuel went to his room at the back of the inn. He would make sure he left at dawn and return to where he was welcome.

CHAPTER 4

SIX YEARS LATER

THE summer sun was beating down on the market stalls in Lake Wood. Once every twenty days a larger market ran which made the village busier than normal. The only two inns were full, mostly by traders and travelling stall owners who would trade with a couple of the more affluent villages in the area. In a few days, they would be trading their wares in either Springfield, Stoney Hill or even further afield in Great Oak. There were also a few out of town folk, coming for necessities. The shops lining the main road through the village were also getting a fair trade, but most people were there for the market, known for the high standard of fresh produce and high-quality goods. The main square had been taken over and was full of market stalls overflowing with merchandise and people haggling. It was a clamour of sounds, from traders shouting their wares, to a small band busking, to bellowing livestock from the nearby farms.

Lara wore a light blue dress which fitted loosely on her slender body, her dark brown plait accentuated her delicate features. She giggled with her friends as they walked around the market, cram-packed with villagers as well as passers-by. Her green eyes focused on the fresh vegetables, inspecting them, and she haggled with the stall owner to get a fair price before placing them in her basket and carrying on. She did not need to get much for her father, but wanted to linger for a while so she could spend more time with her friends. They continued around the market stalls as Lara silently greeted the stall owners and women shopping with a nod of her head. Seeing the usual toy stall, she wandered over. The table was piled high with different types of wooden toys of various sizes. Derwyn loved animals and she always came back with something for him. She had bought most of the small animal collection the stall owner made, and he quickly pointed to the new ones he had recently carved.

One of her friends, Elena, a petite blonde with big blue eyes, grabbed her arm, as she paid the stall owner and pointed towards a tall young man at another stall, inspecting the meat that was on offer. His dark features were very pleasing to the eye, his black hair cropped short and the white shirt and grey trousers he wore accentuated his athletic build. Lara smiled and giggled as they moved from the toy stall.

Her friend said, "That's Yanric. His father owns the farm to the south of here."

He saw them watching and smiled, both girls giggled again. Lara's gaze lingered on him a little longer than was probably appropriate. Her father would not have approved, but there was no harm in having a little flirt.

"Lara!"

She froze and turned to see a tall, slender, blonde woman in a green dress weaving her way through the crowds towards her. Lara relaxed a little. "Hello, Alana. The market is very busy this day."

The woman smiled, observing the young man Lara had been watching. She turned her clear blue eyes back to the teenager. "He's very handsome."

Lara instantly blushed. "Oh, is he?"

The woman laughed and leant forward. "Don't worry. I won't tell your papa. There is nay harm in gazing at a boy. You're still young and should enjoy what life has to give you."

Lara regarded the beautiful woman, pleased she would not tell. She glanced across at the young man again and smiled.

Alana whispered, "He likes you." The woman added. "Why don't you go and talk to him?"

Lara suddenly felt shy. "Oh, nay. I shouldn't. Papa wouldn't approve."

Alana said, "Your papa just doesn't want you to get hurt."

Since her mother had died, Lara's father had become very protective. And when it came to boys, she would have a playful flirt when with her friends, but could never go against her father's wishes and pursue someone without his permission. She smiled at Alana and changed the subject, showing her the small wooden horse she had bought from the toy maker's stall. "I found this for Derwyn."

The woman examined the wooden horse and smiled as she passed it back. "He'll *love* it."

Lara saw her friends waiting for her. "I should go. I will ask if Derwyn can come to play with Peadar on the morrow."

The woman replied, "He'll like that."

Lara weaved her way through the crowds to her friends who were buying fruit from one of the stalls. After buying a pear for herself, they continued. They all had tasks from their parents, but it was also a rare opportunity to meet and talk. Lara glanced back at Yanric and smiled, but when her friends urged her to go over to him, she shook her head and made her friends walk in the opposite direction around the market. She still was not brave enough to talk to a boy.

When Lara entered the large hallway after returning from the market, her features were slightly flushed from the sun. Her father called, "Lara, may I have a word."

She focused on the large imposing door, it was not usually left ajar. Her father never invited her in there unless it was important or she had done something wrong. Lara placed her basket down on the round table in the hallway and bit her lip, realising the majority of the times she was called in the study was when she had not completed her daily chores. She wondered if she had arrived home later than she said she would be. She apprehensively took a single step over the threshold as she pushed the heavy door further open. The large study seemed cramped with all the books squeezed onto the floor to ceiling bookshelves which covered two of the walls on either side of her as she entered. Facing her were two windows, side by side, with views of the main courtyard and stables. There were two more narrow bookshelves on either side of the windows. She turned to her right, to where her father sat behind an imposing desk, and paused.

"You wanted to see me, papa?"

He did not look up from the paperwork he was reading, his loose white shirt masking his athletic frame. Lara stood still in the doorway for a few moments before he indicated to the chair opposite him. Lara sat silently and looked up at the painting on the wall behind her father. It was of her mother, her as a child and Derwyn still just a babe. Lara turned her attention nervously back to her father. Her green eyes focused on his fingers, seeing ink on them from him writing in the leather-bound book which was slightly hidden under the paperwork he was reading. Lara always wondered what was in that book, but she had never dared to ask. She regarded his rugged features, as he sat up and leant back a little in his chair. His black hair sprinkled with grey at the temples, the only clue he was older than he seemed.

He said, "As you know, you will turn eighteen next month. It's a very significant occasion as you will also experience your first transformation."

She nodded, her hands clasped together, her fingers twisting nervously. She was aware the day would come and always worried about it. She glanced up at her father. "Will it hurt?"

He slowly stood, wiping his hands absentmindedly on his dark brown trousers, where faint evidence showed that he had wiped his hands there often to remove the ink from his fingers. He came and crouched beside her taking her hand in his, his kind hazel eyes focused on her green ones.

"Aye. I'm sorry Lara, but the first one is always the most painful. But as you transform more often and get older, the pain will lessen." He paused, getting back to his feet and pulling a chair over to sit next to her, taking her hand once more. "As you know your mama and I can change at will, this comes with practice and will take you a few months to control it fully. But for the first one, you will have nay control. When it comes, you must let it happen, the more you fight, the more painful it will be. Now, my first time was a week before my birthday, whereas your mama's, I believe, was a month after. So you must be ready."

Lara smiled softly, having noticed changes in her body over the last few months; more muscle was developing, and her body felt stronger. But she had also noticed other changes too; with more muscle development, her breasts had filled out more, which made her a little more self-conscious. When some of her friends had developed, they loved the attention it gave them, which was more than she got when she had reached puberty. It had been nice, like today, with the gazes from Yanric, but not the glances the other boys in the village gave her. With the time coming for her first transformation, she had mixed feelings about it. She would have so much more strength and power being a lycan, but that would make her vastly different from all her friends when all she wanted to do was fit in.

But it was her birth right, and something she had to embrace. "Will I have any idea when?"

"You have been developing more muscle of late which hints it will be soon. But the main sign is when you start to get the dreams, there are usually three. This will happen some days before, and they will be of your wolf self as it comes to our world, ready to take their place with you."

Lara leant forward, becoming more intrigued. "So, I will see my wolf self."

"Aye, you will talk with them, as they will introduce themselves to you."

Lara gazed at her father with curiosity. "So, we can talk to our wolf selves?"

"Nay, only in the dreams before your transformation. Afterwards, you will only feel their emotions when you meditate." He raised his finger as he remembered something. "But I know that some elders of the packs could converse with their wolf selves. It is rare, but I have heard of this."

"I see, but it will be nice to talk to my wolf side, even if only in my dreams. Afterwards, once I have had my first transformation, I will feel my wolf with me all the time?"

Her father replied, "Aye, they are you but also not." He smiled gazing up at the painting, lost in thought. "I know your mama was always beautiful, but her wolf form was magnificent."

"Aye. It is you, but also not." He smiled gazing up at the painting, thinking of the past. "I know your mama was always beautiful, but her wolf form was magnificent."

She smiled while studying him. He did not speak of her mother that often these days, but his features always glowed with joy when he did. "I remember seeing mama when you would go hunting, and how large you both were in wolf form."

Samuel studied her. "That's how you tell a lycan from a wolf. Remember, we are stronger too, but we *do not* hurt humans unless they mean to harm us."

"Aye, papa."

He stood, straightening his shirt. "Now back to your studies. But tell me when you have the dreams so we can prepare."

Lara indicated agreement as she stood and left the study, closing the door behind her. After she had taken the basket of produce to the kitchen, Lara entered the library which was next to her father's study. Even that larger room was full of books. Lara was amazed at the amount they had. The ones in her father's study were older, some centuries in age. The family line had always required that they were well versed in demon mythology, the origins of their kind and being aware of other races, good and bad, as well as general knowledge to ensure they were well educated. Her father would always say the same thing whenever Lara asked about the books on demonology, that it was best to be prepared if a situation arose. She was never fully sure why she needed to know the weakness of a demon, but there had to be some logic to it.

She turned her attention to where Derwyn was playing with his new toy, sitting on the floor with the other toys she had bought for him scattered around. His white shirt was untucked from his blue trousers. Her father would always chastise him for looking untidy, but it just seemed to be in his nature. She went up to the seven-year-old and ruffled his black hair.

He gazed up at her and giggled. She smiled. "What are you doing, you little squirt."

He showed her his toy and said, "Thank you for the horse. Will you play with me?"

She contemplated the pile of books on the table knowing she was supposed to be studying. The one she was currently reading was *The Legends of Moonstar* and she was intrigued by the Guardians of the Stone, Swords who vowed to protect Moonstar from evil. Yet playing with her brother for a while seemed more fun.

She sighed and smiled. "Come on then, what do you want to play?"

Her brother's features glowed with joy. "Let's make a farm!"

Lara knelt beside him, taking several of the wooden toys and giving her brother a gentle hug.

CHAPTER 5

L ARA felt someone watching her and glanced up from her
books. Standing at the entrance to the library, shifting
from foot to foot, was a six-year-old boy with short dark
blond hair grinning at her. She forced a smile.

*Why is it that every time Peadar comes here he would follow
me around like a lost puppy?*

He tentatively stepped closer, surveying the books in front of
her. "What are you reading?"

She had been tempted to just say, *a book*. Instead, she lifted
the thick one that was open in front of her so he could see the
cover. "It's about the legends of Moonstar."

He stepped even closer, his hands clasped behind his back,
and swayed from side to side, unable to keep still. Lara
wondered if it had been a wise idea to engage with him. She
may not get any of her studies done with him pestering her. He
stood watching her, his features full of admiration.

She said, turning to face him, her books forgotten for a
moment. "Shouldn't you be outside with Derwyn?"

He grinned, his hazel eyes focused on her. "Aye, but I want
to stay here."

She sighed. The boy was not shy for his age, that was for
certain. She gave him a stern look. "I have to study."

"I'll be quiet," he whispered sheepishly.

Lara went to protest when her brother ran in. Seeing his friend, he snapped, "There you are! Come on."

Her brother grabbed Peadar's arm and dragged him out. The young boy was reluctant to leave. Lara watched them go and sighed with relief. The last thing she wanted was a puppy-eyed boy watching her. She turned her attention back to her book and continued reading, hearing the boys shouting outside the library window. Lara just hoped they did not go climbing the tree again. Last time, they had both ended up with torn clothes and her father and Peadar's parents would not be too happy if that happened again.

Lara regarded what she could see from the library window. She had been studying for what seemed like hours, but the sun was still high in the sky and she could hear the boys still playing. She focused back on the book, the text a blur as her mind wondered if she would ever meet one of the Guardians of the Stone in the flesh. Even though the book was written as a story, she had heard that the group was very real, and still training to save the lands from evil when the prophecy came true. Her thoughts were broken when she heard Alana talking to her father as he invited her into the house. The older woman must have come to pick up Peadar. Leaving the table in the library, she went out into the hall, curious as to what the two adults were talking about.

The blonde woman was stating, "I think it will be fun for Lara. She is now of age, and I will chaperone if you are concerned."

Her father had his arms crossed, and Lara knew that was not good. He was so overprotective and closed off to her having time away from chores and studying.

He pursed his lips. "She has only recently turned eighteen and may have her dreams any day."

Alana responded, "But she may not have them for months, and this is in three days. The celebration of the Spring Goddess is close to my heart. Miriel would always join in the celebration, and it would be fitting that as Lara is now of age, she joins in too."

Lara stepped forward. "Let me go, papa." Her father turned to her, pursing his lips, his arms still crossed. Lara peered up at him pleading. "*Please,* papa. I haven't had any dreams and I may not have them for months."

He sighed, looking between her and Alana. His arms unfolded as he focused on Lara and stated, his features relaxing. "Alright, I am clearly outnumbered. You can go."

Lara rushed to him, giving him a big hug. "Thank you, papa."

He grabbed her shoulders and pushed her back a little so he could study her features and said sternly, "*But* if you have a dream before the night then you must tell me. As it may not be wise to go."

Lara agreed and grinned. "Aye, papa."

Alana smiled. "Thank you, Samuel. And I will watch her closely on the night."

He studied the two, a smile touching the corner of his lips. He had to admit it was nice to see his daughter so happy. "I know you will, Alana."

The blonde turned to Lara. "Do you have a dress in green, white or gold?"

Lara shook her head. "Nay, I only have blue, pink and grey dresses." She glanced at her father. "But I think mama had some."

Samuel took a breath. But he knew that Miriel would have wanted her daughter to have her dresses, and they would not need that much alteration. "Aye, I think she had."

"Thank you, papa."

The witch smiled and thought for a moment. "If it's possible, I will come back later this day. I'll then have time before the celebration to alter it if I need to."

Unable to take in that she would finally be able to go to the celebration in a few days, Lara nodded. She remembered her mother going, and she would wear such fine dresses. Lara had always dreamed that one day she could wear one, and now with her father's permission, she could. She wondered who all would be there, most of her friends would be, and knew it would be fun. Even with Alana as a chaperone.

Lara had been unable to concentrate on her studying, thinking about the celebration. When Alana returned that evening, Lara was surprised to find that her father had laid out all her mother's dresses on her bed in her room. She was beyond excited, and would not stop talking, wondering what her friends would be wearing and who would be there. When she finally went to bed, she was still feeling happy. One of her mother's dresses had been so beautiful, and had only needed a few alterations. Alana promising to make sure they were perfect.

The next couple of days seemed to drag, and her mind was constantly wandering. To the point her father chastised her for it and gave her extra chores as penance. Yet Lara did not mind, as long as he did not stop her from going to the celebration.

Her newly altered green dress was the perfect fit when she tried it on again the evening before the celebration. Alana stated she would come over the following afternoon to help with her hair and make sure she appeared at her best. Alana teased her about the fact Yanric may be there as well and Lara had been unable to stop blushing. When her father had ventured in to see how it was going, he had given her a questioning look when he saw her flushed cheeks. Alana had quickly stated it was because of her excitement. The witch knew not to mention boys, as both were aware how protective he could be, and could easily revoke the permission for Lara to attend.

Unable to sleep being so excited, Lara stared at the ceiling, wondering about the celebrations and then about her dreams. She had not had any yet, and hoped they would not come until after tomorrow. She tried to recall how many her father said she would have before she would have her transformation. She felt sure he had mentioned that it would be three. She sighed and closed her eyes, knowing she needed to get some sleep. It was going to be an exciting, and long, day tomorrow.

Lara found herself walking through a deep green forest. The grass was soft beneath her bare feet. She surveyed her surroundings, it was not a forest she knew. She paused seeing movement ahead. She examined the trees, seeing a clearing and slowly walked towards it.

She stopped when her mother's voice floated to her. "Do not be afraid. Lara, it is almost time."

Lara looked around. "Mama?"

"This way, my darling. She is close."

Lara continued to walk forward, her heart beating faster. She did not feel scared, just excited. As she entered the small clearing of lush green grass, a large wolf entered from the opposite direction. The wolf was bigger than Lara, its grey fur thick and soft, just above its right eye was a silver patch. Lara remembered her father had a similar one near his paw. Lara focused on its green wolf eyes and a female voice floated to her.

"Greetings Lara. I have been sent by the great God Laycain to be your companion till your dying day and will guide you on that day to the everlasting hunting grounds."

Lara gulped, realising she was seeing her wolf self for the first time; this was one of the dreams she had been waiting for. She considered the wolf before her. "When will I change to you?"

The wolf gazed at her, its eyes large and kind. "Soon Lara. Soon we will become one."

Lara swallowed. "Will it hurt?"

The wolf walked up to Lara, towering over her, yet Lara was not afraid. She placed her hand gently into the animal's fur, feeling it between her fingers and also feeling her hand stroking her own back.

The wolf gazed down at her and spoke softly in her mind, "Aye, it will hurt. But you are strong Lara, and I will give you more strength to cope with the first ordeal. When we become one, we will be stronger."

Lara removed her hand from the wolf's fur and the sensation on her back stopped too. It felt strange knowing they were one. She focused on her eyes. "Will I dream of you again?"

The wolf turned and started to walk away. "Aye. It is the will of Laycain." The wolf paused and turned back towards her. "I am honoured to be part of you, Lara."

She smiled and watched the wolf leave the clearing. Lara then sensed another presence and turned around. Lara's eyes welled. "Mama?"

Miriel smiled, walking towards her. "Be strong Lara. Soon you will be very powerful. And with power, comes responsibilities."

Lara smiled softly. "Mama. I miss you so much."

Miriel walked up to her and placed a hand gently on her cheek. Her skin cool against Lara's. "I miss you as well, my love. Remember to be strong."

Slowly, her mother began to fade and Lara held back her tears. "Mama! I love you."

Her mother's voice was just a whisper as she said, "I love you too, Lara."

Lara woke sobbing, still sensing her mother's touch on her cheek. She wiped her eyes looking around the dark room, as she slowly sat up. She bit her lip. That was her first dream, she thought to tell her father, but paused. If she told him, he would not let her go to the celebration. Lara sighed and wondered if she could leave it for a day, then tell him afterwards. A day would not make too much of a difference. She laid back down, closing her eyes, wondering why she saw her mother in the dream. Had her parents seen their parents or grandparents? Lara would ask her father when she told him, but after the celebration.

CHAPTER 6

L ARA smiled, studying her appearance in the full-length
mirror. Her hair had been left down with intricate braids
throughout and tied with white ribbons. Lara felt a pang
of sadness, wearing one of her mother's dresses. The reflection
before her was almost the spitting image of Miriel. Her mother
would have been proud to see her going to the celebration.

Lara turned to Alana and smiled broadly. "Thank you so
much!"

The blonde woman responded, her features glowing in
admiration. "Wait till your papa sees you."

Lara smiled again, but was a little apprehensive. She had not
told her father about the dream she had had the night before,
and felt guilty. She would have two more, before she would
have her first transformation. Lara would tell her father the
following day anyway, so no harm would come of it being
delayed a little. Yet she was still worried that somehow her
father would know.

When they reached the study, her father was beaming. He
gazed at his daughter, his eyes holding a little sadness. "You
look like your mama." He paused, giving her a big hug. "She
would be so proud of you."

Lara smiled softly at her father, knowing why he seemed sad. She gave him a big hug and kissed him on the cheek. "Thank you, papa, for letting me go."

He turned his attention to Alana, still holding Lara in his arms. "Make sure she stays safe."

"I will."

Lara kissed her father and followed Alana from the house. The two walked down the hill, on the warm summer evening towards the centre of Lake Wood. Many others were also heading the same way. On reaching the village, in the market square was a large marquee that had been erected for the celebration. It was full as everyone from the village and the surrounding areas crowded together.

They walked towards it as Alana explained. "This is the celebration of our Spring Goddess, Anoixi. She brings life to the lands and our livestock. In celebrating her, she will ensure a good summer and of course a good harvest."

Lara asked, "And the colour of our dresses?" She glanced at Alana, who was also wearing a green dress with her hair down and decorated like Lara's was.

The woman smiled. "They are the colours of spring and the ribbons are similar to what Anoixi wears in her black hair. Only the females can wear the colours, the males only white and black."

Lara nodded, noticing the men wearing their finest clothes, but as Alana had said, only in black and white. The women were different; all had their hair down and had similar styles like Lara and Alana. They were all wearing finely made dresses in either green, white or gold. On entering the marquee, Lara saw her friends and glanced at Alana, who smiled. "Go and have fun. Enjoy the celebration."

Lara's father had allowed her to go as he had expected Alana to be with her always. Yet the witch was allowing her to have more freedom, something Lara knew her mother would have done as well. She rushed over to her friends, the group of girls comparing their outfits and examining each other's hair. Then all went off giggling as they took wine from the large table at the edge of the marquee, which had goblets of wine and tankards of ale available for all. Other tables nearby held food and more drinks. The centre of the marquee had been left open for a large dancing area. At one end, a band played merry tunes, and the dance floor was already busy with some of the villagers dancing. As the girls tried the wine, Elena squeezed Lara's arm and then pointed to the other side. Yanric was standing with his friends and elder brother.

Lara watched Yanric from where she stood. When he caught her eye, she instantly blushed and looked away.

Elena gasped and grabbed her hand. "He's coming this way." The blonde girl said almost giddily. "He will ask you to dance!"

Lara glanced back to see the handsome lad walking towards them, she shook her head and turned towards Clarisa who was tall and slender with jet black hair. "Nay. He will ask you, Clarisa."

All the girls turned when the tall dark-haired lad cleared his throat. Clarisa gave Yanric her biggest smile. Yanric bowed his head to her, but his hazel eyes were focused on Lara.

He asked nervously, as he brought up his hand towards hers. "Lara, may I have this dance?"

Lara stood frozen to the spot. "I thought you wanted to ask Clarisa."

He smiled nervously, glancing at the raven-haired beauty. "Nay. Vondor is going to ask her."

Clarisa almost turned crimson, all the girls knew how big a crush she had on Yanric's older brother.

Yanric focused on Lara's eyes. "I wanted to ask you."

Lara held his gaze, taking his open hand. He gave her a huge grin, his perfect features glowing and gently pulled her towards the dance floor. The rest of the dancers were almost lined up, Lara and Yanric joined the end of the row and stood arm's length apart. Lara glanced over to the side to see Alana, who gave her an approving smile. Lara was feeling so happy.

The music began. Yanric took Lara's hands, but they remained at arm's length and then with the beat of the music, danced sideways up the dance floor following the others. As they reached the end, they moved together and spun around.

"You look very pretty." Yanric said while they were holding each other closely.

Lara felt her cheeks flushing, but before she could respond the dance moves made them part once more. They locked hands moments later with another couple and they danced in a circle. Lara was unable to stop watching Yanric and blushed every time he grinned at her. Lara had to admit she liked him, and wondered what her father would say. She forced the thoughts out of her mind.

This eve, I'm just going to have lots of fun.

Yanric grabbed Lara's hand. "Come on."

She giggled, a little unsteady after all the wine she had been drinking. They had been dancing and drinking for most of the evening. Lara felt like they had been at the celebration for days. Yanric tugged at her hand and led her out of the marquee and across the market square, towards a side street. The night air was cool compared to the marquee. As they reached the narrow street, Lara, being unsteady on her feet, tripped and fell into Yanric's arms, putting the two in a close embrace. Lara peered up at his flushed face, they had both drunk a little too much. Lara's skin tingled as his hands moved up and down her back, keeping her close. He gently pulled her into the side street and leaned her up against the wall. Putting himself even closer to Lara, he kissed her passionately. Lara melted into his embrace, unable to resist his soft, gentle lips. His hands roamed down her back onto her buttocks. Then further, pulling up her dress while moving her against his firming crotch.

Lara paused, feeling his excitement against her. A kiss was one thing, but she was not about to go any further, she was not like that. She pulled away from him. "Nay, Yanric."

He looked at her, still pulling up her dress keeping her firmly against him. "Why not? There is nay harm in it."

Lara pushed against him, but his arms were locked around her, not letting her go. "Nay!"

He sneered at her, his features suddenly becoming hard. "Then why dress like this? You were asking for this all eve."

Lara was scared, realising they were alone on a side street. No one could hear or see them. She had thought Yanric was a responsible boy, but it seemed with some ales in him, he was different and going along with him had been unwise. She pulled against his iron grip. She pushed harder but not having her lycan strength, she was unable to break free. He continued to pull up her dress. Pushing her against him. Grinding his groin against hers.

Lara snapped, "NAY!"

Suddenly, pain burned through her mid-section. Lara cried out. Yanric still held her tight. Lara felt more pain. Something was not right. She glared at him. "Let me.... *GO!*"

As she said the latter, her voice was more like a growl. For a moment, her eyes changed to be more wolf-like. Yanric's features paled in shock. Then with unknown strength Lara pushed him from her, sending him staggering across the street and hitting the far wall.

Lara folded over in pain and sobbed, "I need to get home."

Yanric stared at her, fear in his eyes. He then turned and ran. Leaving Lara in agony. She collapsed to the ground as pain burned through her body again. Tears rolled down her cheeks. She was going to have her first transformation here. In a side street. All alone.

Yanric ran towards the marquee, bumping into Alana. The blonde grabbed his arm, the lad as pale as snow, and she said with concern, "What is it, Yanric?"

He glared at her. "It's Lara. She isn't *human!*"

Alana's grip on his arm tightened. "Yanric, *where* is Lara?" His gaze was blank, but the witch's grip held firm. "*Where!*"

He glanced back the way he had come. The witch used her skills and focused on Yanric, peering into his thoughts. She saw him making advances on Lara in a side street and then Lara on the floor, hunched in pain. Alana cursed; it seemed his advances may have triggered Lara's transformation. Her wolf self tried to protect her. Alana took a firm hold of his temples, with both her hands and forced him to focus on her blue eyes.

Her eyes glowed slightly, and she said smoothly, "You will forget what has happened here this eve. You had alc and danced with many girls." She paused and then added. "You will not take advantage of naive girls ever again!"

She let go of the drunk lad. Yanric stood still for a moment with a vacant gaze. Then Alana pushed him gently towards the marquee and he wandered back in, in a daze.

She then ran to find Lara.

Alana knelt beside Lara, the young girl's face wet with tears. Her body curled up in agony. The witch said softly, "Oh Lara."

She glanced up at the blonde woman, crying. "I want papa."

Jermer came up behind Alana and gasped. The witch turned to him and said anxiously, "We have to get her to Samuel. *Fast.*"

He nodded. "I'll get horses." Then turned and ran back the way he had come.

Alana turned to Lara, as she grimaced in pain. Alana placed her hand gently on her shoulder, trying with magic to ease the young girl's agony. "We will get you to your papa."

Lara looked up, grabbing Alana's hand. "Yanric . . ."

The witch placed her fingertips gently to her lips. "Don't worry about Yanric. He won't remember anything."

Lara tried to sit up and stated, "I thought he was . . ." She grimaced in pain. "Nice."

Alana studied her, realising Lara had found out the hard way that not all men would be as gentle as she had thought.

Jermer returned moments later with a couple of horses, and he helped Lara to her feet. He turned to his wife. "Lara won't be able to ride on her own in this pain, so I think she should ride with you."

Alana agreed, quickly mounting the horse and helping Jermer get Lara up in front of her. The young girl suddenly had a spasm of pain as they tried to get her onto the horse. Once up in front of Alana, the witch held her tight, chanting a spell silently to help ease Lara's pain. Jermer then climbed on the other horse and galloped quickly through the village back to Lara's home.

CHAPTER 7

W HEN they reached the Tarrenfall family home, Jermer jumped from his horse and carefully took Lara down from the other, carrying her. Alana jumped from hers and rushed to the door. When Samuel opened it, his eyes focused on Lara in Jermer's arms and his features paled.

"What happened?"

Alana answered, "Lara's transformation has been triggered."

He went over to Jermer, taking Lara into his arms, his daughter sobbing, "I'm sorry, papa."

He turned to Alana. "For her transformation to be triggered, something extreme must have happened."

Alana sighed. "There was an incident with a boy."

Samuel snarled, "*A boy!*"

Lara peered up at her father, her arms around his neck as he held her. "Please don't be angry."

He kept his eyes firmly on Alana. "You were supposed to be *chaperoning* her!"

Alana glanced down at the floor. "I'm sorry Samuel. I misjudged the situation. But do not worry, the boy has nay recollection of what he saw."

He barked, keeping a firm hold of Lara as she groaned in pain. "I have more pressing matters to address now. But in the morn, we'll need to discuss all of this!"

Alana responded, "Understood."

Jermer stated as he turned to his horse. "Do you need us to help?"

Samuel snarled, "*Nay!* Now go."

The two concurred and mounted the horses and left. Samuel turned to Lara when she sobbed. "Please don't be angry with them. It was my fault."

He focused on her pain-ridden features. "You can tell me everything in the morn, now we need to get to the barn and get through this." He kissed her on the forehead. "I'm sorry Lara that something had to tarnish this first time."

The moonlight seeped into the stable through its main doors and the windows set high near the roof. The atmosphere inside was quiet, except for the horses shuffling in the straw. At the far end, away from the occupied stalls, Lara was on all fours, naked, her skin covered by a sheen of sweat. Her dress was a crumpled mess near the gate. On the floor covered with straw, Samuel knelt to one side of her, trying to comfort her. Suddenly, a shrill scream of pain rang through the air, her fingers dug into the straw with every spasm. She cried out in pain again. The horses looked on but did not seem to be alarmed. Lara's muscles quivered and twisted, she cried out, then threw up on the ground. The transformation had been slow and arduous as Lara bent over in pain, then her back arched sharply. Tears welled in her eyes. She felt like she was being ripped apart.

Her father took her hand, stopping her fingers from clawing at the ground. "Remember to breathe through the pain and don't fight it."

She nodded, her hair damp and stuck to her forehead and cheeks. She focused on her father as another wave of pain flowed over her body. Her limbs felt like they were being ripped from their sockets. "It *hurts* so much."

He studied his daughter from where he knelt beside her. "Tell me the legend of our people."

Lara glanced at him before realising he was trying to distract her. She focused on what she remembered from the books that her father had insisted she read. "We are descendants of a pack of wolves . . ." She grimaced in pain, took a breath, and continued. "Who were the offspring of the Wolf God Laycain." She paused as pain flowed over her. "It hurts!"

"Breathe through the pain, and it will pass. Tell me more."

Lara clenched her teeth and then continued, "Laycain made it so that . . . to protect them from hunters he gave them the gift to shapeshift . . . into humans whenever they needed to. It protected them . . . from the hunters and over . . . and over the years they came down from the mountains and hid amongst humans." She took a breath, ignoring the pain that was overwhelming her, and focused on her father's eyes.

I can do this. I have to.

The first would be the most painful, if she could get through it, she could do *anything*. She continued to breathe through the pain, her skin clammy and hot. Her body shook as another wave flowed over her, she cried out as her joints began to pop. Her limbs bending and breaking backwards. Her back arched and the pain burned as her limbs elongated. She was finally starting to transform. Then the pain stopped, and there was silence.

She shook her body, it felt strange having four legs. She regarded her father through her wolf eyes. She could hear *everything*. Smell *everything*. So much more than she could before, her senses were briefly overwhelmed. She sniffed her father, picking up his musky scent and growled as he stroked her grey fur with a lighter, almost silvery, patch just above her right eye.

He smiled and said, "You are as magnificent as your mother." He rubbed the patch. "You have a patch just like I do."

She nudged him, feeling his fingers combing through her fur so gently. It felt weird towering over him from his kneeling position in her wolf form. He smiled at her, but his eyes had a shadow of sadness in them. She knew he was wishing her mother could have been present to witness her first transformation, because she was too.

He took a breath, composed himself, then said, "It's time to hunt."

He stood and pulled off his white shirt and black trousers, then changed into his wolf form. Lara watched him shift with ease, and was glad that she would be able to change like that within a few months. She observed the black wolf that was her father. His wolf form was a little bigger than hers. His hazel eyes were intense when he grunted at her. It was time to hunt; together, at last.

Leaving the barn, they ran towards the forest behind their house. Lara felt so strong, all the pain and fear she felt moments before, gone. She loved her wolf form. So free. So powerful. As they ran, she got used to her enhanced senses. Her father had told her that after she transformed for the first time, her newly awakened senses would be permanent, even in human form. That was something she would have to get used to, but after some time, it would be second nature. It was not just her senses that would change. He had also told her she would be stronger. That would take more time and would be gradual, but it was something she would have to constantly remember when with her human friends. She studied the trees, seeing so much further than she could have imagined. Then she saw movement ahead, it was so clear. She ran faster, *food.*

Lara ran after the rabbit, her wolf form so agile weaving in between the trees, and catching up with the small mammal. Her father was close by, going after another. It felt good hunting with him after he had told her how much he and her mother would love to just hunt and be free. When she had caught her prey, she carried it to a small hill that looked across from her home. Her father was already there and had laid down, eating his. She laid beside him and nuzzled his fur. He grunted and sniffed her, then turned back to his kill. Lara turned to hers, biting into the animal, taking in the taste and scent. It felt so good to hunt.

After their meal, Samuel nipped Lara in the ear then took off running, wanting Lara to give chase. When Samuel decided they had enough play time, they trotted down the hill back to the barn. Once inside, they both changed back. It was still painful for Lara, but not as much as when she turned into the wolf. She stared at the crumpled mess of her dress and sighed. Her father passed her his shirt for her to put on, then pulled on his trousers.

As Samuel was leaving the barn, he paused after crossing the threshold. "We will discuss what happened in the study."

Lara swallowed nervously, knowing she would have to tell her father what had happened. She followed Samuel into his study, the house was still quiet in the early hours, but with Lara's new senses, it seemed so loud. She could hear the wooden beams creaking, drafts whistling in through the windows and doors. She could even make out movement coming from her brother's room. He had always been an early riser.

Her father studied her. "So, what happened?"

Lara stood in front of him. Samuel had his arms crossed, and was leaning against his desk. Both were signs that he was not too mad with her and he appeared calm and relaxed. He raised an eyebrow waiting, Lara bit her lip. "Sorry papa, but there was this boy . . ."

"Who?" He asked in a firm voice.

"It was Yanric."

He pursed his lips. "The lad from the farm to the south." He paused. "His father Landor is known to me. He's very vocal against non-humans."

Lara glanced down. "Oh. I didn't know."

Samuel studied her. "Aye. But it's something I *have* to know, being what we are. Why wasn't Alana watching you?"

Lara peered up at him through her eyelashes. "She was, but the marquee was crowded and with all the dancing and drinking."

"*Drinking!*"

Lara swallowed, glancing down again. "Aye, sorry papa."

He took a deep breath and asked, "I need to know how your transformation was triggered, especially with you not having any dreams." He noticed Lara would not look at him, her eyes were focused on the hem of his shirt she was wearing, and her face was full of guilt. "Lara? Have you had the dreams?"

She looked up at him, almost pleading. "*Only one.* Just last eve. But I so wanted to go to the celebration. I was afraid that if I told you, you would have forbidden me to go."

"*And with good reason!*" Samuel's voice rising in anger. "Then this incident would not have *happened!*"

Lara flinched at his harsh tone and glanced up at him, tears welling in her eyes. "Sorry, papa."

He sighed and studied his daughter, his anger subsiding. "I do not need to know what happened, but it must have been serious enough for your wolf self to come forth early. They only do that if you are in danger." He added, raising an eyebrow. "Were you in danger? Did Yanric make unwanted advances?"

Lara flushed. "Aye." She said almost in a whisper.

Samuel clenched his fits, slamming one on his desk. Lara jumped at the gesture. Her father glared at her. "Did he get further than wishing?"

Lara shook her head. "Nay, papa. I pushed him away. Then he went pale. I think he saw part of my wolf self. I'm not sure, but he ran off."

He studied her, relief on his features. He stood and walked over to her, giving her a big hug. "I'm glad you came to nay harm." He kissed her gently on the top of her head. "This is one reason Alana should have been a better chaperone."

Lara slowly nodded, savouring her father's embrace. "Please don't blame her papa. It was my fault."

She felt her father sigh. He kissed her again and then they parted. He gazed at her, and a gentle smile came to his lips. "Enough of the past we cannot change. This is a time of celebration; how do you feel?"

Lara's features glowed, glad her father was changing the subject. She knew in the morning he may ask more questions but for now, he wanted her to have this important part of her life untarnished. "I feel fantastic. I can now hear so much." She pointed upwards. "I can hear Derwyn waking."

Her father chuckled, glancing upwards. "I hear him too, over time and with practice you will be able to filter out the background noise and focus on what you need to listen to. The same with your sense of smell."

Lara nodded, adding, "Us hunting together . . . I never felt so free." She paused. "Or so *strong*."

Her father smiled, studying her glowing features. "That first transformation is the worst one. Your full senses will develop over the next few days. Then we can go hunting again."

Lara asked, "Can I change on the morrow?"

He hugged her. "Nay. For the first few times, leave three or four days between the changes. Your body needs to heal and get used to your new powers. Your extra strength will take a little longer to develop."

"I thought we could heal faster?"

"We can, but remember the larger the injury the longer it takes to heal. With your first transformation, you received multiple major injuries. These will lessen the more you change, but during the first few, your body is still getting used to it. You will ache on the morrow, but it will pass. Soon you will not hurt during, or ache after, a transformation."

Lara inspected the room with her new enhanced senses. "I can see, hear and smell so much more."

They sat down and he said, "The advantage of being a lycan, you will also sense when danger is near. This takes training, and over time you will sense how it feels, but you can almost feel the air change around you." He paused, raising an eyebrow. "The situation you were in this eve would not have happened with your lycan senses." Lara slowly nodded, feeling guilty. Her father continued, "Sometimes you will sense a change, like a pressure change, and, as you grow, and get used to your sense of smell, you will detect pheromones. They signal emotions like fear and love, so you can know if they are friend or foe."

Lara peered up at him concerned. "Foe?"

He replied, "Aye, Lara. You know that our lands are not safe. Not from humans, as with the situation this eve. But also, from other creatures or non-humans. Those books you have been studying tell you about all the creatures that venture in our world."

"I read about vampires and things like that. Couldn't we hunt them if we can sense them?"

Her father focused on her with sadness in his eyes for a moment, he then said, "Aye, we could, and there are hunters out there that do that. I want you to be aware of them so you can be safe. Remember that vampires have an incredibly unique smell; a mix of death, blood, and something resembling lavender. You can smell lycan, as you will know the scent well. Werewolves have a stronger, muskier smell. Then witches have a more human scent, but with them, it is something in the air around them, you will sense the magic. You will notice this more now with Alana. Dwarves have a metallic scent, and elves smell like wood. And then there are all the different demons, those you will detect as they are more unique, but you need to study more to know all of their scents."

Lara frowned. "Really?"

Her father nodded. "But don't worry, hopefully, we'll never come across any that will do us harm. Vampires don't pass this way very often, so just remember, their bite cannot kill us, yet our bite can kill them. Even though humans believe otherwise, our bite will not harm them like a werewolf's bite on a full moon will. Our bite is only harmful to vampires. What is more important than anything is, you must keep what you are a secret. Not all humans are like Jermer, Alana, and his companions. Some think we are as evil as vampires and demons."

Her friends would probably not understand anyway, and seeing Yanric's face, most would fear what she was. "I won't tell anyone."

"Good." He gazed at her with pride. "Go and get some sleep. Nay need to do your chores this morn, you will need to sleep to let your body recover."

She gave her father a big hug, he held her shoulders firmly. "But you will tell me exactly what transpired to bring out your wolf."

Lara agreed, her stomach twisting. "Aye, papa."

He smiled, and kissing her. Then she ran up to her room, feeling happy that she had been able to hunt with her father at last. Yet he would not be happy with what she had done. Lara had learnt from her mistake and she would be a lot more careful when it came to boys. At least she had her lycan strength to protect her.

CHAPTER 8

LARA sat nervously in front of her father's desk. Samuel sitting behind it, giving the impression of being imposing. He had let her have a long sleep but when she was up, he had summoned her to his study. He had also sent word to Alana as well, but he wanted to talk to her before the witch arrived. Lara watched her father nervously.

"So, are you going to tell me all that transpired last eve?" her father asked.

Lara swallowed. The events from the night before already seemed a faded memory, but the severity of them were much clearer to her now. If it had not been for her wolf, Lara knew the situation may have been far worse. "Yanric asked me to dance, and we danced with each other for most of the eve."

Samuel responded, "You mentioned there was drinking, too."

Lara replied, "Aye." She wrung her fingers together nervously. "I did not realise it at the time, but he always made sure my goblet wasn't empty." Samuel nodded his features looking stern. Lara continued, "Then we left the marquee. I was a little unsteady, and he caught me when I tripped. We kissed and well.... he, erm.... he wanted more."

When Lara paused, her features full of concern, Samuel asked, "Where was this?"

Lara peered up at him and bit her lip. "On Smithy Street."

"*Smithy Street?*" Samuel snarled, "That is not a street to be on at night, Lara. I am surprised nay one else became involved!"

She swallowed, flinching at her father's reaction. Realising she could have been in even more danger. "Sorry, papa."

He leant forward studying her. "Where was Alana?"

Lara's features mirrored the guilt she felt in the pit of her stomach. "In the marquee."

"Did she remain with you at all?"

Lara shook her head. "Nay. But I am eighteen now. She knew I would be sensible."

Samuel scoffed, "*Sensible?* Lara, you have shown me from your actions last eve, that you are not *sensible!*"

Lara glanced down and whispered, "Mama would have done the same as Alana."

Samuel glared at her and pointed a stern finger. "Do *not* bring your mama into this!"

Lara flinched at her father's sudden sharp tone. "But none of my friends had chaperones."

"They weren't my *daughter!*"

Lara felt tears welling in her eyes. "I'm *so* sorry, papa."

He sighed, his eyes firmly on her. "Lara, understand I love you, but what happened last eve, could have been far worse. I could have lost you. Do you understand the severity of your actions?"

She looked up at him and nodded but was unable to trust her voice as more tears welled in her eyes. She concentrated on the painting behind her father and felt guilty for letting him down. She swallowed and said softly, "I do papa."

His features remained firm as he said, "Now for your punishment. As you seem to be aware this morn of the severity of your actions, I think hard study will be a good penance." He paused scratching his chin. "Five volumes of the demonology. You will also do more chores. You will help Ida in the kitchen, as well as extra cleaning duties. You will not be allowed into Lake Wood for thirty days." He paused. "Also, not as a punishment, but I will teach you basic sword work. I think it's time that you learn how to defend yourself with methods other than your lycan ones." He turned towards the study door.

"Alana has arrived. I have picked up her scent. You do not need to be here while I speak to her."

Lara nodded and pleaded to her father, "Please do not be too harsh with her."

He sighed, "I will not, but I am displeased she didn't do as I had asked."

Samuel scrutinised Alana as they stood in his study. Standing by his desk with his arms crossed, he said sternly, "Lara has told me of the events last eve, and she is being punished accordingly. What I would like to know is why you didn't chaperone her as I had asked."

She sighed as she stood with her hands clasped behind her back. "What happened was not what was intended, and I am sorry for what transpired. But for my judgement, I believed Lara is a sensible girl and would make wise choices. For most of the eve she did, yet Yanric ensured that she had drunk enough wine to make her judgement impaired. Aye, I should have watched her more closely, but I also believed that Yanric was a sensible boy too."

Samuel glared at her and nodded slowly. "I see. But I asked you to chaperone my daughter. I know that you believed she would be sensible, but it was her first time at an event like that, and I wanted her to be safe. If her wolf self hadn't come forth, I dare not think what would have happened."

"I understand, and I am deeply sorry. As for Yanric, I have wiped his memory of what happened, and I have ensured your family's secret remains safe." Alana explained.

Samuel responded, "I thank you." He paused studying her. "For now, I do not want you to have any contact with my family. I am aware of Derwyn's friendship with Peadar and in ten days I will allow them to have contact again. I do not wish to punish a small child for the actions of an irresponsible adult, but I also want you to be aware of how displeased I am that you broke my trust. As for Lara, you will have nay contact with her for thirty days. That is the length of time I have forbidden her from venturing into the village. But even then, you will remain distant and in time I may let your friendship continue as it once had. She saw you as a mother figure and last eve you failed in that."

Alana bowed her head, her features full of sorrow. "I understand, and again I am sorry for what happened."

The witch left the study. Samuel watched her leave and glanced up at the painting behind his desk. He sighed, "I wish you were here my love; our daughter needs guidance and I fear I am not enough."

He examined the paperwork on his desk and sighed again. He was not in the mood. After the recent events he felt frustrated and helpless. He pursed his lips and decided what he wanted to do. He walked out of his study and into the library.

He saw his daughter reading and said, "Lara, come on."

She turned to put down her book. "What is it, papa?"

He stated as she stood. "Get changed into your riding clothes. I'm going to show you how to use a sword." She smiled, running up the stairs.

He watched her go knowing he had never wanted her to have to train for these particular reasons. Yet after recent events, he needed to know she could defend herself. Having lycan blood made her stronger and faster than humans, but from his own experience, having the skill to use a sword and dagger was always an advantage.

CHAPTER 9

THREE YEARS LATER

THE storm was fierce, thunder rumbled overhead, and lightning flashed across the sky. The house whistled from the wind forcing its way through windows and the rafters. Lara woke knowing something did not feel right, and it had nothing to do with the storm. It was something else. Sitting up, she rubbed her eyes and listened. She could hear her father and knew he must have sensed something too. Climbing out of bed, she ran barefoot in her nightgown to the landing, her father joining her.

He said, his features alert and concerned. "You sensed it too."

She nodded. "Something's wrong." She paused, cocking her head to one side, listening. "The horses seem unsettled, but it's not just due to the storm."

A breeze entered the house from a window which had swung open by the force of the wind from the storm. They both sniffed the air, and she picked up a strange scent. She turned to her father. "Is that . . ?"

He cursed, "*Vampires.*" He turned to her, taking a firm hold of her arm. "I need you to stay here."

"I can help."

He shook his head. "Nay. I need you to stay here in case one comes this way." He paused seeing her concerned features.

"They cannot enter due to that talisman on the back of the door. But they can still damage the house."

Lara focused on the door, eyeing the talisman on the back of it, then watched her father hurry down the stairs, stripping as he went, and run out into the torrential rain. She paced on the landing, nervous. She could still smell the vampires and hoped her father would be all right. She was tempted to run out and help, but she needed to stay here and protect the house, just in case. She jumped as the door swung open from the wind, it seemed her father had not closed it properly when he ran out. It slammed shut, the talisman still on the back of the door. Lara was curious how something so small could keep the vampires from entering. Lightning flashed again, and the door to the house swung open with more force, not having caught the latch when it slammed shut a moment before. Lara bit her lip when she heard a commotion outside. Her father was fighting someone. As the door swung back, she noticed the talisman had gone. Before she could see where it was, the door swung open again, and the rain poured in. Moments later, a huge, wet, mortally wounded wolf limped into the hallway. Her father slumped down on the stone floor as he started to convulse. His limbs snapped brutally in angles that seemed impossible, and slowly, he turned back into his human form.

Lara ran to the top of the staircase and stared in horror. "Papa?"

He focused on her, his naked body covered in blood, his stomach ripped open, and his hands holding the intestines in. He coughed, spitting blood. He shouted through gritted teeth, as he crawled toward the stairs. "Lara! I need help."

She was about to run down to help him when she saw the talisman broken on the floor. Her father saw it at the same moment as he dragged himself closer to the stairs, leaving a smear of blood in his wake. He stopped and turned to her, fear in his eyes.

"*Run!*" Lara hesitated, knowing her father needed help. He glared at her, as he struggled to his feet, trying to hold his innards in. "RUN!"

Her heart was beating fast. Fear taking hold. She wanted so much to run to her father. But he shouted at her again to run, fear in his voice. As she turned, she caught sight of two figures running towards the house. Nothing to stop them from entering now. She did not linger to see what happened; she ran as fast as she could to the smaller bedroom at the back of the house. She heard her father desperately fighting to his last breath, trying to stop the vampires from entering the house. Lara knew what she needed to do. Her father would not like it, but first, she had to get to her brother before it was too late.

Lara ran into the bedroom, the boy still asleep. She studied the ten-year-old, her heart racing. She woke him gently not wanting the people downstairs to hear them. "Derwyn, wake up."

He groaned softly, opening his sleep-filled eyes, his black hair a scruffy mess. "What?"

"Shhh." Lara put her hand to his lips and realised it was shaking.

She heard someone downstairs shout. "There are others upstairs!"

Lara tensed, her throat tight with fear. If they had entered the house that meant her father was dead or too weak to fight anymore. She grabbed her brother's arm. He whimpered when she realised she was holding him too tightly. She did not want to scare him, but he needed to do what she said.

She glared at him. "Derwyn, I need you to be a very brave boy." Tears were welling in his hazel eyes. "I need you to hide in our secret place and be very, *very* quiet."

The dark-haired boy's features were full of fear. "Where's papa?"

She swallowed and tried to not appear as scared as she felt. "He needs my help. You need to hide to stay safe. *Please*, Derwyn, I have to keep you safe and if I know you are, I can help papa."

Tears rolled down his cheeks, but he took a deep breath and roughly wiped them. "I will, Lara."

She studied him intently, hearing someone heading towards the stairs. "Hide now Derwyn and stay quiet." He nodded and ran to the secret passage at the end of the hall.

Lara took a deep breath she needed to lure the killers away. She had no idea how, but she had to protect Derwyn. She closed her eyes and whispered, "Please give me strength, Laycain in this time of need."

Lara pulled off her nightgown and transformed into her wolf form then crept along the landing. Her paws padded silently on the wooden floor. Ahead, she could hear the intruders had almost reached the top of the stairs. Derwyn was safe, she just had to make sure they could not get to the bedrooms. The vampires came into view, a brown-haired man and a woman. Their clothes were soaked from the rain, their faces covered in fresh blood. From the familiar smell, she knew they had fed off her father's dead body. Lara clenched her claws, she had to keep focused. She could morn once they were safe. She somehow managed to stifle the growl threatening to erupt as she sniffed the air. Her father was right about their scent, and she would never forget the smell of vampires ever again.

Attempting a surprise attack, she stuck her large paw between the rails, swiping at the two vampires. They jumped back, missing a few steps as she landed perfectly at the top of the stairs. Before the two could fully get back up, Lara pounced on the closest. Her teeth sliced deep into the flesh of the male's arm, tearing it brutally. His warm, thick blood ran down her throat. Lara grunted; vampire blood tasted so different than animals. She briefly wondered if all blood tasted different. Her eyes focused on his claw-like nails as he cradled his brutally mauled arm.

The female cried out, "*Von!*"

Lara ignored the female as she picked up her father's scent again. It was the blood beneath Von's fingernails. It was he who had inflicted the mortal wound on her father. Lara shook her head. She had to stay focused. Von would be dead in a few days from her bite. She needed to at least bite the other, if she could do that then maybe Derwyn would be safe.

Von staggered back, landing on his rump, the bite already starting to affect him. He whispered, "Levana."

The female vampire screamed then jumped at Lara, pushing her away from her companion. Wolf and vampire limbs entangled as they rolled across the floor away from Von. Lara managed to get back to her feet and realised they were now even closer to the bedrooms. She blocked their path, growling. She had to get them back down the stairs or kill them where they stood.

It seemed to be just pure luck that Lara had managed to disable the stronger of the two. It helped knowing it was the male who dealt the fatal blow to her father. She could only hope that Levana was weaker. Lara tried to make her whole body as big as she could, growling fiercely, and showing her long canine teeth as menacingly as possible.

The female vampire glared at Lara, and the wolf pounced. But Lara misjudged, and Levana bit down hard into her neck, her sharp vampire teeth tore deep into the thick wolf skin. Lara yelped, and before she could fight back, Levana pushed Lara away from her as hard as she could. The vampire was a lot stronger than she had realised.

Lara flew over the bannister, her body twisting around. The fall would have been nothing, but before she hit the ground, her head hit the oak table which stood in the centre of the hallway. Her neck snapped. Lara crumpled to the floor and wheezed trying to breathe. Her body slowly contorted back to her human form. With her dying sight, she saw Levana helping Von leave the house. Her last thought as the darkness took her, was that Derwyn was safe.

CHAPTER 10

A LANA and Jermer rode through the deserted village towards Samuel's house. The fierce storm did not slow their pace. Alana had woken in the early hours to sense something gravely wrong. Her powers had always been useful, able to sense danger or something evil. Yet what she sensed when she woke was something different. It seemed that nature was unbalanced. She felt it in her soul that something was gravely wrong and hoped they were not too late. She had woken Jermer and they had quickly pulled on their cloaks. With no time to saddle the horses, they had ridden bareback through the village.

Her stomach twisted when she neared the house. Lightning flashed, and she could see the door swinging backwards and forwards in the wind. Dismounting, she ran into the house and gasped seeing the carnage. Samuel was dead his neck and midsection ripped open, blood and guts all over the floor. Stopping herself from retching, she pulled down her hood as she examined the room. The talisman she had made to stop vampires from entering was broken and useless. She continued inspecting then her hand went to her mouth in shock, muffling a sound of anguish. Then she heard Jermer inhale sharply behind her. Yet her attention remained on the scene before her. Derwyn was kneeling on the floor next to the naked body of Lara. The little boy was sobbing.

Alana slowly walked over; the little boy gazed up as he was shaking his sister. "Lara won't wake up." He glanced over at Samuel's body. "And papa . . ." His body shuddered with more sobs.

The witch knelt beside the boy. Making sure she blocked his view of the gruesome sight of his dead father. She glanced back to see Jermer removing his cloak to cover the body of their dear friend. She then glanced at Lara, noticing her neck was at an unnatural angle. Then she scrutinised the staircase, the landing above, and the hall. Alana had surmised that Lara must have fallen, breaking her neck on the table.

Jermer whispered, kneeling next to her. "She's gone."

Alana frowned, glancing at her husband. She still felt something was not right and placed her hand on Lara's naked chest, closing her eyes for a moment. With her enhanced abilities, she could sense something flowing through the girl's lifeless veins. That could only mean one thing.

She focused on Jermer, shaking her head. "Nay. I think she's dormant."

Jermer frowned. "Dormant?"

Derwyn stared between the two of them, sobbing, "What's wrong with her?"

Alana gently examined Lara, studying her neck. Then she noticed the vampire bite just above her shoulder and indicated it to Jermer silently. She had been fighting, and with what was moving through her veins, that meant she must have swallowed some of the vampire's blood. Alana looked back at Jermer, with sudden urgency in her eyes. If she was right, there might be hope.

"We must move quickly. I think I can save her."

Derwyn pleaded with tear-ridden eyes. "*Please* save my sister!"

She gazed at him, smiling warmly. "I will. But we must get your sister to my house *now*."

She turned to Jermer, as she stood taking Derwyn's hand. "I need to prepare something. Bring her, quickly."

Jermer grabbed a cloak from near the entrance and placed it around Lara, picking up her limp body with ease. He paused, glancing down at Samuel's mutilated body, covered by his cloak.

He whispered, "I'm sorry old friend." Then quickly followed his wife and Derwyn back to the horses.

Alana was rushing around the kitchen. Grabbing different herbs and bottles from the stocked shelves and reading the labels. Then referring to her large potion book and quickly moving on to the next ingredient. When she found the ones she needed, she placed them on the table near a large pot and a mortar and pestle. She had researched many years before for remedies in case either Samuel or Miriel were ever bitten. Yet, to her relief, she had never had the opportunity to use it, and she could only hope to her goddess that it would work. In theory, the combination of a spell and a potion should work, but reality was never predictable.

Jermer had placed Lara down on the bed in the next room and then took Derwyn to sleep with their son Peadar. He came back to see his wife rushing around gathering ingredients and reading her book.

Alana glanced up at him. Her features were full of hope as she ground herbs in the mortar. "I think I can save her."

Jermer frowned. "How?"

She said, as she poured the ground herbs into the large pot. "Lara was bitten, there is a vampire bite on her shoulder."

"Aye I saw it, but she's dead. That won't harm her now."

She shook her head. "I sense something in her. I believe she fought them. As she is naked, I think she attacked them as a wolf so she would have tried to maul one. If she did, she may . . ." She paused checking a bottle of blue liquid before pouring some into the pot. She glanced back up. "Nay, I *know*, she must have ingested their blood and– "

Jermer gasped. "First bitten, and then she broke her neck in the fall . . ." He paused as he realised, then shook his head. "But she won't survive. The vampire blood will destroy her body."

Alana said, pointing to the pot full of the potion she was making. "But I think this may counteract it and save her."

Jermer probed, "Are you sure? If not, she will be in agony for hours before her body finally tears itself apart."

His wife responded, "If I give this to her now, she will have a fever for a few days, but if she is still with us by morn that means her body is healing. Then I *know* she will live."

Alana closed her eyes and waved her hand gently above the mixture as she whispered a spell. It glowed for a moment, then she decanted the potion into a goblet and rushed into the other room.

"Quick, she must drink this before it's too late." Jermer followed her.

Once in the room, Alana indicated to her husband to lift Lara's head gently. Alana noticed Lara's eyes moving, her neck was still broken, but life seemed to be returning to her. She hoped that soon the injuries would be healed. The witch muttered a second spell under her breath as Lara subconsciously swallowed the potion. Once all the thick liquid had been consumed, Jermer placed Lara's head gently back down, trying to stop it from rolling at an angle due to the broken neck.

As he stood, his wife studied him. "She *has* to survive the night, if she does then I know the potion has worked."

Jermer asked, "But what will she be, lycan or vampire?"

His wife stared at Lara. "She will be both."

"*Both?* But that is impossible."

"She will be one of a kind. What I have given her was something I found years ago for if any of them were in this very situation. I have nay idea if it will work, but all I do know is that she needs to survive the night. If by morn her wounds are healing, then there is a chance she will live."

They both contemplated Lara, Jermer focusing on the scar on her forehead, if it had gone by morning, then there was hope.

Alana placed a hand on Lara's chest and whispered, "You can fight this, Lara. Laycain is watching over you."

Jermer studied his wife and told her, "If it doesn't work, I can't let her suffer."

Alana said sadly, "If that is the case then I will help you to end her suffering." Jermer tipped his head then left the room.

Alana took a seat near the bed, praying silently to the goddess Anoixi and the wolf god, Laycain, if he could hear her. She would stay with Lara tonight and hope she pulled through the fever. The woman looked up and closed her eyes for a moment.

"I promised to always keep your children safe, Miriel. I am so sorry, but Samuel will be joining you in the hunting fields. With you both gone, I will try even harder to look out for Lara and Derwyn. I know Lara has your stubbornness, and she will make it through the night. I pray on my goddess." Alana placed her hand gently on Lara's chest feeling it beginning to move again and smiled softly. "Be strong Lara."

CHAPTER II

WHEN Lara opened her eyes, darkness was all around her. As she slowly began to focus and become aware of her surroundings, a wave of pain hit her, making her softly cry out. She started shivering, even though her body was covered in sweat. Wiping the sweat from her forehead she struggled to try to sit up, but only managed to prop herself up on her elbow. She carefully examined the small room, her eyes had adjusted to the darkness, but her vision was still a little blurred. Her neck twinged in pain. Glancing down she noticed she was not wearing one of her nightgowns.

Where am I? Is this from the fever?

Looking to the side of her, she saw Derwyn lying asleep on the floor next to the bed she was in. Then memories of what happened at the house and her father came flooding back. She placed her hand on her mouth stifling a sob. She felt dizzy, overwhelmed by all the emotions.

She could hear Jermer and Alana talking. *How did Derwyn and I end up at their house?*

She tried to listen to what they were saying, but all she could hear was the slow rhythm of a heartbeat. *Is that my heart?* As she tried to focus on it, she realised it was Derwyn's. She took a deep breath to control the pain burning through her body, making her unable to focus for too long. She needed to listen to the conversation, she closed her eyes and concentrated.

". . . the boy could stay with us; we can raise him with Peadar." Alana's voice came to her.

Jermer responded, "She won't be happy leaving Derwyn here."

"She has to. She can't stay . . ."

The beating of Derwyn's heart became even louder, drowning out the voices. She slumped back down, and pressed her hands against her sweaty temples trying to stop the thunderous sound. *Why is it so loud?*

Lara looked at her brother, her eyes focusing on his neck. She could see his pulse, which made her feel ravenous. Lara turned away feeling disoriented.

What's wrong with me? Why am I in so much pain?

She tried to focus on her breathing as she struggled again to sit up. She had a vague recollection of Alana whispering something and liquid running down her throat.

What had she given me, was it poison? Lara squeezed her eyes shut trying to clear the fog in her brain. *Alana just wouldn't do that, but why was she insisting Derwyn stayed here?* Lara tried to focus on the conversation again.

". . . when the fever breaks, she will have to leave. Alone . . ."

Lara turned to her brother, his heartbeat had faded into the background as she managed to get more control. They could not take Derwyn from her; he was all she had. She had also made a promise to her father to always protect him, whatever the cost. If he had to go anywhere it would be with her, or to a lycan family or pack who would know how to raise him. Not these humans.

Lara flopped back down feeling exhausted, the pain flowing over her again. She had to get them away from the witch as soon as she could, and before the fever broke. *But I can't even sit up, so how can I get us out of here?* Lara took a breath. She had to figure out what was happening to her. She did not feel right, something seemed very wrong.

Lara stiffened, hearing Alana walking towards the room. She focused on the woman as she entered while trying to control the pain that was still flowing through her body.

She whispered to the witch, "What's wrong with me?"

Alana perched on the edge of the bed, placing a hand on Lara's forehead to check her temperature. Lara remembered her mother doing the same when she was a child.

"You are fighting the vampire blood that flows through your body."

Lara's stomach twisted in fear. *Could that be what the feeling was?* She struggled to sit up, frowning that she could only lean on her elbow.

"How?"

Yet as soon as she asked, she remembered what had happened. The fight. The blood flowing down her throat. The pain as her neck broke. Lara felt sick, she had died but she was . . . A sob of anguish escaped from her throat, and tears welled in her eyes.

She grabbed hold of Alana. "Am I?

The woman studied her, her features full of concern. "We believe when the vampires attacked your home . . . during the fight, you swallowed some of the vampire's blood. When we found your body, I saw the bite on your shoulder. So, with these factors, a human would be turned to a vampire, but with a lycan the two types of blood cannot mix, and all usually die." She paused, squeezing Lara's hand. "Yet, I gave you something, and for it to work, you had to survive the night. Which you did. The fever you have now is from your wolf blood fighting the vampire one, and the wolf is winning."

Lara took hold of her arm, with her free hand. She struggled to keep focused as more pain rippled through her body. "My blood feels like it's boiling."

Alana focused on Lara, concern in her eyes. "It will pass by morn," She then glanced towards the little boy sleeping. "I should move him into the room with Peadar."

Lara gripped Alana's arm harder and leant towards her. "*Nay!*" her voice sounding more like a growl. She glared at the woman, her features changing for a second, looking more wolf-like. "He stays with me."

Alana paused, slight fear in her eyes at Lara's reaction. "Alright. But you need to rest, Lara. Let your body heal." Lara took a few deep breaths, letting go of the witch, and trying to control the pain. She watched Alana leave.

Lara frowned. *Am I part vampire, or was Alana just telling me that so I would leave Derwyn with them?*

Lara clenched her fist; she could not think clearly with all the pain. She had to beat it, and she could not wait till the morning. She needed to leave immediately and take Derwyn with her.

A few hours later as Lara lay curled up on the bed still in pain, she concentrated on the house. She could no longer hear any movements and the house seemed still. Jermer and Alana must have gone to bed. It was time to go. Lara struggled to move, her limbs protesting, but she had to.

She leaned down and squeezed her brother's shoulder. "Derwyn, we have to go."

The ten-year-old woke to study her, rubbing his tired eyes. "But you aren't very well."

Lara agreed as she took a breath to stop crying out at the sudden pain in her stomach. "I know, but we can't stay here. They are going to try to take you away from me and I promised papa that . . . that I'd look after you and keep you safe. So, we have to go *now*."

Derwyn nodded, getting to his feet, fear in his eyes. Lara slowly climbed off the bed, the floor ice cold against her bare feet. She took a deep breath trying to keep control, she grabbed Derwyn's shoulder as she tried to find her balance. She gritted her teeth as more pain flowed through her as she forced her body to move, her joints protesting.

She said, "You need to help me, Derwyn. We need to get out of here quietly and find a horse."

Standing up, Lara felt dizzy. Grabbing the headboard of the bed for a moment, she stilled, letting herself get her bearings. Bent over slightly to ease the pain, she slowly walked towards the door of the small bedroom, Derwyn tried to support her as much as he could.

Leaving the room, Lara slowly glanced both ways, one hand on the wall to steady herself. She could see the kitchen on one side, then when she looked the other way, she remembered the corridor led to the main entrance and the courtyard beyond. They moved slowly and quietly down the narrow corridor, the opening to the entrance hall seemed to swim in her blurred vision. Lara vaguely knew the layout of the house having visited before, but with her vision blurry and her senses filled with pain, she was a little disoriented. Lara bit her lip to stop from crying out as a wave of pain hit her. The last thing they needed was to wake anyone. When the narrow corridor opened into the entrance hall, Lara staggered to the door. Derwyn opened it, the night air cool against her skin. To Lara's relief, they were in the courtyard, and the stable was just ahead. As they moved further outside, Lara bent over in excruciating pain. A soft cry slipped from between her gritted teeth.

Derwyn studied her with concern. "Don't die."

Lara took a breath to control the spasms and squeezed her brother's shoulder. "Nay little squirt, you can't get rid of me yet." She focused on the stable across the courtyard. "Let's get a horse and get out of here."

In the darkness, Lara struggled over to the stable, the stone ground cutting into her bare feet. Entering the stable they went to the first stall, the horse snorted at their approach, but Lara gently stroked its neck calming it when it became restless. Lara glanced over at the saddles and then at Derwyn. He was too small, and she didn't have the energy to strap one to the horse. If she was honest with herself, just the walk to the stable left her struggling to even remain standing. But they needed to leave. Taking a deep breath and with sudden strength, she managed to pick Derwyn up and get him onto the horse. She took a few more breaths and with her remaining strength managed to climb up behind him.

She grabbed hold of the horse's mane and whispered, "We have to get somewhere safe."

Derwyn glanced back at her. "Can we go home?"

She sighed, struggling to keep focused, everything was swimming around her. "Nay, it's not safe. We need to head for the den. We'll be safe there for a while." She paused for a second, forcing herself to focus on her brother so she would not fall off the horse from being so dizzy. "Derwyn you're going to have to remember the way. I'm not feeling too good, and I don't know if I can stay awake."

He grabbed the horse's mane. "I'll look after you."

She smiled softly. "I know you will squirt."

Lara leaned against her brother's small body as pain burned through hers. She had to get Derwyn to safety, but wondered if she could do it before she died. It felt like her body was tearing itself apart. She took a deep breath, no, she vowed that she would never leave him alone. She had to protect him. Closing her eyes for a moment, she made a silent prayer to Laycain for strength. What Lara needed was the fever to break, and hopefully, if they made it to the den, she could sleep it off.

Derwyn said with excitement. "Lara, we're here."

She peered up, feeling dazed and disoriented, seeing the small wooden hut ahead, partly hidden in the trees, the forest all around them. Lara struggled to focus and could not even remember the ride. She looked down at Derwyn, he must have remembered the way a lot better than she had thought. They would come to the den with their father when they were younger but had not expected Derwyn to know the way so well.

Her fever was still high, and it still felt like her blood was boiling in her veins. She wondered if it would ever break. Lara tried to climb off the horse but was so disoriented that she fell off, hitting the ground with a 'humph'.

Derwyn jumped down and knelt beside her. "Lara?"

She stared up at him. She was so hungry. His heartbeat was so loud, she looked at his neck, seeing his pulse. Then she could feel her teeth lengthening, but not like her wolf fangs, it felt different.

"*Sooooo* hungry," she whispered as she licked her lips, focused on her brother's neck.

She suddenly froze. *What was am I doing?* She pushed her brother away from her, the vampiric blood was trying to take control. *No!* She would *never* drink human blood, and never her brother's.

Derwyn considered her for a few moments, then suddenly stood, and ran off into the woods. Lara weakly tried to follow, but her body convulsed in pain.

"Derwyn," her voice was barely above a whisper.

She closed her eyes. She had scared her brother away. She was supposed to be protecting him. She crawled towards the den just wanting the pain to end. As she reached the door, Derwyn ran up to her holding a dead rabbit.

"I remembered papa's snares." He dangled the rabbit in front of her. "You said you were hungry."

Even in so much pain, Lara smiled softly. She concentrated on trying to keep in control, she was not going to let the vampire side take hold. Lara's wolf side was stronger, that was why she was in so much pain, her wolf was fighting against it. Food would help. She struggled to her feet so they could get into the hut.

She slumped down on the floor inside and gasped, "Papa had a hunting knife in here, use it to gut and skin the rabbit." She looked at him, trying to keep focused. "Can you set up a fire?"

The little boy answered, "Papa showed me."

Lara nodded slowly. "Good, we both need food."

She could see her brother was concerned for her. Lara took a few deep breaths and tried not to look like her body was trying to tear itself apart. She focussed on the rabbit as her brother skinned it and she licked her lips. Her wolf part wanted the meat, and she hoped with it raw, the blood would stop the vampiric cravings.

"Give me some of the raw meat."

Derwyn passed her some. Lara started to eat it and a wave of delight flowed over her. The raw meat was just what she needed. She slowly laid down, exhaustion from the short trip taking hold, and whispered, "I need to rest, squirt."

He glanced at her, then concentrated on making a fire, in the small fireplace at the back wall. Lara watched him until she could not keep her eyes open any longer.

CHAPTER 12

LARA woke at dawn; the fever had finally broken. She slowly sat up, surveying the hut. The fire from the night before was smouldering and sunlight was coming in through the small windows. She gazed across the room to see Derwyn still fast asleep, the remains of the cooked rabbit near him. She smiled softly, she was proud of him and glad he had managed to eat something. The little boy had coped well with the recent events, a lot better than she thought he would.

Lara took a deep breath. There was no more pain, and she felt amazing. It was strange how only hours before, she thought she was going to die. Getting to her feet, she stretched, her neck still feeling stiff. She needed a run; it always helped her.

Exiting the den as quietly as she could, she squinted at the sunlight, looking up into the trees. Everything appeared so vibrant and fresh. Her senses were much more sensitive. She wondered what else would be different. Lara noticed that the horse had gone, it had probably wandered back to Alana and Jermer's. They still would not be able to find the den, it was way into the forest and Lara was sure only her family knew of it. She looked around then pulled off the grubby nightgown that she had been wearing and changed into her wolf form. It still hurt when her body contorted and changed shape, but over the years she could was able to change as fast as her father could. Compared to the first change, which had taken hours, it only took minutes to fully transform.

Lara shook out her fur. It felt good to be back in wolf form. She ran further into the trees, taking in her surroundings. As well as the heightened senses, she felt different, like she was even more powerful. Lara took a deep breath as she ran, the air seemed so much more fragrant. She could pick up scents, some were extremely old, something she had not been able to do before. She focused on the forest around her, realising she could hear more. From the insects on the branches and leaves of the trees, to sounds that seemed a lot further away than what she could have possibly have heard. She slowed, she had run further than she realised. *Am I faster now too?* It felt like she had not run far at all, she did not even feel tired. She paused, sensing an animal ahead, but it was not just their scent that seemed stronger. Like she had the night before, she could hear the animal's heartbeat. She took a breath and focused. As she got nearer, she could see the badger's pulse even with her wolf eyes. Lara paused again, inspecting the animal. It was as if it were transparent. She could see its blood moving around its body and even see its heart pumping, which quickened when it picked up her scent. That was something she could never see before. *Was this extra sense because of the vampire blood?* Lara remembered the same thing happened with her brother the night before, but had thought it was to do with the fever. She wondered if that was how vampires saw their prey. If that had developed from having vampire blood in her body then she would be so much better at hunting, but what she did not want was the cravings. Yet that seemed to have lessened when she had the raw meat last night.

Lara pounced, snapping the badger's neck, and laid down to eat it. If she could hunt more than she normally did, she hoped it would keep any cravings at bay. For how long she did not know, but she knew over time she would be able to deal with it. She paused, thinking about the recent events, still finding it hard to take everything in. At some point the whole of this would hit her, but for now, she would concentrate on the advantages. She had to remain strong and get Derwyn and herself somewhere safe.

Lara ran back to where she started, shifting to her human form and pulled the nightgown back on. She returned to the den with a rabbit. When she entered Derwyn was awake.

He gazed up at his sister and smiled. "You're alright."

71

Lara sat beside him, putting the rabbit down, and hugged him. "I am."

Derwyn asked, "Why did you have the fever?"

Lara focused on his eyes, wondering what to tell him. It was for the best to be as honest as she could. "What did they tell you?"

"They said nothing to me, but I listened to what they were saying when they thought I was asleep. Alana said something about vampires, and that their blood mixed with your own. Are you going to be a vampire?" He paused looking out the window. "But you didn't burn in the sun, so you can't be."

Lara studied her brother, realising he was right. She had been out in the sun with no effects. "I'm not sure, squirt. I do feel different, and my senses seem so much more sensitive."

"Will you need to drink blood?"

She smiled while studying him, unsure if she would or not, and shrugged. "Nay, I don't think so. But when I hunt in my wolf form, I will be having blood anyway. I think, with all of this, I will have to find out as we go."

"So, what now?" He peered up at her questioningly.

Lara looked at him. He was all she had, and she had to protect him. She sighed, they could not stay for too long as she feared Alana and Jermer would still try and take Derwyn from her.

"We will need to leave." She glanced down at the slip which was grubby and smelled of her sweat from the fever. "I need to get clothes and we need supplies," she told her brother. "Stay here and cook that rabbit for your breakfast, I've already eaten. I'm going down to the house. I will sneak in to get clothes and other things we may need. Be ready to leave when I return."

He agreed, gazing up at her. "Please be careful."

She smiled, ruffling his hair. "I will, squirt. We must stick together now, and I will make sure you are always safe."

Leaving Derwyn at the den, Lara ran down the hill to the back of the house, confident she could sneak in without anyone knowing. She paused as she entered and listened, the house was deathly quiet. Taking the back stairs, she ran to her room. When she entered, she found her clothes chest was open and her riding clothes were gone. She cursed, wondering what she was going to do. Wearing one of her dresses was not very practical, but she may have little choice. While she thought of what to do, she went to Derwyn's room. His clothes chest was open too, but there were still some clothes left behind.

What she needed was a satchel, weapons and she still needed clothes. She walked towards her father's room, wondering if she could use some of his, they would be a little big but still more practical than a dress. If nothing else, he would have some sort of bag and possibly weapons. Or those items could be in his study. Lara was not sure and entered the large bed chamber. She paused, her father's familiar scent invading her nostrils. Lara's heart ached and she fought back the tears. She wished her father could be with her and tell her what to do. She sniffed and quickly wiped a stray tear from her cheek. She had to be strong. She found her father's satchel behind the door, the one he used when he went riding, and she stuffed Derwyn's clothes in it. She scanned around for weapons then she paused, gazing at her mother's clothes chest, and realised that those clothes would probably fit her.

Lara felt guilty opening the chest, but her mother and father would understand. She pulled out a few dresses, her mother's scent still on them. Tears welled in her eyes again, realising how much she still missed her. Lara took a deep breath, she needed to concentrate. Near the bottom she found riding clothes. She pulled out trousers, a shirt, and a leather jerkin. She paused, under that was a sword and dagger. She picked up the sword and pulled it free of the scabbard and froze. It was made with silver, the workmanship was of high quality. The swordsmith had to be skilled, as from what she had read, silver swords were hard to make. With too much silver, they would be too soft, and too little, would not make them effective. *Why would mama have a silver sword?* She frowned. Her parents were not demon hunters, which was more than likely with there being no rune markings on the blade. She pursed her lips, remembering everything her father had told her. He knew a lot about vampires and demons and wanted her to be aware of everything non-human. *Could mama have had the sword for self-defence?* It would be effective against rogue wolves, and other magical creatures that silver was deadly to. Her father had said they needed to be aware of those creatures to be safe. Lara shrugged; it was not the time to figure out what secrets her parents had kept from her.

She needed to get them somewhere safe, and they needed protection. The sword and dagger, especially the sword designed for smaller hands, would be perfect for her. Placing the weapons and clothes on the bed, she scanned the room and found her mother's riding boots in the corner. They had gathered dust, but otherwise, they looked in good condition. She placed her bare feet against the bottom, they would fit. She moved to her father's trunk, tracing her hand over the symbol of two swords crossed over each other behind a wolf head, all on a simple shield. The Tarrenfall family crest. She hesitated before opening it. His scent was strong inside, but when she looked through his things, she could not find any other weapons. Glancing over at her mother's, she felt relief having found those. Lara looked back at his clothes and took a couple of his shirts as they would be good as spares even if a little big.

She listened carefully; the house still sounded empty. She quickly stripped, wanting to get rid of the nightgown she had been in for the last few nights. Lara gave herself a quick wash with the water that was in the jug by her father's wash bowl. Then she pulled on her mother's clothes and boots, surprised by how well they fit. She glanced at herself in the mirror, her mother almost looking back at her. Lara took a deep breath, holding onto her emotions as tears welled again. There was no time to break down, there was too much to do. She took a deep breath and cleared her head, she needed to get some supplies; not wasting time thinking of the past. She fastened the sword to her back and placed the dagger in the satchel with Derwyn's clothes and her father's shirts. She took one last inspection of the room, not seeing anything else that could be useful, and headed out.

She then walked towards the landing, the night of the attack came back to her. But when she got to the top of the stairs expecting to see her father's body, nothing was there. She could smell the old blood, but the floor had been cleaned. Lara frowned, from the faint smell of the blood, several days had passed. *How long had I been in the fever?*

She ran down the stairs and paused outside her father's study. It was strange to see the door open. She bit her lip feeling she was disobeying her father's wishes in entering, but she had to. Walking in, she found things had been moved and his sword was gone. Someone had made it seem like they had left, and ensured there was no sign of what had happened. Lara didn't like this, wondering why. She turned to the bookshelves, she wanted to get some of his books. Finding the ones she wanted, she put them into the satchel. She hoped she could find out more of the effects of vampirism. It would help her to know what she would have to expect. She paused before pulling out the book on Laycain. It was her father's most treasured book, and she could not leave it. She quickly put it into the satchel too.

Moving to the desk, she found her father's purse full of coins in one of the side drawers. She took it as they were going to need currency. She then remembered his strongbox, which she found hidden in the bottom drawer, but it was locked. Lara regarded the desk, knowing he kept the key close. She checked all the drawers, two were locked, and the others held inks and paper. One drawer seemed looser than the others, she pulled it further out and found the key hidden at the back. Quickly opening the strongbox, she found another purse full to the brim. She placed both in the satchel, which was now full. At least they could pay for inns and food. Lara took a breath; she had no idea where to go, but it had to be away from Lake Wood. There was a map in the library on the wall and she quickly ran in there. Pulling it from the wall, she rolled it up. It may prove useful.

As she ran to the kitchen, she saw the riding cloaks and quickly grabbed a couple. Entering the kitchen, she found a couple of saddlebags off to the side. She grabbed all the staples she could carry, knowing that at least Derwyn would need the food, then she paused to examine what she had. *Would I be able to eat any of it or would I have to keep to fresh kills?* She took a deep breath, she had so many questions, but first, she needed to make sure she got everything. She paused, remembering sleeping blankets and bedrolls and found them in the chest near the door, along with sword oil and leather. All of these would be useful as they wouldn't be sleeping in inns every night and the oil would maintain the sword if she needed it. Knowing there was nothing else she needed from the house, she then walked briskly to the stables, ladened down with all the supplies.

All the horses were still there, which surprised Lara after seeing things missing from the house. She quickly found hers and Derwyn's saddles and prepared her horse and his pony. Lara fastened the sleeping blankets and bedrolls to the saddles, then secured the saddlebags on Derwyn's pony. She looked around the stables, thinking of anything else they may need to take. She paused when she picked up Jermer's scent. He was downwind, and he caught her off guard.

"Lara!"

She was tempted to just climb on her horse and gallop out, but she needed answers. She glared up at him. "What are you doing here?"

He held his hands up slightly, his brown eyes full of sadness. "I'm not here to hurt you, I was just hoping you were alright."

Lara nodded. Feeling tense, she studied him in his black shirt and trousers. There were no weapons in sight. "You aren't taking Derwyn!"

He shook his head. "Nay. We thought it was best for him to stay with us. But when you had gone, we realised that we should have discussed things with you more."

Hoping she gave the impression of being in control, Lara responded, "He's better off with me."

Jermer said, "We know. It's just you're different now. We wanted to make sure you were both safe."

"Derwyn *will* be safe with me." She pointed towards the house. "Did you take the items from in there?"

He nodded, "Aye, but it's not what you think. It was to make sure you were safe."

Lara frowned. "Safe?"

"We thought it was best to hide what happened. We thought if people found out, they would hunt you down, Lara. This way it looks like you have all left. I'm going to say your papa went north to see the pack up there."

"There's a pack to the north?"

"Aye. Your papa knew the alpha. They may be able to help you."

Lara studied him, fear in her stomach, but she needed to know. "I need to ask, what did Alana give me?"

"A potion. She said that it would stop the vampire side from taking hold."

Lara's eyes filled with tears, her emotions getting the better of her again. "What am I?"

He glanced away from her accusing eyes. "Alana thinks you're both."

"*Both*?" Lara's hand went to her mouth trying to stop the sobs, which threatened to escape. Tears slowly rolled down her cheeks.

Jermer gazed at her softly, his body language showing how he was forcing himself not to hug her. "Aye, but your wolf side is the most dominant. Usually, lycans would die from a vampire bite or the process of being turned, but with her potion she had managed to make both sides combine. It has made you unique. But you must still be careful. She doesn't know what will happen now. You may live years or ...." He glanced down.

"Or?"

He shrugged, looking back up, his slim face full of guilt. "She doesn't know. You may have months, years or centuries."

"*Centuries!*" Another sob broke free.

Jermer's hand reached out and touched her arm gently. "You died that night, Lara. When a human is turned, they become immortal like a vampire. But with you, she doesn't know."

Lara glared at him, wiping away her tears angrily, she could not take it all in. *Could I be immortal? What would happen to Derwyn?* She bit her lip; it was even more important she found a pack or lycan family.

Taking a deep breath to regain control of her emotions, she stated clearly to Jermer,. "I am taking Derwyn to the pack up north. Thank Alana, but you will never see us again."

Looking sad, he said as she mounted her horse, "Be careful Lara." He passed her a leather-bound book. "This was your papa's. It will tell you where the pack is. I took it when I came to clean the house and I was going to give it to you when the fever broke."

She nodded, taking the book. She recognised it as the one her father was always writing in, and placed it in the satchel. "Thank you."

Jermer added, "I also buried your papa. Up in the woods next to your mama."

She smiled at Jermer, realising they were not the enemy. "Thank you, that means a lot."

Jermer smiled sadly. "He was a good friend and a kind man. He would be proud of you."

She focused on his slender features. "Goodbye."

Holding the reins of Derwyn's pony, she trotted out of the stables heading for the den. She glanced back at Jermer, as he watched her go. She turned her attention ahead, she needed to think of a plan and hoped that the pack was willing to take Derwyn and herself. She would have a read through of the book and hope it gave her all the information she needed. Everything Jermer had told her; how she may be the first of a new type of creature, was still sinking in and she needed time to process it all. But she would keep her secret and her fears from Derwyn. What he needed was stability, and to know he was safe. That was what Lara was going to ensure he got.

CHAPTER 13

L ARA rode back up the hillside towards the forest, the mid-
morning sun warmed her back. Entering the trees, she
stopped at the hut, fastening the horses outside. She
looked back at her home, seeing it through the foliage of the
trees with her improved sight. It seemed Jermer and Alana were
only helping, and what she had heard had been out of context.
Yet it was still in her and Derwyn's best interest to head for the
pack in the north. The two meant well, but a pack would give
them what they needed, especially Derwyn. When she went
inside the hut, with the bags, she found that Derwyn had
managed to gut and cook two more rabbits from their father's
snares.

Lara smiled proudly; he smiled back, glancing at the bags as
she put them down. "Did you get everything we need?"

Lara said, "Aye. I have food, money, some clothes for you and
some books of papas, so I can find where the other packs and
lycan families are. I took the map from the library too to help
us."

He gazed up at her eagerly. "There are other packs and
families like us? Where are they?"

Lara sat on the floor beside him, crossing her legs. "There's
one north of here. We'll stay here, but on the morrow we need
to set out and find them. I'm going to read papa's books to find

out where they are. It will be a few days' travel, so we need to make sure we have all that we need."

The ten-year-old responded, "I'll find the ropes papa used for the snares. I know he kept them here."

Lara nodded, knowing they would be helpful, but if needed she would be able to hunt for them both.

They stayed at the hut while Lara sorted her father's books. The leather-bound one that Jermer had given her was incredibly old, which drew her curiosity. She would see her father writing in it whenever she was summoned to his study. She wondered if it mentioned anything about why her mother had a silver sword and if there was information about other packs and families too.

She considered the leather cover; there was a crest on the front. Lara recalled seeing it for the first time as a child on the lid of her father's chest of belongings in his bed-chamber. She smiled, at the recollection of him telling her it was the Tarrenfall family crest of his ancestors. She closed her eyes in remembrance, tracing her fingers over it.

She focused on the book again and opened it. The first page in the book had different handwriting, and the ink had browned with age. The book had been around for generations, giving details of alphas and packs from all over the land. The very early entries were locations and the names of those that had joined the Tarrenfall pack through marriage, as well as the main family lines from the other packs. Lara recalled that her father had once told her they had been part of a northern pack. She skimmed over the next few pages; more information had been added giving almost a full history.

For hundreds of years there had originally been three large packs in the northern territory. The one that her family had been a part of, and had been very influential in, had split over two hundred and seventy years before. The Tarrenfalls, along with some other families, had headed south. The group had spread over the southern part of Moonstar, believing it was better to be smaller family units than one large pack. From what Lara could tell, her mother's family, Greenforge, and the Tarrenfalls had moved to a village called Stoney Hill. Then there had been a feud between the two packs, and both insisted one should leave and cut all ties.

When they had separated, her father's family had set up their home in Lake Wood. The journal reported that they had been left to live their lives, keeping to their traditional roles as protectors. Lara frowned. *Protectors of what?*

Further on in the book, the writing changed to that of her father's. No other mention about the rest of the pack, apart from him meeting her mother. She pursed her lips noticing some pages had been ripped out, before and after the documentation of her's and Derwyn's births. Lara was curious as to why. There was no mention of her mother's riding accident either. She wondered if that had been on the pages that had been removed.

In another entry, Samuel reported contacting the northern pack and the main family, the Stonelances, who lived near Crowling. He had wanted to resolve the almost three hundred years old conflict and bring the packs together. She paused after reading that it had been her grandfather's dying wish. That was why the book had been left with her father; it had been her great-grandfather who wrote the earlier entries. From what her father had written, her grandfather had wanted the rift to end and Samuel had contacted the Stonelances soon after Derwyn's birth, yet nothing else was mentioned after that. Then more pages had been removed.

Her eyes widened and she reread the next entry. There were negotiations for her to marry! To help bring peace to the families, her father and the northern alpha had agreed for her to marry the alpha's son. Lara sighed. *Was that why he was so disapproving of me being friendly with the boys in the village?* She doubted that agreement would stand now. *Would they want to marry an immortal lycan, if that's what I've become?* She sighed. She really did not care. What mattered was Derwyn, if they wanted nothing to do with her, so be it. They just needed to want to help Derwyn when the time came.

She skimmed the book again, trying to find more about the southern pack that her family was part of, but there was little information, only that they had scattered. There was no other mention of the Greenforges, nothing that confirmed they were still at Stoney Hill. Her only choice was to head north and find the Stonelances. Since Samuel made recent connections with the northern pack in Crowling, at least Lara knew they would be there.

She unrolled the map from the library but found the map had little detail and only showed the larger cities including Adnama, Naverac and Kerlish to the north, and the capital, Great Oak, and the city of Bay Light to the south. Many lines were drawn between the cities which had to be main routes, but nothing more. Lake Wood was only marked because her father had added it some years ago when she had asked where they were on the map. But there was no indication of Crowling. She had seen this map so many times and should have realised the lack of information on it, yet it could be useful and she could add more information to it.

Lara studied her brother, and wondered if she could leave him with another family or pack. She already knew he would not want to stay without her. She sighed, thinking of her conversation with Jermer and how she felt inside. But till she knew what she was able to do and could control it, she worried if he would be safe with her. Lara had no idea what to do and wished her father was around to help her. She had promised that she would always look after Derwyn, passing him over to a pack or another lycan family was breaking that promise.

She pursed her lips, closing the book. They would find the Stonelances, from her father's notes they were located near Crowling. She would see what they were like, and then she would decide. Lara hoped that when they got there, the pack would accept them both with open arms. Yet if that was not the case, then she would have to think of something else. Derwyn would not have his first transformation for another eight years, maybe then would be the time to think about a pack. *But would I be alive that long?*

Lara sighed, placing her head in her hands, trying not to cry again, especially in front of Derwyn. She was going to have a long life, maybe not centuries but longer than the average lycan. Since the fever broke, she had never felt so powerful and felt positive about that. It was just everything else; the future weighed on her shoulders, and hers alone. A big responsibility, but her father had brought her up to think wisely. Even though a lot had happened over the last few days, which she was still processing, she was strong enough to make the right choices. There had to be positives in finding the Stonelances, as her father was hoping to get her to marry one. It could be worth finding them.

Lara glanced across at Derwyn, who was reading the book on Laycain. There was another issue; she had only ever travelled out of Lake Wood once. It had been the year before, she was with her father and she had not been paying that much attention then. She was too busy talking to her father about things that now seemed so trivial.

She rubbed her chin. *Could we find Crowling on our own? It was north, but where exactly?*

The map from the library, rolled out on the floor before her, was useless. Lara had good tracking skills. Her father had taught both her and Derwyn from an early age how to use nature to find where they were and to know the lay of the land. From talking to market traders, they had told her many times what towns and villages were north of Lake Wood and Crowling was mentioned; but a good twelve-day ride, at least. They just had to be careful, and at least try to find the northern pack. Of course, the main routes were well used, and if nothing else she could always ask about Crowling, as there were other villages and inns along the way. She should not go too wrong by keeping to the main routes.

By mid-afternoon, Lara wanted to see her parents' graves and Derwyn would need to also say his goodbyes. She needed him to understand that they would possibly not return for a long time, and it was best to see them before they left. Leaving the hut, they walked up further into the forest and made their way through the trees to a small clearing. Off to one side was a large oak tree, and before it was two mounds of earth, one fresh. They both stood next to the tree, studying the graves in silence. Lara held Derwyn's hand while they both thought of their parents, tears rolling down their cheeks. She whispered a silent prayer to Laycain and her parents, hoping for courage for what lay ahead.

Derwyn wiped his eyes and peered up at his sister. "I don't remember mama."

Lara smiled, wiping her own eyes, kneeling beside him. She had only been eleven when their mother had died and found it hard to remember at times, too. She gave her brother a loving kiss and said, "She was very kind and beautiful. She would have been very proud of you."

His bottom lip quivered. She pulled her brother close and whispered, "You will need to be very brave now, as we are going to have to travel further than either of us have done before."

He looked at her with tear-ridden eyes. "Will the pack be nice?"

Lara smiled, hoping they were. "Of course they will be." She studied his hazel eyes, wiping away the tears from his cheeks. "But whatever happens we will be together, and I will keep you safe. I made a promise to papa to always take care of you."

He nodded; his features less sad. "What do you think we will see when we travel north?"

Lara smiled, seeing the determination in her brother's eyes. "We will meet a lot of people. But remember, they must not know what I am or what our family is. Not everyone will be like the people you know here, and some people don't like lycans."

"I know Lara. Papa told me never to say."

"Good." Lara smiled, ruffling his black hair. "Let's get some dinner, then sleep and we will set off at dawn. Remember, we may not find shelter every night when we sleep, but when we can, I will make sure we get a room at an inn."

He nodded. Lara glanced back at the graves, wondering if she would ever see them or their home again. She slowly regarded the woods with tear-filled eyes. She glanced up at the sky through the leaves, clouds billowed overhead, it looked like a storm was brewing. As they left the clearing, she gazed across, making out the village in the distance through the trees. It was all she had ever known. Lara took a deep breath and wiped the tears rolling down her cheeks and headed back to the hut. She felt scared, but also invigorated. It was both, a new beginning and an adventure. She had no idea what they would see or what the Stonelances would be like, yet Lara knew their future would be positive.

CHAPTER 14

A S predicted by the clouds rolling in, a storm developed
overnight, yet they were warm and dry in the hut. Derwyn
slept soundly, but Lara was disturbed by vivid dreams,
the storm reminding her of the night her father died. She woke
with a start in the dark hut, stifling a cry. She placed her hands
over her mouth trying to muffle the uncontrollable sobbing
caused by the dream, and everything else that happened over
the last few days. The last thing she needed was to wake
Derwyn and for him to see the one person he was relying on,
broken. Getting to her feet she quietly left the hut, instantly
becoming wet from the rain of the thunderstorm. Lara ran up
to the clearing where her parents were buried, tears rolling
down her cheeks.

She stopped by the graves, taking a deep breath to stop the
sobs and control her emotions. She dropped to her knees
studying the two graves. "I don't know if I can do this, papa."

She focused on the freshly turned earth of her father's grave,
hoping for an answer that would never come. She angrily wiped
her eyes and took a breath and spoke to herself, "I can do this.
I *have* to." She gazed at the storm-filled sky. "Give me strength,
Laycain, to get through this, and keep my brother safe."

Lightning flashed, and Lara closed her eyes for a moment
getting a hold of her emotions. The rain ran down her face,
hiding the tears. Her parents had brought her up to be strong

and she needed to be even more so now. She kissed her fingers then placed them on her mother's grave and did the same for her father's. Slowly standing, soaked from the rain, Lara took a deep breath, a sense of strength flowing over her. She could do this and would protect Derwyn till her dying breath.

By the early hours, the storm had eased and by dawn, it had gone. A mist rolled over the hills, making it seem so peaceful again. Lara woke early, her clothes still damp, except her shirt as she had changed it for one of her fathers, that hung near the fire to dry. Her doubts and nightmares were almost forgotten. Leaving the hut quietly, she went to check the horses and make sure the sleeping blankets and bedrolls were secured to the saddles. As she came back in to sort out the rest of their supplies, Derwyn woke up. Not long after that, they had left the small hunting hut behind.

The sun rose higher in the sky and burned the mist away. They rode northward across the hills, Lara had hoped it would be the quickest way to the main route out of Lake Wood. As they rode, she glanced back, making out their home in the distance and wondered if they would ever see it again. She turned to Derwyn, he would feel bereft more than she, and she would try and keep his spirits high. When they reached the main route, which snaked around Lake Forest, it was muddy from the storm. It would slow them a little, yet she was hoping if they kept a good pace, they could still reach Little Stump to the north-east within about four or five days. She had heard it had an inn but before that, they would have to sleep in the open. They would not want any storms like the night before, but she could ensure they camped off the route, with as much shelter as they could. That would, hopefully protect them, not only from the weather, but from no one finding them as well. It was the best way to keep Derwyn as safe as possible.

They made a good pace on the first day, the weather remaining dry and pleasant. As dusk fell, Lara and Derwyn left the main route and camped on the fringes of the large woods, called Fern Wood. It had other names that Lara did not want to think of, but if they kept to the outer edge of it, they would be safe. She picked a spot that, with the help of the large fern trees, would shelter them if the weather turned. It also gave them some privacy from passers-by. Once the camp had been set up, both settled down with something to eat. Yet when Lara tried to eat the food, she found it tasteless. Her mouth went dry and she was unable to swallow it, the thought making her gag. She watched Derwyn, as she spat the food out into her hand, as discreetly as she could. He was eating with no issues and seemed to be enjoying it, so it could not be anything to do with the food. Right then she realised that was the first time she had tried to eat anything other than a fresh kill since she woke from the fever.

Am I now unable to eat normal food?

The thought of it turned her stomach, but she seemed to have no issue drinking water. The more she thought about it, Lara did not feel hungry. She had passed her brother food earlier in the day as they rode, but she did not take any, only water. She had only been eating something because her brother was. She took no more of the food, knowing it was better to leave it all for Derwyn as he would need it. But she would ensure there are no issues with the fact she was not eating; and if he asked, she would just smile and say she would later. She did not want to make it even more evident that she was no longer a normal human and scare him.

Lara leant back against her saddle and focused on the trees above them. She wondered when the best time would be to go and hunt, but decided since she did not feel the need, to wait at least another day. She pursed her lips, hoping that a fresh kill would ensure her vampire side was kept at bay, which seemed satisfied too, and the raw meat she had at the hut did seem to do something. Lara took a deep breath. She would need to see how long she could go without hunting, and as they were nowhere near anyone else, it would be a good time to see how long she could last. She also realised, when they did reach a village or town, it would be harder for her to hunt. The more she got used to keeping the cravings under control, the less likely she would be to weaken with people around her. She glanced at Derwyn; it was a risk with it just being her and her brother, but she had to know her limitations. At least out on the road, if she lost her restraint, she would be able to find a wild animal quickly.

After four days, they reached the small hamlet of Little Stump. There were a few cottages, a farm, a blacksmith, and an inn, the only one for miles. It was situated in the centre of the hamlet, with a large stable next to it. They stopped outside the long, stone building, the inn's sign had faded over the years, and it was hard to even tell what its name was. As they climbed down from their mounts, a young lad in a well-worn shirt and trousers, ran out nodding his head to them both. "Are ya goin' for board?"

Lara answered, "Aye."

His toothy grin grew wider. "Then I can stable ya horses for ya. Let me par know when ya go in."

She agreed and they removed their belongings before the lad led the horse and pony into the stable. She turned her attention to the stone-built inn, looking forward to a night in, the warm and dry. She glanced down at Derwyn knowing her brother needed it more than she did. The weather had been mostly good on the journey, but on two of the mornings, they had woken to a fine drizzle that had made the ride not as comfortable, and their clothes still felt slightly damp because of it.

When they entered, Lara's senses were bombarded by the many scents from the occupants, as well as the food, and the smell of wood burning in the fire. There was a strong buzz of conversations, which reduced slightly when they entered, clattering from the kitchen, and the general sounds of a busy inn. Lara forced herself to focus, realising it was the first time she had been round a group of people since the attack, she needed to stay in control. She had managed to do it when she first got her lycan senses, and knew she could do it again with the more heightened ones. She just needed to practice. As they travelled, she learnt that if she hunted about every third night she would have very few cravings. Even though she felt that she could have lasted longer, she did not want to take the risk with them reaching their first busy inn.

Lara walked over to the main counter, holding Derwyn's hand.

The overweight innkeeper studied them both with a sour look. "Can I help ya?"

Lara smiled, trying to not let his unwelcome spirit put her off. "We were after board for the night. Your lad has taken our horses into the stables."

He nodded, studying her for a second with his grey eyes, then peered down at Derwyn making the boy nervous. "Ya can, but the boy will 'ave to share ya bed."

Lara replied, "My brother would want to be with me, anyway, thank you."

The man regarded them both, still looking sour, and Lara realised it was just his natural expression. He peered under the counter then passed her a brass key. "Ya 'ave the Stone Room. Get a table over there and me wife'll bring ya and the lad the dish of the day, which is stew and ale."

Lara turned, seeing the one remaining table in the corner that he had pointed to. A few of the occupants were watching them, but soon turned back to their conversations when Lara and Derwyn just went and sat down quietly. She got Derwyn to sit down on the bench by the window, then made him shuffle over so she could sit next to him. Seated that way, they would not have their backs to the dining area, something her father had always told her was wise to do. She slowly and secretly observed the room, picking up everyone's scents and, as she had with the rabbit, seeing their blood flowing through their bodies. She had learnt over the last few days that if she relaxed, she could see them normally once more. She hoped with more practice it would become more natural, but for the time being, she had to force herself to stop seeing *everything*.

She felt like she was constantly in a hunting state. That could be why vampires were always on the move and wanted to hunt. Yet as a wolf, that was controllable and she only felt the urge to hunt when it needed to feed. Maybe that was how she was able to control the vampire side, her wolf self was able to keep it in check. Her father had shown her after her nineteenth winter, how, if she focused, she could almost communicate with her wolf. It was not the same as in her dreams before her first transformation. The link between her and her wolf were more like emotions. Over the last few days, with everything that had happened to her, Lara could only sense faint feelings, yet it did feel her wolf was in control. Another thing Lara would have to get used to was being amongst people; as the more they travelled, the more people they would meet, especially when they reached a big town or a city. Lara would have to try and meditate, and hope her wolf was in control as much as she felt it was.

A short, well-endowed, red-headed woman with a kind face walked towards their table with a tray laden with food and drinks. She smiled warmly at the two as she placed two bowls of stew and two pot beakers of ale down.

She said, "'Ere ya go me lovelies, some fine stew and mild ale." She paused before taking the rest of the contents to the other tables that were waiting. She leant forward. "It's not safe for a lass like ya and a young'un to be out on these roads."

Lara smiled, seeing the genuine concern in her features. "We'll be alright."

She focused on the sword Lara had removed from her back and leaned against the bench they were sitting on. "Hope ya can use that dear." Lara nodded, and the woman added, "Just watch out, there can be some unsavoury characters about."

Lara replied, "We'll be extra careful. Thank you."

Someone on the other side of the inn shouted for their stew and the woman smiled at Lara and then hastily left to serve the food. Lara turned to her brother to see him already eating his stew and enjoying every mouthful of a well-cooked meal. Lara pretended to have a bit of hers, noticing that the smell did not even make her feel hungry. She took a sip of the ale which, to her surprise, she enjoyed. She surveyed the inn again, everyone was busy with their own business. She turned back to the stew to see Derwyn had just about finished his. She slid her bowl over to him. "You can have mine too."

He scrutinised her. "Are you sure?"

"You need it more than me, squirt." He smiled and dived in.

She leant back and turned her attention to the conversations in the inn, most of them were about the price of leather, the ridiculous taxes or bedding a fine woman. It seemed no one was interested in a young boy and girl on their own in the inn. There also seemed to be no mention of troubles on the route. She wondered if the woman had been trying to scare them, but from the woman's features, she was just concerned and there was no ill intent in the warning.

Lara's senses prickled when she smelt wolf. She focused on the door as two entered, a tall well-built man with a sword strapped to his back and a teenage boy, also with a sword on his back. Their riding clothes were covered in dust from a long day's ride. They had similar features, their dark hair cut short, and more than likely, were father and son. As she took in the scent, she realised it was just a wolf and these two were human. They probably had a wolf trained to help in their hunting or from what her father had told her - as these seemed to be Swords - that Swords for hire used wolves to track their bounties. She took a sip of her drink watching them without being obvious. There was suddenly tension in the room and Lara could tell some of the occupants were not happy to see them. She heard the man asking for a room for the night and food. Lara focused on a couple of men at the back of the inn, who had become extremely tense. They seemed to have something to hide and after a few moments left the inn, not wanting any trouble.

She looked back toward the innkeeper to see the teenagers' blue eyes focused on her. He smiled, his handsome features glowing. Lara instantly flushed and glanced down at her ale; she had never been able to react well when a boy flirted with her. When she looked back a second later, the lad was still eyeing her and smiling. Then she saw the man glaring between his son and her and she instantly felt uncomfortable. His scarred features looked mean. The man suddenly clipped the lad on the ear, snapping him out of his trance. The boy turned to him, a flash of fear in his eyes, as the man whispered, "Keep focused, lad!"

Lara could not help but smile when he sheepishly turned away and followed his father to a table on the other side of the inn. Hearing Derwyn yawn was the perfect time to escape to their room.

While Derwyn slept soundly from a full belly in the large bed in the small, yet clean, inn room, Lara sat by the window using the moonlight to read. She had found more information about the Stonclances. Her father had visited them and it seemed they were in Crowling, not near it as stated in an earlier entry. Her father had been talking about the arrangement of the marriage and keeping their towns and villages protected. Lara paused; that was the second time 'protecting the village' had been mentioned in the entire book. She read the entry again, and wondered if her father protected Lake Wood and if that was why her mother had a silver sword. From what she was reading, that was what lycan packs and families did, and the reason why her father was in discussions with them. Yet there was still too little detail.

Lara was even more intrigued about meeting the family. But she would need directions. She had heard of Crowling, but was not sure if it was north-east or north-west of Little Stump. And with the woman warning her to be careful on the road, it would be wise to make sure they were heading in the right direction. Glancing at her brother, she decided she would be able to leave him alone for a little while, and quietly left the room heading down to the bar area.

The sour-looking innkeeper studied her. "And what would a young lass like ya, be wanting to go to Crowling?"

Lara regarded him, the inn was just about empty, and the occupants had gone home or had taken board at the inn. There was just a couple in the corner, lost in each other, and a very drunk old man sitting by the fire, hunched over his tankard of ale.

She told him. "It's a family matter. Can you tell me the quickest route?"

The innkeeper answered, "Aye. Head north-west from 'ere, keep straight. Ya will get there in 'bout three days, or ya can take the well-trodden routes to Hangman's Cross but add on another fifteen for that way. Most traders will go the long way, as they can pick up customers at the inns and villages, but just interested in Crowling, most head across the country. The route is clear, just not well-ridden. Can be a bit open in parts so make sure ya have good cloaks and blankets."

Lara responded, "Thank you for your help."

"Ya welcome." He placed a concerned hand on her arm and studied her. "Just be careful. A young lass like ya with only a small boy for company can be easy pickin's. If ya wait a few days, ya may be able to ride with a trader."

Lara smiled, the last thing she needed was to ride with strangers. He meant well, but Lara would be unable to hunt. "Don't worry we'll be alright."

He replied, his features stern. "Well, just be careful. I don't want to 'ear about ya falling by the wayside from a passing customer." Lara nodded, realising that even with his sour look, he was a kind man.

She headed back up to the room, still wondering about the fact her father may have been the protector of Lake Wood. She wanted to read more of the journal, but also, they would have an early start and she could read more that evening when they made camp. But in all of it, she was seeing her parents in a new light and wondered why they never told them.

Lara had a restless night, the dreams had returned. Luckily, Derwyn was a heavy sleeper, so when she was unable to sleep, she sat at the window studying the clear night sky, tears rolling down her cheeks. She had not had a dream like that since leaving Lake Wood and knew it was from reading the book and wondering what her father had hidden from them. *Had that been the reason why the vampires were there that night, or was it just fate?* It was something she would never really know. She sighed and wondered why her father never told her. Then again, he had never been the same after her mother's death, the light had faded in his eyes. He was still a loving father, but something had always been missing. She would catch her father brooding sometimes when he thought he was alone. Lara wondered if she should have asked Jermer, but she had not known anything till she had started reading the book, and why were there pages torn out. Lara sighed again and glanced back at her sleeping brother; he was her main concern. What was in the past was gone, and there was nothing she could do. She turned back to the window and closed her eyes for a moment, focusing on her wolf side, feeling her warmth in her heart. Lara smiled softly, glad to feel her wolf there giving her comfort. Wiping the tears from her cheeks she returned to the bed and tried to get some sleep.

CHAPTER 15

LARA woke early, rolling over, she found Derwyn was still sleeping. She did not want to wake him, as the next few days would not be as nice as sleeping in a good bed. Getting her boots on quietly, having slept in her clothes, she left the room and walked through the deserted inn. She went to the stables to get the horse and pony ready so they could set off quickly. As she went to enter the stables, she could smell wolf and knew one was close by. She paused, observing the stables, none of the five horses seemed unsettled. Then she saw a lone wolf curled up sleeping, near two black horses at the back, near the stall where her horse was situated. She carefully entered, yet the further she went in, its ears pricked up, waking. It sniffed the air and started watching her. As she got closer, it began to growl, getting up slowly, making itself as big as possible. Lara stood still; slowly, her features became more wolf-like and she growled back, exposing her wolf fangs. The other wolf froze, it sniffed the air and considered her for a moment, then slowly became submissive, as she focused on it. Her features returned to normal as she strolled over. Lara knelt beside the grey and white wolf, combing her fingers into its soft fur. The wolf focused on her and licked her hand. She continued to fuss over the animal as it relaxed more in her presence.

"So, a kindred spirit."

Lara froze, the wolf looked up, glanced at her, and then trotted towards the voice. She stood and turned to see the teenage lad from the night before. His young features were even more striking in the morning sun. The wolf was sniffing his hand and then moved to stand by his side.

She smiled. "He's a fine animal."

The lad glanced down at the wolf, then grinning at her, showing perfect teeth. "My pa trained him from a pup. Not many people can get that close to him. It has only been myself and my papa."

She smiled and shrugged, trying to appear relaxed and not show how tense she felt. "What can I say? He must like me."

He studied her intently, like he had the night before but also regarding her with a little suspicion. "Hmm, could be."

Lara walked towards the entrance, knowing this was attention she did not need. "Well, I better go and pay the innkeeper for my stay. Good journey."

The lad watched her leave, and when Lara glanced back, he gave her a big smile, making his features glow. She smiled back. He was a nice-looking lad, if a little young, and she could see him becoming a very handsome man. She had to admit, it did feel nice to see him smile. Yet what concerned her was that he might tell his father about her, as he did not seem to be a man to cross paths with. Her instincts were telling her that if he did tell his father, they may then follow her and Derwyn, and that was the last thing they needed. When she entered the inn, much to her relief, no one was about so she quickly walked to her room, deciding to wait a little while before they set off for Crowling. She did not want to have to explain herself to the lad's father, and hoped by the time they did come down, the two would have gone.

Carn had woken with a thud, opening his eyes to find himself on the wooden floor of their room. He looked up groggily to hear his father grumble. "Get up lad! Those horses won't saddle themselves."

He slowly sat up on the floor, glancing up at the bed and rubbing his side. Carn cursed in his head knowing it was not wise to let his father hear him sounding disgruntled. As he got to his feet, pulling his trousers up, he had been surprised his father had let him share the bed. Then again, his good moods never lasted long. Carn slowly walked over to grab his shirt and boots, his father made a rasping cough then snorted. "Don't dilly dally lad!" He paused then added, "And I won't hear any more moaning about wanting to join that guild again. I've told you; nay son of mine is joining that cult!"

He glared across at the large man's scarred back and pulled a sour face, saying under his breath. "The Guardians of the Stone are not a cult."

His father muttered, turning. "What was that lad?"

Carn quickly pulled on his white shirt. "I said I was on my way."

His father grunted. Carn fastened his shirt; he would be glad when he could go off on his own. Then he could join the guild if he wanted to, and his father could not stop him. He focused on his father's back again. At the moment he seemed more like a servant to his father than a partner. Grabbing his black boots, he pulled them on before he left the room.

Carn wandered down to the stables still half asleep, tucking his shirt into his black trousers. He left the inn feeling grumpy, his shoulder ached from the fall. *Why didn't pa just wake me, instead of kicking me out of bed?* He sighed, that was his father, mean-spirited and never in a good mood. Well unless he had had a few ales, like last night.

Carn's thoughts were broken when he saw the girl from the night before stroking his father's wolf. No one had ever got that close to it; it had taken months for it to be calm around him. Carn watched her for a few moments wondering who she was to make a wolf so calm around her.

He then stated, glad he would be able to talk to her. "So, a kindred spirit."

He saw the girl tense by the movement of the long plait of her brown hair snaking down her back. The wolf looked towards him and then trotted over after a moment's hesitation. Carn wondered if he should have said anything at all, and just hid till she had gone, but it was too late. The girl stood and turned towards him. He took a deep breath, she was so stunning, but he needed to seem like a Sword, not some teenage boy with a crush.

She smiled at him. "He's a fine animal."

Carn glanced down at the wolf, suddenly feeling nervous. He took another breath and then smiled at her. Informing her that his father had trained it from a pup, and that not many could get close to it.

The girl smiled and shrugged. "What can I say? He must like me."

Carn gazed at her, her green eyes were amazing, he could lose himself in their depths. He swallowed and thought. *Snap out of it! Why was the wolf so calm with her?* He wanted to pull his eyes away from her, but instantly fixated on her lips, making his ache. He tried to keep cool and look like a Sword, so kept his features neutral. "Hmm, it could be."

As the girl passed him leaving the stable, Carn lost focus, picking up a scent of lavender. He did not hear what the girl said before she walked towards the inn. Carn watched her leave, unable to stop gazing at her and hoping she would turn back. When she did, his heart skipped a beat and he gave her a big grin. She smiled back and Carn wanted to jump up and whoop but he had to keep his cool. She turned back and walked inside the inn. Carn's eyes lingered on the doorway for a while, long after she had gone. The wolf grunted and drew his attention back to the task at hand. Carn walked over to the horses with a little spring in his step. He may never see her again, but she smiled at him and that was worth it. He started to check on the horses and get the saddles ready, yet his mind kept wandering. He was not going to say anything to his father, he had moaned at him all night just for looking at her in the inn. He was not about to tell him he had spoken to her. His mind wandered again as he saddled the horses. He would not forget that smile for weeks.

With the horses saddled he went back inside to see his father paying the innkeeper. The large man picked up his saddlebags and cloak, Carn's were left on the floor.

His father asked, "Ready to go?"

Carn's stomach grumbled. "What about breakfast?"

"Took too long in the stables lad!" Grunted the man, as he left the inn.

Carn sighed. He glanced up when the innkeeper got his attention with a low whistle, and threw him an apple. "That will tide ya over lad. Ya can't ride on an empty stomach."

Carn smiled at the innkeeper. "Thank you."

The man winked and went back to cleaning some mugs. Carn picked up his things and bit into the apple as he went back outside. Securing his things on his saddle, he mounted his horse and followed his father onto the main route heading south. He glanced back at the inn wondering where the girl was headed but with his luck, he would never see her again.

CHAPTER 16

WHEN they came down for food as well as to pay for the room and board, the inn was almost deserted. As Derwyn ate, Lara sat beside him and studied the quiet inn. There were what looked like a couple of locals, but all the travellers from the night before had gone. As for the man or his son, she could barely pick up any scent. When they finally went to the stables, the two black horses were gone, and the faint odour of the man and his son headed towards the south. Either the teenager had said nothing, or if he did, his father was not concerned. Much to Lara's relief, they were not heading for Crowling. The chance of bumping into them again and having to explain anything was very slim. She sighed, remembering the lad's smile, and part of her would have liked to see him again as he did seem nice. She glanced at Derwyn, flirting with boys or getting their attention were the least of her concerns.

Once the horse and pony were saddled and everything secured, they rode north-west. As the innkeeper had told her the route was not well used and was very exposed with it snaking through open moorland. Lara was glad they had thick cloaks against the chilly winds, but was concerned when she could not see anywhere in the distance for shelter, and hoped to Laycain that the weather would not turn. She considered their surroundings as they rode, and Lara wondered where she would be able to hunt. She would need to before they reached Crowling, as she did not want to risk having any cravings while in a large town. She could make a kill sustain her for several days, so she would have to time it right. Knowing roughly how long the journey would take them, it would be better to wait a day or two and then try to hunt in the dead of night. The fact that she could run a lot faster, meant she would only have to leave Derwyn for a short time. With the route not being too well used, some tracks were about a day old and whenever she glanced ahead or behind, no one was in sight. The chance of meeting someone was fairly low, which gave Lara mixed feelings. It would have been good to know there were others on the route if needed, but also with no one about, meant she would be able to hunt in peace.

It took them four very long days to reach Crowling, and it had not been the most pleasant of journeys. They had been all right for the first day, but by late afternoon on the second, the wind picked up across the moorland. It had turned bitter and unforgiving. Not long after came the snow, and due to the winds, it had brought visibility down to almost nothing. Lara got Derwyn to tether his horse to hers so that he would not get lost. Because of the weather conditions, they had little choice but to slow down. They did not want to lose sight of the trail which was quickly getting lost under a light layer of snow, and soon only the stone markers were visible. By the time they needed to make camp, the snow had stopped, and the wind had slowed, but it was still bitterly cold. They had not covered the distance Lara had hoped, but they needed rest. When they set up camp, she had been unable to get any fresh wood and the few sticks she had in the saddlebags were a little damp. Yet Lara managed, with the very little tinder that was still dry, to light a fire but it was weak, making more smoke than heat and barely warmed Derwyn's hands. Lara gave him some food but she needed to hunt. After nightfall, she reluctantly left Derwyn, wrapping him in all their cloaks and blankets. On her return, they could then share body warmth as the fire was not enough against the bitterness of the night.

Lara had returned in the very early hours and snuggled up with her brother once she was dressed again. Then just an hour later, the rain came pouring down. With it coming at night, they had not been prepared and it soaked them through. Lara was unable to make a shelter so did the only thing she could think of. Stripping again, she turned back into her wolf form. Her large lycan body was able to shield Derwyn better than her human form could, and she did her best to keep him dry and warm. But at dawn, she had reluctantly turned back, putting her soaked clothes back on.

They had to continue, but the rain, and the return of the bitterly cold wind, made the journey unpleasant. Derwyn started crying and saying that he wanted to go home. Lara had tried to keep his spirits high, but she was struggling with the conditions too. That night, the rain had eased but both were wet and chilled to the bone. Derwyn had also caught a cold. Lara decided to continue riding, knowing they could not make a fire to keep warm. She hoped that if they continued, they would be able to catch up on the time they had lost the day before. When they finally reached the outskirts of Crowling, by late afternoon the following day, the rain was still coming down. Derwyn was riding with Lara on her horse, and she had fastened his pony's reins to her stirrup, so it followed with ease. Derwyn was coughing and sniffing, full of a head cold with a slight fever. Lara had pulled her cloak as far around him as she could, while trying to keep herself sheltered from the rain as well. If not for her wolf and vampire blood she would more than likely have had a fever too.

As they rode through the busy market town, the road was a mass of sticky mud, making horses, carts and any people braving the weather struggle to move. They needed somewhere to stay for a few days so Derwyn could recover while she searched for the pack. They reached the nearest inn, The Tipsy Tulip, just up from the main square. Lara climbed down, landing in a big muddy puddle. She cursed, even though her boots did not leak, she was annoyed that they were covered in mud. Lara secured the horse and pony to the hitching rail, next to the main entrance. She then helped Derwyn down, making sure he was on the boardwalk before grabbing their belongings. She glanced at Derwyn who looked so weary, his eyes and nose red from the cold. Lara hoped a good warm bed and hot food would help him fight the fever. A few days' rest would do him good and hopefully raise his spirits.

Entering the inn, the wall of warmth was welcoming to their chilled bodies. It was not too busy within, and Lara hoped there would be rooms available. Keeping a firm hold of their supplies and Derwyn's hand, Lara walked over to the main counter and spoke to the slender blonde woman in a green dress, serving ale to a customer.

"Are you the innkeeper?"

The woman turned to her and smiled warmly. "Aye, I'm Olena. How can I help you?"

"Can we have a room for several nights please?"

The woman nodded, her blue eyes focusing on Derwyn when he sneezed. "My poor lad, you don't look well."

He shook his head, his features sullen. Lara sighed. "We rode across from Little Stump and didn't have much shelter."

The blonde regarded the weather out of the inn window. "And with this rain, you poor loves will be soaked and chilled to the bone." She took a brass key from under the counter, shouting for hot water to someone in the back kitchen. "Come with me. I can help you get him settled."

Derwyn started coughing, looking very poorly. Lara moved the bags round on her shoulders and picked her brother up with ease and then followed Olena to the back of the inn and up some stairs to where the guest rooms were. The innkeeper unlocked a room and let Lara and Derwyn enter first.

"This should be perfect for you; it has its own bath too. Hot water is already on the way up."

Lara pondered the nice medium-sized room with an open fireplace, a large bed that they could share, a bath in the corner and a table with a bowl and jug under the window.

Olena followed them in and started to sort out the fire as she stated, "Once I have set this for you, I will get some herbs for the bath, and hot stew and herbal teas, which will help fight the cold." She stood up, brushing her hands together to get rid of any dust from them, as the fire took hold. "I would get the young lad sorted first to make sure he's kept nice and warm."

"Thank you."

The woman squeezed her shoulder. "Don't worry, lass, he will be fine in a few days. You're lucky you haven't caught it too."

Lara smiled, knowing she would not but said, "Well, there's time yet."

The innkeeper pulled out the bath that was stored to the side, just as one of her staff arrived with two large jugs full of hot water, and then rushed off to get more. Olena left to get what she needed, while Lara placed their bags down to one side, then got Derwyn to sit on the bed. She pulled off his boots and then waited while the bath was being prepared. Olena returned with a tray of two bowls of hot stew and two mugs of steaming herbal tea.

She placed it on the table and said, "Here, this will do you both good." She glanced at Derwyn, who sat on the bed sniffing. "Eat the stew and drink all of the tea, lad. You will soon be back to normal."

He smiled at her and took the tea that Lara passed to him. He wrapped his small hands around it and started to drink it carefully as it was so hot.

Lara turned to Olena. "Thank you. We left our horses. Well one horse, one pony, tied up outside."

The woman smiled. "I'll get my stable lad to take care of them. You both get yourselves warm and dry."

She then pulled out a small bag of herbs from her pocket in her dress and sprinkled some into the bath as the staff member poured in the hot water. Once the bath was ready, they left them in peace, Olena leaving the key on the side and closing the door behind her.

Lara turned her attention to Derwyn and took his drink from him, then helped him get all his wet clothes off before helping him into the bath. She then laid the garments by the fire to dry and placed the stew next to them to keep warm. As he sat, letting the hot water stop the chill, Lara took off most of her wet clothes and placed them to dry too. She then turned back to her brother, and scrubbed off all the dirt and grime from their journey. Making sure he got a good clean while the hot water warmed him through. Once he was clean and warmed to the bone, she helped him out, got him dry and into some almost dry clothes from the saddlebags. Once he was tucked under the covers in the bed, she passed him the rest of his warm drink and his stew. Lara took a sip of her herbal tea and then stripped getting into the bath herself. Her skin tingled; she would not need the herbs to stop a cold, but the bath was still very welcoming. She leaned back, closing her eyes for a moment, realising this was the first time she had truly relaxed in days. She glanced across at Derwyn seeing he had devoured his stew. Climbing out of the bath, she passed him hers knowing it would do him well. She left him eating while she tried to comb her hair from the scraggly mess it had become on the journey and drinking the herbal tea which warmed her through.

Realising her only set of clothes needed time to dry, she donned one of her father's shirts. Then Lara retrieved the journal before laying on the bed next to her brother, savouring the scent of her father on the one shirt that was the driest of the bunch. Derwyn had eaten both bowls of stew and was now tucked under the blankets and slowly falling to sleep. The herbs from the tea and the bath had cleared his airways so he could sleep more easily. She glanced down at him and then turned her attention to her father's book about the packs. All her father had written was that the alpha lived at a house with the name Stonehaven but had not said where in the town. She pursed her lips, she would need to ask around, even Olena might know. Lara read through the entries again trying to find more about protecting the village, but did not find anything. She wondered if there was anything back at the house that would give more information, but Lara sighed knowing that she might never get an answer. She wondered if the Stonelances would know and decided it was worth asking when she found them. Noticing Derwyn was sound asleep, Lara quietly climbed from the bed, pulled on her trousers and boots, and went to talk to Olena.

"Hmmm," Olena pursed her lips. "I think Stonehaven is the large stone-built house at the end of the main street. I think some influential family lives there." She paused for a moment. "I think they are the Stonelanes? Why do you ask?"

"Friends of my papas. Is the name Stonelance?"

Olena said, "Aye, that's it, I know they seem to like to keep their privacy. None of my business really, but just be careful lass, this town has some unfriendly folk. Not as bad as the cities though. There, I hear, they have groups of that hunt down demons."

Lara smiled, it was nice that people were concerned for her welfare, but little did they know she was more dangerous than anyone else in the town. Well, apart from the family of lycans which, like any others, kept themselves private.

She responded, "I will. Could you keep an eye on my brother in the morn while I go and see if they are there?"

Olena studied her warmly. "I can lass. You just be careful."

"Thank you, and I will."

As she headed back to the room, she wondered what the Stonelances' response would be and she hoped it would be positive. If they refused them, then she was not sure what they were going to do.

CHAPTER 17

LARA woke early, after a restless night. She had been wondering about the Stonelances and what their reaction would be when they met her. She rolled over to see Derwyn still sleeping and appearing a little better. She wanted to find the family and hopefully, later, meet them, but she needed to do it without Derwyn as he could become too overwhelmed by it all. Climbing out of bed carefully to not disturb her brother, she was relieved that her clothes had fully dried. Once dressed, and her hair tied back into a long plait, she left him a note informing him not to worry about her, and that she would ask Olena to bring him breakfast.

Heading into the main area of the inn, it was noticeably quiet, and Olena was cleaning down the tables, getting ready for her first customers of the day.

Lara went up to her and smiled. "Good morn."

Olena responded, "Good morn, how's the lad?"

"He's sleeping, and better than last night. Thank you for your help. I was hoping you could check on him, I'm leaving to find Stonehaven."

Olena placed the cloth she was using down on the table in front of her and folded her arms. "And see your papa's friends?"

Lara replied, "Aye. Could you make sure Derwyn has some breakfast."

"Don't worry, I will, and make sure he stays in the room to rest." Olena asked, "Don't you need breakfast too?"

"I will get some food while I'm out."

Olena nodded and turned back to cleaning the tables. Lara left the inn to be welcomed by a dry, sunny morning. She looked around to see if she could find the house called Stonehaven. The town was still incredibly quiet. The only activity was the market traders as they set up their stalls for the day's trade a little way up the still muddy road at a small square. Asking a couple of the stall owners, she soon found out which was the main street. It was no wider than any of the others, but was the only road that spanned the entire town, hence the name. Her wolf senses told her to head towards the northern end, so she made her way up the deserted street, inspecting the buildings as she passed.

The town was slowly coming to life as Lara walked along the main street, she looked ahead and soon saw a large grey stone-built house. It did not seem to be anything special, but that had to be the one. As she got closer, she started to pick up the scent of a lycan. She turned her attention to a fair-haired man who was walking her way, wearing a black shirt and trousers, which accentuated his muscular build, and wore highly polished boots. His scent invaded her nostrils from the light breeze that blew in her direction. Lycan.

At first, she thought he was just walking down the road then realised he was walking straight toward her, his broad features cold and stern. She saw his nostrils flare as he took in her scent when he got closer.

He stopped in front of her and said, "We don't want your kind here, whatever you are."

Lara glared at him, disliking him instantly. Wondering how she knew she was a stranger to the town, but then remembered, like her father would have, the alpha was probably aware of her arrival last night.

"I'm here to talk to someone from the Stonelance family."

He glared at her with disdain. "What are you?"

Lara glanced around, the street getting busier, and luckily there seemed to be little interest in their exchange. Her scent would be different, but the last thing she or he needed was to make a scene here. "Are we going to discuss this here, in the street?"

He took a firm hold of her arm with his rough, large hand, turning towards the house. "Then let's talk in private." He leant towards her. "But if you do anything, I'll kill you."

Lara glared back, pulling her arm free and stopped. "I am here to talk, nothing more, but I will defend myself if need be."

He studied her, then gestured to her towards the house and they walked side by side. As they got closer, she could pick up at least three other lycan scents. But she was not going to let any of them, especially the alpha, intimidate her. Her wolf senses grew uneasy, telling her that the meeting might not end well. She just hoped she would be able to leave without causing an issue.

Reaching the house, the alpha entered first, as Lara followed him, two men, one a lot younger than the other, and a woman came out into the large front room. The older man had similar features to the alpha, so Lara hoped these were the Stonelances. All were glaring at her, the tension in the air was almost suffocating. She focused on the one about her age with similar features to the woman yet, he also closely resembled the alpha, he had to be their son. The alpha led the way, keeping his family in check. Lara stared them all in the eye, never lowering her gaze. She was making sure they knew she would not submit to any of them as she followed the alpha into a spacious study.

The room had a large desk near a fireplace, and three of the walls were covered with bookshelves, packed with old books. She felt a twinge of sadness as it reminded her of her father's. The alpha stood at his desk, arms folded and eyeing her with suspicion, his grey eyes cold.

"So, what are you?" He sniffed the air. "I smell lycan but also death."

Lara inquired, ignoring his statement, "I am presuming you are the alpha to the Stonelance family?"

"I am Handrel Stonelance." Then sneered. "What are you?"

Lara's distaste for the man was growing by the moment. "That's a nice way to talk to someone who was supposed to be marrying your son."

Handrel frowned. "What?"

Lara folded her arms and said, "My papa was Samuel Tarrenfall of Lake Wood."

He pursed his lips. "So, you're Lara?"

She answered, "Aye."

"But your scent isn't right for a lycan, it's off. There is a faint aroma of . . ."

"Lavender," Lara said.

He frowned. "But that's impossible."

She smiled without any emotion, trying to appear in control, knowing he was the first person she would be telling her secret to. "Well, maybe. But I survived."

Handrel studied her intently, leaning against his desk. "If you think I will honour your papa's agreement now, I'm sorry but nay. We are a pure line of lycans, something like you will not be welcome. Your papa, coming from the Tarrenfall line, would know that."

Lara glared at him, knowing how far back her father's family line went. But only herself and Derwyn remained. "Well, he's dead. I only found out about the agreement with you a few days ago."

His voice and features softened. "I am sorry about your papa; he was a fine man."

She nodded to him and unfolded her arms. "I'm not here about the arrangement my papa and you were making."

Handrel raised an eyebrow, studying her. "If that is the case, why are you here?"

Lara responded, "You are the closest lycan family that I know of, and from what my papa's notes say, once we were one pack. My brother Derwyn is still alive, and I was hoping when he gets to age, you could help him know what he will become and help him through his transition."

Handrel took a seat opposite her at his desk and gestured for her to sit. Lara slowly sat as he did. He rubbed his chin studying her. "I see. You have nay contact with the southern families or packs?"

Lara shook her head. He pursed his lips, studying her, his features cold again. "We can take your brother. I will raise him like a son, but he will have nay rights to become an alpha. Then once of age, I will assign him to one of the larger packs in the northern cities. He will also have nay contact with something that is nay longer a pure lycan."

"*Really?*" Lara spat, feeling his hostility at what she was. "I vowed to protect him. I will not agree to leave him while he's so young and to sever all ties."

"Then we cannot help you. He either becomes one of our pack members fully, or there is nay way we can help you."

Lara pursed her lips, slowly standing. "I see."

The man added, placing his hands on the desk. "And whatever the outcome, I want you to leave Crowling by the morn."

She raised an eyebrow. "I see. For a family my papa thought could be allies, you are not what I thought."

He glared down at her as he stood. "*Things* like you die within hours for a reason."

Lara snarled, exposing her wolf fangs. "Glad to disappoint."

Handrel tensed, then scrutinised her as she turned her teeth back to normal. "Nay lycan can part change like that."

Lara responded, "Well, I'm nay ordinary lycan." She headed for the door, glancing back at him. "Don't worry we will be gone by the morrow, and I hope never to cross your path again."

The family members outside tensed as soon as she opened the door and left the study, she glared at them in turn. The woman went to move towards her. Lara let her claws slowly grow, ready to defend herself.

Then the alpha snapped from behind her, "Nay, she's leaving."

They all stepped back, Handel's son said, sniffing her scent, his grey eyes as cold as his father's. "Good riddance."

She glared back at him, her eyes turning red, her anger fuelling the vampire side. Her claws fully formed now. "Good thing I don't have to join a family like this or have to marry you."

The alpha's son frowned but before he could say anything more, the alpha stated firmly, "Nay pack will have you, Lara and all will say the same about having your brother. You should reconsider my offer, as it might be the only one you will get."

Lara reached the door, her eyes slowly turned back to normal and her claws receded, as she regained control. She stopped turning to face him. "*Never.*"

She turned on her heel and left the house, hearing the eldest male lycan say. "What an abomination. *It* should be destroyed."

Tears welled in her eyes, never feeling so unwelcomed before in her life. She kept walking, knowing she could not get angry, it would give her vampire side too much control, and she might do something she would regret. Lara found herself heading out of town, she needed to run and clear her head. With what they had said, she also needed to think of another plan. Or could she sever all ties and agree for Derwyn never to have the opportunity to be an alpha that would be his birthright. Lara took a deep breath and wiped her eyes. She was trying to find a solution that would help her brother, and being in a family of lycans or a pack, would. *But would he consider never seeing me again and giving up his right to become alpha?* At ten years old, he would not be able to make a proper decision. Yet, she also did not want to leave her brother with a family that seemed so cruel.

Reaching the edge of a forest of thorn riddled trees and shrubs, she stopped and took a deep breath. The last thing her brother needed, having just lost their father, was to lose her as well. She needed to clear her head so she could think straight, not go by an emotional reaction. Yet, just from the walk here, Lara realised they were better off staying together.

CHAPTER 18

LARA slowly walked through the town, in the early afternoon, lost in thought. She had run for miles, but her head still was not fully clear on what to do next. She felt so much pressure, if her father had still been with them, he would have known what to do. But she was alone having to make the decision, that of a sister and as a parent. What the alpha had said still lingered in her mind. *Would any pack or lycan family accept me? And due to that, refuse to help Derwyn?* If Derwyn had been older, then the decision would have been easier, but Derwyn was just too young. It had been hard to separate her feelings as a sister, but she had made the right choice for them. Lara sighed, she could not think too far ahead, she just needed to figure out their next step. Her wolf instinct was telling her to head north, she just was not sure where.

Upon returning to the busy inn, Olena smiled at her as Lara headed to her room. When she entered, she found Derwyn sitting on the bed reading her father's leather-bound book. He looked up, put it down, and ran to her, giving her a big hug. "Lara, where were you? Did you see the family?"

She nodded, savouring her brother's loving embrace, something she realised was what she needed after the morning's events. "Aye, I did. I see you have been reading papa's notes."

The lad responded, a little sheepish, "Sorry."

Lara shook her head. "Nay don't be. It's your family history too. Now that I have met that family, I'll tell you what they are like."

"And?" He peered up at her eagerly.

Lara sighed, walking her brother to the bed, where they sat next to each other. "They are a very strict family, and would help you with your transition, but they wanted you to become part of the family and pack now and remain with them."

"That's not too bad."

Lara studied him, taking his hand. "But you would also lose your right to become an alpha and have to sever all ties with me. They will not let me join them with what I am now."

Derwyn focused on her with hurt in his eyes. "Then I am staying with you."

Lara said, "But they could help you become a good wolf and provide the guidance you will need."

He shook his head, tears in his eyes. "Nay. Papa would want us to stay together, to help each other." He squeezed Lara's hand. "You're my sister and my alpha, Lara. I will always stay with you."

Lara took a breath, trying not to cry. He was right, they were their own little pack and would take care of each other till the day they died. That was something her father had always taught her and something she would never forget. She ruffled his hair and smiled. "You're right, squirt, we do work well together." She stopped studying him. "How are you feeling?"

"A lot better, why?"

"We'll have to leave in the morn because that family of lycans doesn't want us to stay, and I don't want to cause any problems."

He agreed. "I understand, and can't wait to see more of the land."

Lara smiled. "It will be *our* adventure."

They snuggled up on the bed together, Lara needed the time with her brother more than she realised. Once Derwyn had fallen asleep, Lara headed back down into the inn, she would ask Olena where best to head. But the inn was remarkably busy with the early evening customers, so Lara ordered ale and took a seat at the only remaining empty table near the door.

She sat lost in her thoughts, going over every possible option she could think of.

After a while, Olena had time to come over to see Lara. Olena studied her. "You seem a little lost, lass."

"I'm just wondering where to go from here."

Olena sat opposite her. "So the meeting with your papa's friends didn't go as planned?" Lara shook her head, and Olena sighed, "I'm sorry to hear that, love."

Lara responded, "It wasn't what I had expected, so I need to think of something new."

"Why aren't you heading home?"

Lara said sadly, "That isn't an option."

The woman squeezed her hand. "I'm sorry. You are welcome to stay here with me for a while."

"Thank you." Lara looked up at her. "But it's for the best that we leave."

Olena nodded, "So be it, but if you are ever this way, you are always welcome." She paused and then smiled. "I would head north to Naverac. My brother, Feroy, has an inn there, called the Black Bull. Naverac is almost a city, it's three times the size of Crowling, so you may be able to find something there, where you could get some work and board. If not, my brother may be able to employ you or know someone who could. And I know he will find something where you will be safe."

Lara responded, "Thank you."

Olena glanced towards the bar and said, "I should serve my customers."

Lara watched Olena return to the counter and then focused on her ale. It was nice just to sit and watch the customers. The ale was strong, but the alcohol did not seem to affect her, yet she did feel good, a little like the buzz she would get from fresh blood.

As the evening progressed the inn quieted down. Lara sat at her table, undisturbed by the customers and with Derwyn asleep in their room, it gave her time to decide what to do. The best option, as she trusted Olena, would be to head to Feroy's inn. There did not seem to be any better place to go, and at Naverac, at least there would be someone there they could trust.

Her thoughts were broken when someone entered the inn. She glanced up to see a slim man, wearing smart black boots, dark purple trousers and an elegant black jerkin. His scent had a hint of lavender. She carefully watched the dark-haired, moustachioed man as he walked up to the counter.

Olena smiled broadly. "Fashor, your usual?"

He responded with a broad smile and a nod. Lara stayed seated. Even though he was a vampire, to everyone else, he seemed to be just another regular customer. Then she remembered that sometimes vampires hid in plain sight and with a family of lycan in town, she could see why he was keeping a low profile. He scrutinised the inn and focused on her. Lara glanced away taking a sip of her ale. When she looked back, he was heading towards her table, smiling. He glanced at the empty chair opposite her.

"May I sit?"

Lara made a quick nod. Olena seemed to know him so she would be friendly for the time being and remain neutral.

He sat and gazed at her for a few moments with his light purple eyes, and then leaned forward. "This is an interesting feeling. I have the agonising pain in my stomach I get from being in the presence of a lycan or werewolf. But I am also getting a faint scent of lavender."

Lara smiled slightly while studying his slender features. She had not been this close to a vampire since the attack. "I'm a lycan. So, the scent is lavender?"

He smiled, leaning back a little, his finger playing with one tip of his moustache. "Well, my dear, nay one knows for sure, but it is the closest description to give it. If I correctly remember the difference between a lycan and a werewolf, it is your wolf form?"

Lara relaxed a little. "It is. We are also not locked to the lunar cycle. When we transform, we are a large wolf, not a humanoid wolf like the werewolves are. So, what is a vampire doing in a town with a lycan family?"

He chuckled, taking a sip of his wine. "Treading very carefully. What about you, my dear? I am intrigued to know how you survived. Most die within hours. I think I heard one managed to last a day before their body tore itself apart."

Lara sighed, "I must be the lucky one."

He smiled again, lifting his goblet. "Well, I salute you, my dear. You are the only hybrid in this land, and I have been here an exceedingly long time."

"How long?" asked Lara.

He leant forward. "I have lost count, but think about eight hundred years. You will find it hard for the first hundred, but you will learn not to make too many ties."

Lara swallowed, having not thought she would live that long. "Oh."

He placed his slender hand on hers, his feeling slightly cooler. "Sorry my dear, I feel that is something you have not thought about." Lara shook her head, and he smiled. "I think you probably still have a family. Do what you see fit, but understand they will age, you, if you do take after a vampire, will not."

Lara swallowed and studied Fashor. "Do you think I could live that long? Being what I am, I didn't think I would."

He shrugged, leaning back, playing with his moustache again. "Maybe you will not, but a vampire's life usually is not short." He sighed and smiled leaning forward, raising a perfect eyebrow. "But what am I to know? With your wolf blood, you may just live your normal long lycan life."

Lara focused on his light purple eyes, remembering reading something about the eye colour being a trait of a vampire being a pureblood. "Can I ask you something?"

"Anything my dear." He smiled, his slender features seeming so friendly.

"The cravings, how do you control them?"

"Are you struggling?"

"Not too much. I hunt every few days which keeps it at bay, but if I can't hunt . . ."

He glanced down at his goblet. "You would like to know how long? Well, good, strong red wine can keep the cravings at bay. I believe it has something to do with the alcohol. As for when I do need blood, I prefer not to feed off humans if I can truly help it." He glanced back towards Olena who was serving a customer. "Especially people I see as friends."

Lara leant forward. "So how does the alcohol work?"

He smiled showing perfect teeth. "It seems to mimic the same feeling as with blood. You see, we don't need that much to live, we aren't alive anyway. And we can survive for an awfully long time before we start to mummify." He took a sip of his wine, raising an eyebrow. "Something I wouldn't recommend. The blood sustains us as well as helping us *appear human*, and to be honest from my experience, it can be any blood. Human blood is; oh so *wonderful*. Like a fine wine." He closed his eyes for a moment. "But blood from an animal is just as efficient. As you have found with your wolf side you can hunt, and a fresh kill sustains you for days."

"Aye. I am trying to see how long I can last."

"Well, with some training, you can last a surprising length of time before the mummification starts, but if you wish to sustain the option to turn to your wolf form, I think you better hunt regularly. Alcohol can curb the urge to feed, but you will need sustenance to help you to be able to change. We do not get tired like we did when human, well in my case, I think you lycans have a lot more stamina than a human has, but you are still using energy. Well, more like magical energy, and even a hybrid like yourself could end up exhausted."

She explored his features and smiled softly. "I never expected to have a conversation with a vampire."

"Nor I with a lycan. It seems we are not all as the other kind portrays us as."

Lara nodded, tapping his goblet with her mug when he held his up towards her.

Olena walked over. "I hope Fashor here is being on his best behaviour, Lara."

She smiled, glancing up at the innkeeper. "He is."

Fashor turned to Olena, placing a hand on his chest. "You hurt me, Olena. I can be quite the gentleman when I want to be."

Olena chuckled, raising an eyebrow. "Very true, but she's a young lass taking care of a little one, so not someone to take advantage of, or I will have words with you."

Fashor smiled and glanced at Lara raising an eyebrow. "I see. Family is always important."

Lara looked at him. "Very."

Olena smiled. "Well, I will be closing up soon, but you can stay a little longer if you wish Fashor, as Lara has board here." She gazed at them both. "That's if you are still talking?"

Lara nodded, wanting to get as much information from this friendly vampire as she could. "We are."

Olena smiled and left, Fashor watched her leave and then turned back to Lara. "How old is the lad?"

"He's ten."

Fashor considered her and placed his hand on hers again. "You will be fine for several years. When they get a lot older, and yet you have not aged, there can be some resentment."

"I thought as much. But for the time being, he will have to stay with me. Once he's a grown man, I will give him the choice."

"Wise words." He gazed at her, his eyes warm and kind. "I feel you have more questions?"

Lara glanced down. "Aye, sorry."

He smiled. "Nay, nay, my dear, I am happy to help."

"I have read a few books on vampires, but was wondering are you always alone or in small numbers?"

He leant back. "Ahh, well, as we do not age, we never like to stay in one location for long. This is so we do not arouse suspicion. But there are covens out there where there are several together. They like to keep to themselves, and it is usually the older lines that like to keep our species *pure*."

"Oh. Are there many of these covens?"

He played with his moustache again, almost lost in thought. "Not many that have purebloods. I was part of the northern one for some time." He raised his eyebrow. "Over two hundred years, I believe. But they were so much on tradition and I disagreed with most." He leant forward. "Better be careful my girl. They will not like the fact of a hybrid, much less one walking around who is very much alive."

"Well, it seems the feeling is mutual with the lycans."

He sighed, "But from what I know, the lycans do not have trained assassins."

"Lycans will work together in packs if anything threatens their lands. But nay assassins, why?"

He studied her intently. "Unfortunately, vampires do. These vampires will not just protect their covens, they will track down anything that is not pure or vampires who are going against the rules. They call them Cleansers and are highly trained." He paused and sighed. "Centuries ago, there was unrest between the covens and the lower-class vampires, ones sired by servants. And the Cleansers almost wiped them out."

Lara frowned. "Servants?"

He pursed his lips and then indicated with his fingers. "There are four classes of vampires. The elders." He curled one finger down. "Then purebloods, who are sired by the elders." Another finger curled down. "Then servants who are sired by purebloods." Another finger down, he gazed at her for a moment. "Then there are the others. These are the lower classes. They are sired by servants and each other. Those are the most common vampire humans see and they are also the most ruthless." He took hold of his goblet, taking a sip of wine and continued. "For centuries, there was unrest between these classes. Of course, after a time and the use of the Cleansers, it was squashed, but there is always tension. The Cleansers are still used and the elders hope to wipe out the others and anything not pure. So, I suggest you keep clear of them, my girl, as they will see you as an abomination."

Lara smiled, sipping at her ale. "Then I will stay clear of vampires. Well except yourself," she flirted.

Fashor smiled while studying her. "You are a very striking woman. I think in a few years we will cross paths again."

Lara raised her eyebrow. "Really?"

He chuckled. "I find it hard not to flirt with someone pleasing to the eye."

Lara smiled. "I see, and thank you for helping me understand more about my vampire side."

"Well, as your lycan side is just as magical, I think you would be a formidable ally."

She said, "I do feel a lot stronger than before, and so much faster."

He responded, "Vampires can move extremely quickly when we wish. And both our species are far stronger than humans, so maybe the combination in your system will make you even stronger. I think I would feel sorry for the Cleansers if they ever did cross paths with you."

"Well, hopefully, I will never have to find out."

Fashor gulped down some of his wine and Lara started to ask him where he had been on his travels. It was good to find out as much as she could, as she would be travelling for some time.

CHAPTER 19

FIVE YEARS LATER

THE Black Bull was one of the most popular inns in Naverac, selling the best ale and good food. It was used mainly by the locals and Swords for hire whenever they were in the city. Then there were the market days which made all the inns in the city busier than normal with all the traders that were there to sell or buy wares. Lara wore a simple blue dress, her white apron stained by ale from earlier, when a trader lost his balance, unable to hold his drink. It would take a good scrub to get it fully clean and with it being so busy she had not been able to change it for a clean one. Lara hoped Feroy did not scold her for that fact. He liked his staff to be tidy and presentable, he would always state that he had a reputation to uphold, being the best inn around. Lara even started to tie her hair back in a low plait, as a bun would not always stay as neat after a busy day. Yet when the inn was packed, it was hard to maintain a proper appearance.

After they had left Crowling and travelled on to Naverac, Lara had contacted Olena's brother, Feroy. He had been as helpful as his sister and had given them both a roof over their head and he gave Lara a job in his inn. He also paid well. Feroy was a demanding boss, but also a kind-hearted man. Derwyn and herself were safe at the inn and could stay for as long as they wanted. With the money she earned, she would go to the well-stocked bookstores in the city, and with Feroy's help, had ensured Derwyn had some sort of education.

Lara focused on the tray ladened with tankards of ale, she would get them to the customers and then hopefully she would have time to change her apron. Lara weaved her way through the tables, picking up the pace to take the new order of ale to a table of burley Swords. They cheered when Lara arrived. She smiled at them and placed the tray in the centre of the table so all could grab a drink. One tried to get a little too friendly with her and slapped her behind as she leaned over. Lara turned and glared at him. He smiled and tried to grab her. Lara bent away from his drunken grasp and shook her head.

The large man gawked at her. "Come on lass, join us."

With a tight smile she shook her head, but the man was not about to take 'no' for an answer and went to grab her again, this time more aggressively. The man was not a regular and as soon as he made the unwanted advances, the others around the table and nearby, went quiet, knowing the man had crossed the line. Lara glared at him and with lightning speed, grabbed him around the neck almost pulling him out of his seat.

She snarled, "The answer is *nay!*"

The man's features grew red and astonished, surprised at Lara's strength. Choking, he put up his hands showing he surrendered and blurted out. "Sorry, lass."

Lara let him go, just as Derwyn came over, to see what was happening. The lanky teenager, wearing a dark blue shirt and black trousers, a little big on his slender frame, tried to appear tough.

He asked, "You alright Lara?"

She looked at him and smiled. "He won't do it again."

Derwyn glared at the drunken man who was rubbing his neck and giving Lara a worried look. The man glanced at Derwyn, and the teenager just smiled and turned back to his sister.

"You haven't had anyone do that in a while."

Lara shrugged. "Aye, most know not to."

She had had to toughen up a lot on their journey to Naverac and while working in Feroy's inn. Lara could not complain; he took care of them and wanted the best, but also customers would get a little rowdier as the ale flowed. But Lara showed Feroy that she could manage it with ease, and it did not take long before the locals realised it was best to leave her be.

Derwyn scanned the inn. "Not seen it this busy in weeks."

Lara studied her brother. When he turned fifteen, Feroy had given him work in the inn as well. He liked it and would help with serving drinks, or in the stables when they were not as busy. Lara found it hard to think of him as a young man, yet in the last couple of years he had grown tall, but was still skinny. Most thought he could not handle himself, but Lara had made sure he knew how to throw a punch and use a sword, even if only a cheap, short one from the market.

Lara said, "I need to change my apron, can you check the tables to see if there are any more orders?"

Derwyn nodded, and as Lara turned, she glanced across at the empty table in the far corner. Horas was supposed to have returned by then and wondered if she should be concerned. After what he had said he was going to do, she did not know if she should be worried more that he would succeed, or if his luck had finally run out.

Derwyn leant towards her and said, "You know Feroy doesn't want you talking with men like Horas."

Lara eyed her brother wondering what he would think if he knew the real reason for the huge argument between Feroy and Horas several months ago. Yes, Feroy did not want her talking to Horas as he would be a bad influence, but it was due to him catching her leaving Horas's room in the early hours. Feroy meant well, but she had argued with him because he was still treating her like a child, instead of someone in their mid-twenties. Even though Feroy was concerned for her safety, it was Lara who was far more dangerous than Horas.

Lara smiled at her brother. "Well, I don't think he will be coming back anytime soon."

Derwyn said, "I heard Lorn telling Feroy that Horas had been arrested."

Lara responded, "When? This morn?"

Derwyn nodded.

She glanced around not seeing Lorn in the inn but knew that it was probably the truth. Lara turned to her brother. "Well, I think Horas will leave a few broken hearts if he has."

Derwyn raised an eyebrow. "And you?"

Lara laughed. "Not me." She paused and asked, "Can you lock up this eve?"

"You need to hunt?"

Lara replied, "Aye, need to sneak out so I was going to go up early."

Her brother gave a quick nod and then his attention was drawn to a table near the back as the customers shouted for ale. He placed a hand on her arm and smiled. "Don't worry, I can lock up."

She smiled back at him and carried on with her work. They had come up with a plan early on so Lara could satisfy her need to hunt. She had managed to last a good four to five days without feeding. After some trial and error, she started locking up early to sneak out, but with Derwyn being older, it made it even easier if he did the locking up. Then Lara could sneak out from her room window, get out of the city and hunt and be back before dawn. Feroy was never the wiser.

Lara laid on her back, in her room, having changed out of her dress into her shirt, trousers and boots, ready to go hunting. She thought about Horas, when he left, she had a feeling that she would not see him again. She smiled recalling how she would always serve him whenever he came in and linger to hear his new tales and adventures. She thought about his handsome features even with the jagged scar down his left cheek, but what drew Lara had been his clear grey eyes. She could lose herself in them. But it was his air of confidence that drew most people. Her smile softened thinking of his very flirtatious nature that made him very popular, and some of the women would get jealous. But Lara never did, it was just something fleeting for her. Yet Feroy had seen her being drawn to him, and had warned her that Horas was a bit of a womaniser and had a dubious past. Feroy meant well, and she told him not to worry. At first, she would just listen to his stories but over time, Horas and she became closer. He had been the first man that she slept with. She sighed, remembering again the disapproving talk Feroy had with her when he had caught her leaving Horas's room. Lara had snapped at him, telling him he was not her father. They had such a big argument that they did not speak for a good week, and Derwyn had to calm the waters between them. From then onwards, Derwyn was always watching her and Horas. Yet neither he nor Feroy knew that she still saw Horas, as she did enjoy his company, but a lot more secretly.

Lara thought about what Derwyn had overheard and it did not surprise her what Lorn had said. Horas was not the most law-abiding citizen and some of what he did was dangerous, so if he had been arrested, she was not surprised in the slightest. She took a breath, she had to stop thinking of the rogue Sword and focus on the matter at hand, hunting. The inn seemed quiet enough, and Feroy would not come and check on her, so she opened her window slowly and jumped down into the side alley next to the inn. Lara surveyed the area, it was dark, thick clouds blocked out the moonlight which would help her get across town without being seen. Keeping to the back streets and side alleys, Lara ran quickly and quietly across the city, heading for the northern gate. She only had a few hours, but once out of the city walls, she could get to her spot where she would strip and then run freely into the woods. It was getting there that was the tricky part. There were always some people about, as well as the occasional night demon or vampire, and she had to always tread carefully.

Lara paused seeing a couple of drunkards ahead blocking her normal route. She cursed and quickly took a different side alley near the non-human quarter. She usually tried to avoid the area, she did not want to bump into anything that could be far worse than the odd drunkard. Yet tonight, Lara took the risk, knowing she could skirt around the next street. She did not get far when she picked up a vampire scent. Lara saw someone ahead and quietly crouched out of sight behind an old cart. She peeked around the side and peered up the alley, the vampire was female from the attire, and was feeding on a drunk. Lara senses informed her that he was too near death to help him, and it was best to keep out of sight till the vampire moved on. Luckily, she was upwind so she would not be detected. The clouds broke apart for a moment and Lara could see the vampire's features. She froze. She would never forget that face, it was the vampire, Levana, who sired her! Lara cursed, she had come out to hunt so had not brought her sword. Yet, Lara could not let Levana slip through her fingers again. She pursed her lips wondering what to do. She could face the vampire, or follow her to see where she lived and return tomorrow with her sword and deal with her then. Or she could just let her be. But Lara could not do the latter. Just seeing her again, she knew what had to be done. Lara leant a bit further forward intensely watching Levana and knocked something on the cart, causing noise, the vampire suddenly turned in her direction. Lara quickly hid and cringed hoping she had not been seen.

Levana said, in a thick sultry voice, "I know someone is watching me, don't be shy."

Lara cursed; it seemed her choice had been made for her. Lara slowly stood, brushing the dust off her trousers, she moved out from behind the cart and smiled sheepishly. Levana strode towards her, her red dress accentuating her womanly figure, and paused when she saw Lara's face, recognition dawned on the woman's features. "Well, well, well, you managed to survive. What an abomination you are."

Lara's face wrinkled in disgust, all her memories of that night and her father's death, returned as if it was yesterday.

The vampire pursed her blood-stained lips. "I will have to make sure I finish you off this time."

Lara stood her ground, letting her hand transform into wolf claws, and smiled without emotion, wishing in the back of her mind she had her sword. "We will see about that."

Levana lunged at her, with her claw-like nails. Lara jumped back, the claws barely missing her, tearing her white shirt. Lara lunged forward, her wolf claws finding their mark. The vampire hissed as they slashed across her chest, ripping the bodice and the skin beneath. Yet Levana was fast and plunged her hand into Lara's mid-section. She cried out in surprise, feeling the vampire's nails slicing into her innards as Levana slowly moved her hand up towards Lara's heart. Lara grimaced and coughed up blood. She grabbed the vampire's arms as pain burned through her mid-section. Lara glared up at the woman, Levana's broad face full of glee at her pain and shock. Lara gasped. *Is this it? Could Levana kill me again, but this time permanently?*

The vampire smiled, her features pure evil. "You really think I would let you get away with Von's death. This time you will be nothing but dust."

Lara coughed up more blood, feeling the hand moving up, getting closer to her chest. Nearly at her heart. She was in so much pain she was unable to stop Levana. After years on the run and keeping Derwyn safe, a chance encounter in an alley may be the end. Lara wondered if she should have done anything differently, but could only wish she had killed Levana that night all those years ago when her life had been turned upside down.

Lara suddenly heard barking and then shouting behind them. She tried to turn, just able to see a group of large men with two hounds on leashes heading their way. One of them shouted, "Vampire!"

Levana's features contorted, cursing, she yanked her hand free of Lara. The vampire turned back the way she had come, cackling. She jumped onto the nearby roof and ran off.

Lara made a muffled cry, grabbing her bloody mid-section. She staggered forward slightly, no longer having the support of the vampire's arm. The men ran past, the dogs having the scent of Levana, pulled them along. Neither hound seemed to notice Lara's scent which was probably masked by all the blood. One of the men slowed, looking at Lara with concern. Another shouted, "That one's a goner. Leave her."

The men carried on, leaving Lara for dead. She stumbled away, needing to heal, and could feel her vampire side trying to take hold with humans being so close. She could smell the human blood. It was intoxicating. With all her strength Lara staggered off into the night, holding her mid-section, feeling broken after letting the vampire slip through her fingers.

Lara glanced up groggily at the dawn sky, she had been curled up in a side alley for hours letting her body heal. She felt so weak, and she needed to hunt, but did not have the strength to head out of the city, let alone change to her wolf form. Once she was strong enough to stand, she tried to find Levana's scent, but to no avail. She had lost her. Lara cursed under her breath, angry with herself that the vampire got the upper hand. She should have been faster and stopped her. But Lara had not fought a vampire since that night and did not know they were that fast. She paused for a moment, feeling dizzy. Luckily the streets were still deserted. Lara's shirt was torn and covered in blood, her chin was also stained from what she had coughed up from the injury, and her mid-section felt tender and sore. Lara slowly continued then saw the inn ahead, Derwyn just coming out from the side alley. She staggered towards him.

As soon as her brother saw her, he ran over, concern on his teenage features. "By Laycain! What happened?"

Lara glared at her brother, frustration, and tears in her eyes. "I lost her, Derwyn."

He frowned, glancing around quickly making sure no one saw them. He directed her towards the side alley as he asked, "Who?"

Lara snarled, "The bitch that sired me."

Derwyn froze, turning to face her, both standing in the side alley. "What?"

Lara answered, tears welling in her eyes. "I found Levana last night by accident. We fought and she nearly killed me. Then I lost her."

Derwyn gazed at her with sadness. "I'm so sorry sis." He paused. "So, you didn't hunt?"

She shook her head, looking more exhausted. "Nay."

Derwyn focused on her eyes. "But if that vampire nearly killed you, you need to get blood and hunt."

Lara peered up at him, her features forlorn. "I'm just too tired, it took most of the night to heal." She paused. "I'll go this eve."

Derwyn glanced around looking worried. "You're pale Lara, and your eyes are a little red like when the vampire side takes hold. You need blood now." As they reached the side entrance he added. "Listen, Feroy isn't up yet, sneak up to your room and rest. I'll get you something to stop the vampire side from taking hold."

Lara nodded distractedly, all she could think about was Levana. Derwyn grabbed her shoulders making her focus on him. "Promise me you won't go after that vampire."

Lara glared at him, tears now rolling freely down her cheeks. "I was supposed to protect you, and that bitch made me into this!"

Derwyn did not release his grip on her shoulders and reminded her, "Lara, you *did* protect me, and you *still* do. But you can't go after her when you are severely injured. I may lose you *forever!*"

Lara glared at him, her face full of anger. "I didn't realise how much I hated her till I saw her, Derwyn. She must die!"

Derwyn snapped, "Lara, nay! You aren't thinking clearly. If you want to deal with her, then fine, but we do it *together* and when you are at full strength. What you need to do now is to rest and feed!"

Lara paused, staring at her brother; he was right. Her head was clouded by her vampire side trying to take control in her weakened state.

She turned to the doorway and sighed, "Alright." She paused, sensing his blood, her vampire side trying to take hold. She gripped the door frame, almost breaking it. Her fingernails growing longer like the vampires, she glanced back at Derwyn. His face paled, as she added. "I'm sooo hungry."

Derwyn suddenly felt scared, he had not seen Lara like this in years. He needed to act fast before the vampire side took over. He grabbed her arms as tight as he could.

He snapped, "Lara focus." He looked around, he needed to get her out of sight. "The stable now!"

He half pulled her from the doorway, walking briskly to the stable, he needed to get Lara blood and fast.

Lara staggered and licked her lips. "I can smell blood."

He turned back towards her to see her eyes turning red. He cursed; the vampire side was taking hold. He did not have his lycan strength yet, and hoped, with Lara weakened, he could be of help to her. He looked around again, then back towards the street, the town was slowly coming to life. The last thing he needed was other people about. He may not be able to keep her under control once she got the blood lust. He was never scared of Lara and what she was, but when the vampire side took hold if he did not act, he could lose his sister, and that scared him.

Reaching the stable he pulled Lara in, and examined the area not letting her go.

Why is it that when I need a rat, I can't find one?

There was a sudden movement near the back, which had to be varmints. Keeping hold of Lara, he dragged her towards the noise and managed to grab the rat before it ran off. He turned to his sister, shoving the writhing animal in her face and ordered, "Feed!"

Her almost red vampire eyes focused on his neck. Derwyn held up the rodent, blocking her view of him. "Feed on this!"

Lara seemed to get control for a moment. Grabbing the rat, she bit down on it eating the rat raw, the blood running down her chin. Derwyn let go of her; she seemed to be a little more in control, and searched for another rat then passed it to her as she dropped the carcass of the first one. Derwyn searched for a third, knowing that would be enough for her to regain control, then he would ride her out of town to hunt. Not ideal in the daytime, but he had little choice.

Lara dropped the remains of the third rat and gazed at Derwyn. She was still very pale, but her eyes had returned to normal. Derwyn had placed a harness and saddle on one of the horses and turned to Lara. "Come on, let's get you out of the city, so you can hunt."

Lara peered outside the sky a clear blue. "It's too risky."

Derwyn gave her a stern look, as he mounted the horse. "Less risky than being in an inn full of warm-blooded customers. Now come on."

She paused. "What about Feroy?"

Derwyn grabbed her, pulling her up behind him. Suddenly, for the first time since they had left their home behind, he was the one taking charge. "Feck Feroy. Let's get you better, and then we can deal with him."

Lara held tight to her brother and whispered, "Thank you, Derwyn."

He glanced back at her. "You're my alpha Lara, and we will always take care of each other."

She smiled, holding tight as Derwyn rode the horse out of the stable and went at a quick trot towards the northern gate. He wanted to do a full gallop but that would draw too much attention.

Feroy glared at them. "I had to set everything up *and* deal with two customers' horses!"

Both Derwyn and Lara stood silent in the kitchen at the inn, the large, blond man seethed at them both. He frowned at Lara shaking his head and was about to say something.

Derwyn said, "I'm sorry, but I stayed out longer than I should have, Lara only came to find me to make sure nothing bad had happened to me."

Feroy glared at Derwyn, then turned to Lara and snapped, "Is this true? As you are the one that usually tries my patience."

Lara glanced at Derwyn and then at Feroy, her mid-section still ached but at least since she had hunted, her strength had been restored. On the way back, Derwyn had insisted that he would take the blame since Lara had been in bad books with Feroy recently with the argument about Horas. She did not like it, but Derwyn would not take no for an answer.

"I went to find him this morn. Sorry, I should have said something and not just taken the horse without asking."

Feroy pursed his lips and sighed while considering the two. "I'm glad I don't have children of my own, I think I would be bald from all the stress by now."

The two smirked and studied Feroy, the innkeeper smiled. Lara would always see Olena when she regarded him, especially around the eyes. They were a handful for the man. Lara half wondered if she should tell him everything, but it was for the best he did not know the full truth. It was safer that way.

He folded his arms then sighed and eyed Derwyn. "Muck out duty for two days." He turned to Lara. "Dawn duty for you. I want this kitchen sparkling."

Both nodded and Feroy glanced toward the door into the inn. "Right. Back to work. Luckily the inn is a little quieter this day."

Both returned to their duties, Lara glanced at her brother and smiled at him, and he returned the gesture. If it had not been for his quick thinking this morning, she was not sure what would have happened. She had made a vow to forget about Levana for the time being. She realised if she wanted to face her again, she needed to be prepared. Vampires were fast, but Lara could be faster.

CHAPTER 20

THREE YEARS LATER

LARA leant back savouring her wine, her attention on a barmaid, at the far side of the inn, having to listen to a very overweight man complain about his food. Lara felt sorry for the girl and glanced at her brother who had scraped his bowl clean and was now on her bowl of sausages and beans, which meant it could not be that bad. She glanced back at the girl who was trying to tell the man that no one else had complained, then Lara's mind wandered, remembering when she had been in those shoes.

They had stayed at the Black Bull Inn for nearly five years. It was a good life there and Feroy had been like a father to them both. Yet being in a city, Lara found it hard to be able to hunt, having to sneak out at night and hope she did not get caught. Luckily, and with Derwyn's help, she never had been. There were a few close calls, but otherwise, it had worked out well. Yet she was also concerned as to what they would do when Derwyn reached eighteen. They needed somewhere he would be able to transform for the first time in safety. Even if they had that, there would be a time with her immortality, that Lara would have to move on. She discussed those factors with Derwyn and he agreed that it was time to start fresh somewhere new. With reluctance and heavy hearts, Lara and Derwyn left Naverac and headed further north.

They travelled for about a year, exploring, and taking on the odd job or favour where they used Lara's skills with the sword or their experience at Naverac to get extra money. But they needed some stability, somewhere, before Derwyn turned eighteen. He would need privacy for his first transformation and somewhere he could learn how to hunt. After a time, they found a vast evergreen forest to the far north. It had been called the Venomous Woods, due to the fact of it being so old that mostly non-human lifeforms lived there, some being very dangerous. The locals gave it that name hundreds of years before to discourage anyone from entering. Yet some were still lured by the adventure. Most of the dangerous demons seemed to keep to the far north where it was much denser in the oldest part of the forest, and that was where the glory hunters would usually try their luck. The southern part of the forest was less dangerous but still not safe for humans. Yet, for a couple of lycans wanting a homestead, it was perfect. In a small clearing, they built their cabin, away from as many of the non-humans and humans as possible, but there was still a village somewhat close by.

The small fishing village of Yarl was about half a day's ride away. When they came for supplies they would always take a room at the inn and return the following day. She had learnt everything about her capabilities and was in full control of her cravings. She could spend several days in a town if ever she needed to. Lara did like their trips to Yarl, either together or on her own, as they could interact with the locals and keep abreast of any news that could affect them.

Lara turned back to her wine and surveyed the rest of the inn. Her slightly loose shirt, wide black belt and dark brown trousers accentuated her figure, and with her brown hair up in a soft bun, her features were also more noticeable. She noticed that a few men were glancing her way, but they did not approach. The sword at her side was one deterrent. The other was reputation. All in the village knew she was not someone to mess with, even with her delicate features.

The inn this early evening was not too busy, most of the customers were traders passing through and local fishermen, most of whom she knew by sight. She noticed the young barmaid walking back to the kitchen, after finally dealing with the awkward customer, and how the young girl's eyes lingered on Derwyn. Lara glanced at her brother, oblivious to the girl as he finished off the second bowl of food, scraping it clean. He had changed so much in the last year, from a lanky teenager to a young man. He had filled out with muscle and even his voice had fully broken. He also seemed unaware of how handsome he had become. From the physical changes, his transformation could not be far off. His body was preparing for the extra strain it would experience when turning into a wolf for the first time.

Derwyn looked at her as he drank his ale, then said, "So the sword will be ready first thing?"

Lara affirmed. Derwyn did not always come into the village with her, but on this occasion, it was to ensure he got a fitting sword. Not some cheap one of the likes they found at the Naverac market. She had been training him, and he would have skills in his wolf form, but there were times when using a sword for protection was a must.

"We can collect it on the way back to the cabin."

He asked, "Do you think I'll have my transformation soon?"

Lara leant forward studying him, putting down her wine. "Have you had the dreams yet?" He shook his head. "When the dreams start, we will need to prepare. Till then, it's a waiting game. Mine came just after my eighteenth birthday, papa's were about a month before, and mama's were months after."

He asked, his features a little apprehensive, his fingers playing with the handle of his mug of ale. "Will it hurt?"

Lara smiled; she had asked their father the same question. "Aye the first time is the hardest, but the more you change, the easier and less painful it will become. But even now it hurts me when I change."

Derwyn took a deep breath. "At least I have you to be there to help me."

Lara placed a hand on his shoulder. "I will, as papa was there for me."

Derwyn nodded, studying his sister. "How long did the first one take?"

She smiled softly, staring off into the distance, it seemed so long ago. She glanced at her drink, she had never told her brother that her transformation had been triggered by being foolish and she was not going to now.

"It felt like days, but it was only an hour, maybe two. But after that, the more you change the quicker it becomes."

"You change so fast."

"True." Smiled Lara. "The more your body gets used to it, the easier it becomes." She glanced at his ale. "Drink up. I want an early start."

He nodded, downing his ale. They both stood and headed up to their rooms, leaving the chaos of the busy inn behind.

Lara slumped down on the bed and undid her wide belt, before pulling off her black boots. She would be glad once Derwyn had a decent sword. The old one had been all right when he was a lanky teenager, but his full strength was developing and he required a sturdy, strong sword. He would need a bit of practice with a longsword, but he was a good swordsman already and he would pick it up quickly. Standing again, she pulled off her trousers and cream coloured shirt, then laid back down on her bed. She sighed, feeling wide awake. Talking to Derwyn about his transformation brought back memories of hers. It had been a long and eventful night. She still squirmed when she thought about Yanric, she had been so naïve then. That was the first time her wolf side had protected her. She took a deep breath focusing on the transformation instead, the pain was now a faded memory. But she would never forget the thrill of her first hunt and the many more she had with her father. Her heart ached thinking of him. She realised she had not thought about her father in years, not even after she had started adding to the leather-bound book. That was not entirely true, she would be reminded whenever she looked back through the pages and saw his handwriting, but she had not even done that lately. After they had reached Naverac, and having read everything in it, she felt it was her duty to continue filling it in. There had not been many entries, but she had ensured all that had happened since they left Lake Wood was documented. Even the fact the Stonelances at Crowling were not welcoming. She had even updated the map from the library.

Lara sighed, unsure who would read any of it but knew that Derwyn would pass it on down the line when he had a family. She closed her eyes, wondering if Derwyn would want a family. She shook the thought from her mind, knowing that he would. She thought of the book entries again, not wanting to think about the future too much. The book had been an interesting read, there had been nothing more other than what had been mentioned a couple of times about protecting the village. Yet from what Lara had read elsewhere, and from talking to witches on their travels, it seemed most lycan packs or families were protectors of a village, town, or area. She was certain her mother and father did something similar, and maybe with Jermer and Alana. It was something she may never know. She did still wonder what was on those torn-out pages. She rolled over and sighed, staring out the window at the night sky. She had to stop dwelling on the past and focus on Derwyn. His transformation would be soon, and she needed to ensure he was prepared.

Derwyn woke early, scratching his head, his black hair a little longer than he liked it. The summer sun was creeping over the horizon and gave the room a warm glow. With the light entering from the window, he was eager to get his sword, as he had been using a cheap short sword for far too long. He was nearly eighteen and it was time to be able to protect himself, and his sister if need be, with a decent sword he could call his own. His sister could take care of herself, but it felt like it was his duty as she had been his sister, mother, and father for so long. It felt right that he could return the favour fully, and they could protect each other.

He stretched his lean muscular limbs, got up and glanced out the window. It was hard to believe he would soon be having his first transformation. The dreams had not come yet, but he just had this feeling that it would not be too long, and it excited him. He noticed he had developed more muscle since the lanky teenager he had been the year before. He also felt stronger and could not wait to fully embrace his wolf abilities after his first transformation. Over the last few months, he had been reading the books they had on lycans. It seemed the males had more difficulty with becoming a wolf and the amount of aggression they would have to deal with. Yet, even though he would not have the guidance of a male, Derwyn felt that he would be able to cope with it all.

Putting on his black shirt and grey trousers, his hazel eyes staring back out the window as he tucked in his shirt, he wondered how it would feel to turn into a wolf. He sighed, and pulled on his boots. One thing he did know was, it would hurt. He headed down to get something to eat, hell he was always hungry, even more so of late. He sat at a table in the quiet inn and ordered waffles.

Derwyn thought about his sister. He had been wondering for years why Lara's appetite, which could be as insatiable as his, seemed to have gone. A few years ago she had finally told him that since she was turned, she could no longer eat normal food. He suddenly understood why she would always pass the food to him when he was younger, telling him she was not hungry. It had been so he would not be scared of her change. Yet he would never have been scared. She was his sister, and would never have harmed him. They had been in a couple of scrapes over the years where he had seen the vampire side surface, and he had still seen her as his sister. As for the food at the inns, it seemed to have become a habit, and even though he knew the reason now, she would still order the food as if it was for herself. He smiled, he loved his sister dearly and he would miss the act they always did at the inns with the food and hoped it never stopped. He took a breath, it had been hard since their father's death, but they had got through it and they were happy with a life of their own.

He smiled when Lara came down from her room. She sat opposite him and said, "You are eager for that sword aren't you."

He swallowed a mouthful of food. "You have been protecting us for too long, and now we can protect each other."

She smirked, studying him, and replied, "I should have got you a decent sword earlier."

He smiled, placing a hand on hers. "Nay it's alright. The time seems right."

Once eaten, he left Lara to pay the innkeeper while he went to sort out the horses. Once saddled, he waited outside with them. A young girl, who he had found out was named Isla, walked by in a well-fitting yellow dress, giving him a broad smile. Derwyn instantly felt awkward, turning his attention to his saddle as if there was an issue with the strap. He had been trying to talk to her for months, but never had the courage, yet she was smiling at him.

Why am I suddenly all awkward?

He was missing the opportunity he had been waiting for. He looked back up to see her talking to her friends. They glanced his way and giggled. One he knew was Calisa, they had kissed in the barn many months before and she was a nice girl, but Isla was always the one he had really wanted to know. He

137

hoped Calisa had not told Isla what had happened between them, and she did not seem to be that type of girl. She smiled at him and turned to Isla whispering something in her ear. Isla's eyes lingered on him for a little longer and smiled, then she suddenly looked away. Before Derwyn could even wonder why, he heard a movement and turned to see Lara taking the reins of her horse. She glanced between him and Isla and raised an eyebrow. Derwyn smiled and started riding towards the blacksmith. The opportunity had gone, yet he was glad that he had some interaction with Isla, maybe next time he was in Yarl he would talk to her. Or if he saw Calisa, ask her to arrange a meeting.

As they rode across town, Taul, the owner of the general store, and Lara smiled at each other. Taul's gaze lingered on her for a few moments. Derwyn glanced between the tall, slim man and his sister; they seemed very friendly. He wondered if that was the man she would see when she went to the village on her own. He knew she was seeing someone but had never asked. Yet seeing how Taul looked at her, he had to be the one.

He turned his attention towards the blacksmith ahead and thought back to Naverac. To this day, he had thought there had been more than she would say with that rogue Horas. Feroy had been furious with her about him, more than her just talking to him too much. Derwyn had always wondered if they had been lovers, even if only fleeting.

That's another thing, could we truly connect with anyone?

He liked Isla, but like with Calisa, it would only be fleeting as he could not tell them what he really was. For Lara, it would be even harder to tell Taul or Horas.

They stopped outside the blacksmith, hearing him working at the back. Derwyn glanced at Lara, whatever her relationship was with Taul it was not his business. What frustrated Derwyn more was she had never been open to him about anything.

Was that because she was trying to be a parent more than a sister to me?

Derwyn just wished, since he was older, she would be more like a sister and talk to him as a friend. He sighed, maybe one day she would, he just had to be patient.

Tying the horses to the hitching post they went round to the back where the blacksmith was working. The large, muscular man smiled and put down his hammer. "'Ave ya come for ya sword, young man."

Derwyn smiled. "I have."

The blacksmith wiped his dirty, sweaty hands on an old cloth that had been stuffed in his pocket and walked over to the shop going in through the back door, the two following. Inside was full of samples of armour, swords and daggers of different shapes and sizes, either displayed on the wall or over countertops. The blacksmith went over to the longest counter where a scabbarded longsword lay waiting.

He smiled proudly, picking it up. "Ave a go with it, lad."

Derwyn pulled the sword free; the gleaming steel singing at its release, it had a good weight, and felt comfortable in his hand. He could not help but grin, showing Lara. "Look at the workmanship."

Lara examined it, then turned to the blacksmith. "This is fine work. Thank you."

The blacksmith gave a short nod before taking the small bag of coins from her when she passed them over. "I always ensure me customers are 'appy and 'ave a good service. I may not be one of those fancy swordsmiths, but me work is always a high standard."

Derwyn sheathed the sword, unable to stop smiling. "It is magnificent. Thank you." He turned to his sister and gave her a big hug. "And thank you, Lara."

"It was something papa would have done, so I wanted to make sure it was perfect."

Derwyn gazed at her, feeling a little sad that it would have been a father-son moment, but with Lara arranging it, it meant even more. He took his sword, and they left the blacksmith to his work, securing their swords to their saddles, they mounted their horses and rode out of the village. Derwyn could not wait to try the sword once back at the cabin.

CHAPTER 21

T HE cabin was dark, and a trickle of moonlight from the windows illuminated the open area near the fireplace. Derwyn was on all fours in front of it, naked and covered in sweat. His muscles and limbs quivered from the pain. It felt like his body was trying to tear itself apart. His features contorted and he gritted his teeth, as he convulsed again.

Lara knelt beside him. "Don't fight it."

Derwyn glared at her, his dark hair plastered to his sweaty forehead, his features full of pain. "It *fecking* hurts!!"

Lara placed a hand on his shoulder, studying him. "This is the hardest one. Just breathe and let the pain flow over you."

He gritted his teeth, knowing he could do it; his sister had, his father and mother all had, so he could too. He had woken with excruciating pain in his stomach in the early hours. Bent over, he walked to Lara and woke her, telling her he was in pain. Lara was instantly up and got him to strip, telling him that it was time. It had been well over an hour, Lara had told him that hers had taken over two, so it would not be too much longer. Then his body convulsed again, but it was different. He felt his joints pop and move into inhuman positions. Then his jaw ached and started to elongate as his features started to change. He cried out in pain as muscles tore and bones snapped.

The pain suddenly stopped. Derwyn observed Lara with his wolf eyes, she smiled broadly. He took a deep breath. He could smell the forest outside. Lara's scent, and the food in the storage. He felt amazingly strong. His hearing had become more acute and could hear the animals nearby and the forest trees moving. He shook his black fur and felt Lara stroking his neck.

"I knew you'd do it, squirt."

He glared at her and growled. He hated her still calling him that, he was not a little boy anymore.

Lara said, "Sorry, I promise not to call you squirt anymore." She stood raising an eyebrow. "Ready to go on your first hunt?"

He shook his fur again and stretched his legs, it felt so natural to be in this form. He had dreamt of running as a wolf these last few days and now he was actually going to. He glanced away when Lara stripped off her nightgown, she then opened the cabin door, and he trotted out. Once they were both outside, she closed the cabin door and changed, shaking her grey fur. Derwyn knew she always loved to be in her wolf form, and now in his, he could see why she felt so powerful and free. He scrutinised the trees, seeing further than he had been able to before, and with the moonlight, it seemed as bright as daylight. It was his lycan vision and something that he would still have when in human form.

He gazed across at Lara, studying her wolf features for the first time with his wolf eyes; her green eyes, still so piercing, and the spot of silver fur above her right eye. Derwyn remembered there was a similar silver patch on his left ear when he had seen his wolf self in his dreams. He had even seen their father, which had upset him more than he had thought. The morning after when he told Lara, she informed him she had seen their mother in hers. He focused on Lara again, she had always seemed so big as a wolf, but in his wolf form, she was a little smaller than him. She grunted at him, and sniffed the air, then ran off. Derwyn grunted and gave chase; he had been looking forward to the moment they could hunt.

Derwyn loved this new freedom. He stared ahead, Lara was so fast! He realised she had slowed to let him catch up; he was going full speed, but forgot that Lara said she was so much faster when she turned. He saw her sniffing the air, Derwyn did the same catching the scent of some rabbits. She stopped then glanced at him, Lara was letting him have the first kill. He ran off in the direction of his prey, he could still hear Lara following at a slower pace. He could sense the rabbit ahead and felt his stomach grumble then when he saw it, he pounced. His canines dug deep into the animal's neck breaking it, the blood running onto his tongue. He looked across to see Lara get hers, he then followed her to a small clearing where they ate their kills in silence.

Derwyn loved hunting and wanted to do it again and again. But he would need to rest a few days first. Lara had spoken to him the night before, informing him they would camp in the forest after his first transformation. She would ensure Derwyn knew how to hunt; quick and sure, without making a sound. The forest was huge, so they would be safe, but Derwyn and his sister knew they were not the only occupants. To the north-east, and further, were other supernatural creatures. Most kept to themselves, but some of the demons were very territorial, and Lara wanted to make sure he did not run into any situations when he went hunting. He remembered the time Lara had chased a badger through the forest and ran into a demon's territory. It had taken them weeks to ensure it did not venture their way and destroy their home. Lara had to take dominance over it to ensure there were no further issues. Derwyn hoped he did not run into anything like that, and Lara was going to make sure he knew the safest places to hunt. The forest, with its reputation locally, had been perfect for them to keep their privacy, but it was always good to be on their guard and prepared. He would need to learn to hunt wisely so that he was as undetected as possible, not only by his prey, but also from humans, and demons. But for his first time, he did not care, he just wanted to run.

CHAPTER 22

THE forest was quiet, a few birds twittering nearby, but otherwise, all seemed still. The early morning sun was breaking through the trees' foliage, giving the forest floor a dappled effect. Lara walked slowly between the trees, seeing Derwyn ahead. He had kept concealed well enough, then she caught his scent on a light breeze.

She muttered softly knowing he would hear her, "You're downwind. Move."

She saw the wolf stop and change direction. It was supposed to be his first solo hunt, but she wanted to see that he remembered everything she had taught him, so kept him at a safe distance. He would moan at her later, but she wanted to be sure that he did not make any mistakes. Lara continued following him and was pleased that over the last few weeks he had taken to his wolf self so well. She had been worried that, without the guidance of a pack or lycan family, he would have struggled. It was known for the males to have more issues with controlling their emotions, but it seemed with the two of them working together, he was coping. He was a strong wolf too, as large and foreboding as their father had been. Lara smiled softly; he was black like their father too. He had even inherited the silver patch. Lara always wondered if their father had inherited his from his father or his mother. *Was it a trait of the*

Tarrenfall line? She smiled knowing wherever it came from, it made them unique.

With their size, the forest was the perfect place to hunt and would give them the cover they needed. Yet they would still have to be careful, as they did not want rumours of wolves in the area spreading to the local villages. Due to the forest's nature, glory hunters wanting to hunt down a demon or two would always venture through. That was what they had to be most careful of, more than a local hunter. She had to ensure Derwyn could hunt on his own and never be spotted, as well as keep out of the way of the other creatures.

Lara stiffened, and stopped, picking up a new scent. She slowly scanned around and saw someone hiding in the shrubs ahead of her. Luckily, they would have been oblivious to her being there but wondered if they had seen Derwyn. She could make out a man's broad back through the foliage. *Is he here to hunt?* Not many ventured this far into the forest for just a bit of hunting. She had to make sure he did not head in Derwyn's direction; glad she had got him to move upwind. Slowly, she crouched, and moved round to creep up behind the man. As she got closer, she could see his sword was still in his scabbard on his back, and no other weapon visible. She instantly knew he was not hunting deer. She stood and quietly pulled her sword free then moved up behind him, making very little sound. She placed the tip of her sword against the man's back.

He stiffened as Lara asked amicably, "Can I ask what you are doing here?"

The man slowly stood keeping his hands open, his arms slightly out from his sides, to show he had no weapons as he turned. He was a good foot taller than her, with black shoulder-length hair. His hazel eyes focused on her green and he said, with a deep gravelly voice. "I'm wondering how you managed to creep up behind me."

She studied him. He had no bow, only a sword, and from his stance, he was not a hunter, more a fighter, but kept her observation to herself. Instead, Lara raised an eyebrow, keeping her sword steady on his chest. "There aren't many deer in this part of the forest to hunt."

He smiled, studying her, his eyes lingering on her waist and then her chest. Her figure was accentuated by tight leather trousers with a wide corset-like belt, and her shirt was open at the neck.

His smile broadened as he said, "Well I heard *there* are deer in these parts."

Lara raised an eyebrow, he was built like a warrior, his black leather trousers and black leather jerkin fitting his athletic build well. "Really? I haven't seen any."

"Really," he repeated. "I feel sure I saw something over in that direction." He nodded his head to the north, roughly where Derwyn had been some moments before.

Lara kept her eyes firmly on him. "Funny, I didn't see anything."

He raised an eyebrow with a sly smile on his face. Lara sheathed her sword knowing Derwyn would probably have headed back to the cabin to change. The man had to be a glory hunter, probably searching for demons that may have strayed from the north. She was half tempted to just deal with him, but she was not sure if he had seen anything, and she would not kill someone who was not a threat.

He cocked his head to one side. "Can I ask what a fine young woman is doing out here?"

Lara responded, "You could, but that doesn't mean I'll respond."

He chuckled. "Very well."

There was a movement in the trees and Derwyn strolled over, looking serious. The man tensed and glanced between Lara and Derwyn.

Her brother stated, "There you are. I have found the pup. He had been chasing rabbits. He's secured on the cart."

Lara smiled, then turned to the man. "Well, good day."

Derwyn glared at the man for a moment, sizing him up. Derwyn was the same height and almost as broad as him, giving an air of authority that he seemed to possess since his first transformation. "Are you lost?"

The man shook his head and looked towards the south of the forest. "I came to do a bit of hunting." He turned back, studying the two. "But it seems I will be leaving empty-handed."

Derwyn gave him a cold smile and then turned, heading back the way he had come, Lara close behind. She paused and glanced back to see the man heading south, glad it was away from their cabin.

She caught up with Derwyn and raised an eyebrow. "Pup?"

He shrugged. "I had to think quickly. But it worked, didn't it?"

Lara replied, "Aye, it looks that way."

She glanced back to see the man had gone. They had people venture into the woods before, either for a glory hunt, after the odd deer, or just plain lost. Lara hoped that was the end of it. To ensure the stranger would not follow them, they took a roundabout route to the cabin

Lara gently scolded her brother. "You didn't need to come over and help."

He snorted. "I was actually coming to moan at you for watching me, but then with that man there, I thought I'd better make up something. It was probably my fault for being downwind, especially if he was a good tracker."

Lara smirked, glancing down at her feet feeling guilty. "I was just making sure you remembered everything." She paused and added, "Anyway, I'm not sure what he was, I think he may have been a glory hunter."

"Really? We haven't had many of them for a while."

Lara responded as she observed the area, "I know, and we have been careful, yet the other creatures do venture too far sometimes."

"There are a lot of them further north-east of here."

"I think we best keep our hunting to the west for a while."

Her brother asked, "Do you think it could become a problem?"

She shrugged. "I don't know. But I didn't feel there was a need to deal with him, and he was nowhere near the cabin. If we run into any trouble, we can deal with it. Till then we are better off doing nothing. We don't want stories starting that the forest is even more dangerous than it already is."

Derwyn said, "Wouldn't that help? It would keep people away."

"Not glory hunters. They would come in droves to catch some mystical creature and be a hero."

He folded his arms across his chest. "Didn't think of that."

Lara gazed at her brother. "I'm heading into Yarl in the morn, I'll ask around to see if there have been any issues. Meanwhile, don't hunt till I'm back." He nodded and Lara glared at him intently, knowing what he was like. "I mean it, nay hunting."

Derwyn smiled, holding up his hands. "I promise."

The following day Lara rode to Yarl. As she got supplies that afternoon, she had several conversations with the market traders and store owners. There did not seem to be anything noteworthy about the forest, apart from the usual rumours. Once she had requested her supplies, she had time to visit her lover, Taul, the local store owner. Over the years they had become quite close, yet it would never become anything serious. He did not know what she or Derwyn was, and as far as he knew, they were living in the forest to try and find out about its mysteries. With her knowing him well she could be less vague in her questions, but even he had not heard anything.

When she asked if he had seen any strangers, he mentioned there had been one, but he left that morning. Taul did not know what the stranger looked like, he just heard something in passing from one of his customers. It was possible the hunter she had seen was just passing by, on the off chance the stranger was the same man. It was known locally that the forest had something suspicious about it, and Lara would not be surprised if he had heard something in passing and had decided to take a chance. Of the ones that did try their luck with the forest, not many ventured into Yarl. They usually headed to the forest directly and then on to Spor, which was further south, had larger inns and a brothel.

After spending time with Taul, Lara went to the local inn for the night. She took a table near the back wall, and being such a regular, the innkeeper bought over a large goblet of wine before she had to even ask and left her the key to one of his rooms at the back. Taul always offered for her to stay at his place, but Lara felt it was best not to. He was a nice man and a good distraction, but nothing more. Suddenly staying with him whenever she came to the village seemed too much of a commitment, and would also raise even more questions. She sat back, having removed her sword and placed it beside her, and watched the customers come and go. She made a quick nod in greeting to the other regulars, but all knew that she liked to drink alone.

Suddenly someone was standing to her right, and said in a gravelly voice. "Well, if it isn't the silent woman."

She peered up, and froze, she had not picked up his scent, he made sure of that. It was the man from the forest. The stranger Taul had heard of was not the same man. Without asking, he sat opposite her putting down his mug of ale.

He leant forward; his eyes steady on hers. "Nay one has ever managed to creep up on me without me knowing."

Lara took a sip of her wine, trying to seem as relaxed as possible. "Well, we all have off days."

He leant further forward, studying her, his features stern. "What are you?"

Lara's muscles tensed, maybe she should have dealt with him in the forest after all. "What?"

His gaze did not waver, and he repeated, "*What* are you?"

Lara glanced around the quiet inn, everyone was focused on their conversations and lives. She turned back to him and leaned forward, her eyes slowly turning red. "Someone you don't want to mess with."

Suddenly, one of her hands started to burn. She glanced down to see him holding an expensive dagger, the tip of it against her skin. To burn her, it had to contain silver. Only one type of person would own an expensive weapon like that, and it would not be a glory hunter. This was one for hire. He placed his free hand on her other hand, pushing it hard into the table. Lara's eyes started to turn red as she struggled to control the vampire blood from the pain of the silver. She slowly let her wolf claws form, on the hand that was burning as that would control the vampire side.

He glared at her, looking from her eyes to the claws that had grown from the ends of her fingers. He snarled, keeping his voice low as they were both trying not to draw attention. "What the *feck* are you?"

She pulled her hand away from the silver dagger and slowly placed her claw against the tanned skin of his hand that was holding her other one firmly against the table. She pushed the claw down slowly making it draw blood and she snarled, "As I said, someone, you don't want to *feck* with. I suggest you let go, otherwise, everyone in this inn will be dead before you can draw your sword."

His grip was not loosening, and he just sneered at her. Lara needed to think fast before they drew too much attention. She could easily slit his throat with her claws but that was the last thing she wanted, especially in public. There was another option. In one swift movement, she slammed his head into the table, breaking his nose and knocking him out cold. Then seconds later, knocked his ale from the table, it was so fast that everyone only heard the smash of the mug. When people glanced her way, Lara's eyes had returned to normal along with her claws.

She sighed, raising an eyebrow. "It seems he can't manage his ale."

People smirked and turned away, believing he had just passed out from too much alcohol. Lara casually took a swig of her wine, and regarded the unconscious man for a moment, wondering if that had been a planned encounter or not. She looked over at the innkeeper, he would have said something if a stranger was asking about her. Maybe it was just a coincidence that their paths had crossed again. She grabbed her sword and got to her feet, trying to remain relaxed. Lara headed to her room. She could feel her wolf self, it was unsettled, and there was a sense of uneasiness. Those feelings were never wrong. Once in her room, she left money on the side table and climbed from the window, landing on the ground outside with ease. She had to get back to the cabin now.

Quickly saddling her horse, Lara rode back through the forest in the dead of night, which was not wise, but she had little choice. She just hoped she would not have anything else to deal with. She thought of the stranger and wondered if he had been hired, or if it was just bad luck. Not many knew what she was, only the Stonelances and a witch in Naverac.

Could they have hired him?

She shook her head, it had been too long, especially with the Stonelances. The encounter was more than likely just a coincidence. Whatever the reason. She was glad she had been in the forest watching Derwyn, but she did regret not dealing with that man there and then.

CHAPTER 23

DERWYN rubbed his eyes as he sat on the side of his bed in the early hours. He had been pulled from his sleep by his sister when she shook him awake. Yawning, he slowly stood and regarded her as she paced the cabin then got some water. She seemed concerned as well as exhausted. She would never normally ride through the forest at night even though most of the mystical creatures gave her a wide berth. Something had happened and the look on her face worried him.

He yawned again. "What's wrong?"

Lara continued pacing the cabin as she gulped down the water. She then stopped and studied him. "Seems that man wasn't just any type of glory hunter. He's a Sword."

"Are you sure?" asked Derwyn, concern etched on his features, his arms folded across his chest.

Lara showed the burn mark on her hand. "Silver is the only thing that will leave a scar this long. Only someone who knows about killing demons would own a silver dagger or sword." She glared at him. "He wasn't scared of me, so he's encountered non-humans more than once."

"He could be just a random glory hunter."

"Nay the dagger was expensive. Glory hunters don't make enough coin to have anything that ornate."

"So, what do we do?" asked Derwyn. He had not seen his sister so tense in years.

Lara sighed. "Head south. I think we leave the area for a while."

"Why didn't you kill him?"

"I could have," responded Lara. "But then we would be hunted by all of Yarl!" She crossed her arms and continued. "When I asked around, nay one seemed to have seen or heard anything, not even Barac, and we know what a gossip he is. I think he was hired by someone out of the area, maybe to find or kill a specific demon, like a Zenfus. Their organs take a fair price on the black market. Or . . ." She paused. "We have been seen."

"Are you sure? We have been very careful. Not many know what you are."

Lara pursed her lips. "I know, and I really think it is just coincidence."

Derwyn sighed, knowing this day would have come. "But you think it is best not to take the risk."

She nodded, regarding her brother. "At some point, we would have to think about moving on, or at least I would."

Derwyn studied her, she had so many times mentioned leaving and every time he had refused. "Nay, we have had this conversation before, and I have told you, *we stick together.*"

She smiled while gazing at her brother with affection. "But there will come a time when you will look more like my papa than my younger brother."

Derwyn sighed and regarded his sister aware of the fact that they seemed closer in age than they actually were. "Very true, but that's years away. We still stick together. I have told you so many times, and it's still the same now."

She nodded. "Alright."

Derwyn raised an eyebrow, leaning against the wall. "So, if we leave, where should we go?"

Lara rubbed her face for a moment as she went over options in her head. She peered up at him. "I think we head for Kerlish."

He stood up straight, already thinking about what they needed to pack. "What if he heads that way?"

Lara responded, a little sheepish. "Well, not for a few days."

Derwyn raised an eyebrow, wondering what his sister had done. "Let's hope he doesn't hold a grudge."

Lara shrugged, "We may never know. But if we head off, we will have a head start and our trail will have gone cold." She paused and sighed, her features looking conflicted, like she was doubting herself. "To be honest, I could be overreacting, he may not follow us. He will probably go and get whatever is on his contract, and that will be it."

Derwyn responded, "True, but what does your instincts tell you?"

"My wolf self feels uneasy."

"Then it's time for us to move on as she's never wrong." He placed a hand on her shoulder. "I sooner we are wrong than still be here and regret it."

Within an hour they were heading south, ensuring they did not ride on the main route until they were a good distance from the village. As they left, Derwyn glanced back at the cabin. They had secured it as best they could, all their belongings, which was not much, were in their saddlebags. The cabin would be a good base if they were ever back in that direction, and with it being in the depths of the forest, the chances of anyone finding it were slim. Once they were a good distance from Yarl, they rode across to the main road which headed south to Spor. They hoped to reach the large market town within about three days.

Derwyn missed the times when they used to travel and was looking forward to it once more. Even with the uncertainty over the Sword. He gazed at his sister, he knew she would do anything to keep them both protected, and he hoped that it was just a coincidence. At least this time they could watch each other's backs. Derwyn was as good with the sword as his sister, and if they came across any trouble, they had the strength and the skill to protect themselves. After years on the run as a child, being a man meant Derwyn could do his part.

Derwyn surveyed the horizon ahead. After Spor, it would be another five days to Kerlish. He could remember Naverac and how busy it had been, and Kerlish would be just as big, maybe bigger. It would be good to see a city once more. He had liked it at Naverac, and had been reluctant to leave, yet it had been a wise choice. He had got used to a quiet life in Yarl, but even their busiest day would be nothing like the chaos of a big city.

That would take some time to get used to. But also, they could get lost in a big city for a while, which would give them time to decide their next move. He glanced back towards Yarl and wondered if he would ever see the village again.

CHAPTER 24

LARA and Derwyn made it to the large market town of Spor within three days. Most of the journey had been warm and pleasant, but as they reached the town there was a chill in the air. Both knew the weather was on the turn, a storm brewing to the east from the coast. They fastened their horses outside one of the inns in the town and when they entered the large stone building, they were greeted by a warm open fire and the gentle buzz of conversation. The inn was not too busy, the town's main market day had been a few days before, but Lara's senses were still invaded by new and old scents. After years of practice, she could tone them down with ease. She went up to the main counter to ask for rooms, while Derwyn went to find a table. As she waited for the innkeeper, she leaned against the counter and glanced casually around the large open room. Tables scattered throughout, some occupied.

As she scrutinised the room, a familiar scent invaded her nostrils. She turned towards it, it was a human with a smattering of wolf in the mix. The same she had picked up all those years ago at Little Stump. Her eyes focused on a dark-haired, athletically built man sitting on his own in the corner, drinking his ale. From his physique and manor, he was probably a Sword. She focused on him a little more closely without making it obvious.

Could that be the teenage lad from all those years ago? He resembled the older Sword, but if it were the lad, he would be in his mid-twenties, and this man seemed to be about the same age. A smile curled across her lips, remembering when he had been clipped around the ear by his father for gawking at her, then him smiling at her in the stables. It felt strange to be crossing his path once more after so long. His hair was not as short and his features seemed rougher, but still strikingly handsome, probably even more so from age.

Her attention was drawn back to the innkeeper when he finished with his other customer. She asked for a couple of rooms and food and drink.

The innkeeper passed her room keys. "Me girl will be over with stew and dumplins, as well as your ale and wine."

Lara gave a quick nod and then headed over to the table Derwyn had acquired. She removed her sword and sat down next to him, both able to survey the inn.

Derwyn looked around and then said, "It will be further to get to Kerlish. What do you want to do when we get there?"

Lara responded, strumming her fingers on the table, wanting her drink. "Get board for a few days, not sure where after that. But Kerlish is a busy city. We can lay low for a while, and I may make some enquiries about local Swords in the area."

Derwyn raised an eyebrow. "Is that wise?"

Lara shrugged. "Maybe not, but I am curious to know why he was there."

A tall, slim, black-haired girl came over with a tray carrying two large bowls of piping hot stew and dumplings, a mug of ale and a goblet of wine. The two thanked her, then Lara noticed the girl's eyes lingering on Derwyn a little longer than normal. She smirked as her brother nodded a thank you to the girl before taking a sip of his ale.

Lara whispered, "She likes you."

Derwyn just smiled, seeming a little awkward. Lara chuckled and took a sip of her wine. Derwyn's attention soon turned to the food. She leaned back and watched the room. Her eyes lingered on the Sword again who was still alone in the corner, mirroring her actions. Their eyes locked for a few moments, both glancing away at the same instant. Lara took a sip of her wine and carefully glanced back up, to see him getting to his feet and picking up his ale.

Lara turned to her brother when he said, "He looks like he could be trouble."

She smiled. "It's just a harmless flirt."

Derwyn nodded in the direction of the Sword as he ate. "Well, he's heading over."

Lara turned back when the familiar scent became stronger, the tall, dark-haired man smiled as he stopped at her table. His black trousers and brown jerkin fitted his body well, accentuating his lean build. He smiled broadly, causing dimples in his cheeks, and showing perfect teeth. He said in a deep soothing voice, "May I join you?"

Derwyn looked up, instantly disliking the Sword. As he said no, Lara said yes. The man stared at the two of them, raising an eyebrow. Derwyn felt Lara kick his shin under the table.

She said, "Sorry, ignore my brother. You're welcome to join us."

Derwyn glared at her, his eyes opening wide, mentally saying, *Really?*

His sister ignored him and smiled at the tall man as he sat. "So, what brings you to these parts?"

The Sword gazed at his sister intently, making Derwyn dislike him even more. He could smell Sword's testosterone and was now picking up Lara's pheromones. Lara was definitely attracted to him.

The man stated, "I'm travelling south." He leant forward a little, his blue eyes focused on Lara's. "This may seem odd, but I feel sure we have met before."

Derwyn choked on his ale. What a bad chat up line. He then felt Lara kick him again on the shin. She focused on the handsome man opposite her. "Really? I don't recall." She smiled. "I'm Lara. This is my brother, Derwyn."

He did a quick nod to them both. Derwyn glared back at him, yet the Sword's gaze never faltered. The Sword then turned back to Lara. "I'm Carn."

Lara glanced at the sword on his back. "So, are you a Sword for hire?"

Carn smiled, glancing at hers, leaning against the bench beside her. "I'm on my way to pick up another contract. And you both seem to be well-armed."

Lara responded, "Just for protection. You can't be too careful these days."

Carn's eyes lingered on her. "Aye, very true."

Derwyn eyed him with suspicion, not liking how Carn was gawking at his sister. The sexual attraction between the two was becoming suffocating. "So do you take *any* job, or do you refuse if they are a little *unethical?*"

Lara raised her eyebrows glaring at her brother, whispering under her breath, "Really?"

He smiled at her, then turned his attention back to Carn waiting for his answer. He was not intimidated by the cocky Sword and would soon put him in his place.

Lara smiled. "Sorry for my brother."

Carn focused on Lara for a second before turning to Derwyn. "I do pick and choose my contracts. Which I can't say is the same for other Swords."

Derwyn pursed his lips. "I see." He kept his gaze steady on Carn's and asked, "So what was your last contract?"

Carn responded, his gaze as steady as Derwyn's. "A bounty, on a couple of robbers. They were stealing from a merchant at Fish La."

Derwyn nodded, knowing if Carn tried anything, he would knock him out cold. He glanced at Lara as she joined in the conversation, his sister could do so much better than some cocky Sword. He may be taking more ethical contracts, but Derwyn still did not trust him. Carn was just too sure of himself. What made matters worse, they were trying to avoid one Sword and this stranger may even have connections to the one at Yarl. The last thing they needed was getting involved with anyone when they did not know if he could be trusted.

After a while Derwyn wanted to head to bed and as he stood, he tried to get Lara to go with him.

She smiled. "Nay. I'm fine for a while longer."

He glared at her. It seemed his plan to get them away from Carn was not working. "Don't we have an *early* start?"

"Aye, but I'm alright. Go to bed."

Derwyn looked at her for a moment and then at Carn. The teenager grunted, it seemed his sister was not taking the hint, and if he stayed any longer, he may do something he would regret. He grabbed his room key, turned on his heel and left. Derwyn glanced back seeing the two lost in each other's gaze. *Is Lara seriously flirting with a Sword when we need to keep a low profile?*

Reaching his room, he slumped down on his bed. He will have a word with Lara in the morning and tell her how annoyed he was about the situation. Then again, once on the road, Carn would become a forgotten memory. He was not sure why Carn was rubbing him up the wrong way.

Is it the fact that I have never seen my sister flirt so obviously in front of me before? He took a deep breath, focusing on his wolf self, feeling its annoyance with the situation. Carn was the first alpha type male he had crossed paths with. *Is my wolf trying to force dominance?* Derwyn smirked. It was not jealousy, he could beat Carn in a heartbeat. *Could it be more a protective gesture with Lara being my alpha?*

Whatever the reason, he needed to keep his wolf side in check. Closing his eyes, he focused and he felt the wolf's emotions calming. He needed to keep control and not let his emotions get a hold. He was still getting used to all his new feelings and abilities. From what he read, that was an issue for young male lycans. Until the situation downstairs, he had felt like he was in control. The journey was definitely going to test him. But if he meditated like his sister had shown him, he would keep his wolf side in control. Leaving Yarl behind and being on the road would be challenging, but Derwyn could keep focused.

Lara watched Derwyn reluctantly leave, she would have to have a word with him in the morning about his attitude. From what she had read about young lycan males, she wondered if that was one of the issues she would have to deal with.

She turned back to see Carn also watching him leave. He focused back on her, his eyes never wavering from her green. "He's very protective over you."

Lara smiled coolly. "He knows I can take care of myself."

Carn raised an eyebrow. "Well, older brothers can be very protective."

Lara was about to correct him, but realised that to anyone regarding them both, there was little between their ages. With Derwyn being taller, it seemed that he would be the older sibling and not the younger of eleven years.

Lara shrugged. "Maybe, but he shouldn't be overprotective."

Carn focused on her features, his eyes only on her. "I know I would be with a beauty such as you."

Lara found herself lost in his gaze. His eyes were so clear she could easily lose herself in their blue depth. She was right about him becoming even more attractive with age. She could not help but be drawn to him, even more than all those years before. "Really?"

"Really." His hand slid across the table, his fingertips brushing hers.

Lara's skin tingled, feeling his rough skin against her own. It had been a while since she had met someone new. It felt good to have an innocent flirt and possibly a little more. The thought of which made her whole body shiver in delight. She glanced down at his hand, her fingers lacing into his. "Soo, do you have an early start?"

"Not too early," he responded, raising his dark eyebrow.

Lara smiled lost in his gaze. "Good."

Lara continued to kiss Carn as he fumbled to unlock his room door. One of his hands was firmly on her waist, keeping their bodies close. Once the lock clicked, he pushed the door open with his back, pulling her in. Once they were in private, Carn having kicked the door shut with his foot, they started to undress each other. Lara threw clothes to the floor as she directed Carn towards the bed, while they continued to kiss. By the time his legs hit the side of it, they were both naked. He picked her up in his lean arms with ease. Her legs wrapped around his waist, her groin next to his, feeling it grow. Carn climbed blindly onto the bed not wanting the kiss to end. Lara let her senses go, but kept her vampire side in check. She took a deep breath of Carn's musky scent, filling her lungs. She had been drawn to him all those years before, and the attraction was still there. She was not at all surprised they were having sex in his room.

He paused, studying her features. "I wasn't expecting this when I came over to your table."

Lara smiled at him then kissed his lips, straddling him. "Strange, as I did."

He gazed at her, grabbing her firmly around the waist. "Love a woman who knows what she wants."

She grinned and then she felt his phallus against her thigh, moments later he entered her. Her loins shuddered in delight as he pushed deeper. She gazed at his lean, muscular torso as their bodies moved in unison. Her eyes focused on a couple of scars, one on his side, the other on his shoulder.

As he held her waist while their hips moved, he whispered, "You are amazing."

Her fingers traced the scar on his shoulder, she leant forward and kissed him, flicking her long hair out of the way. "Less talk."

He deepened the kiss and breathed, as their bodies continued to move in rhythm. "Not going to argue with that."

Lara arched backwards, letting his penis go deeper, her body buzzing. Carn's firm hands moved to her hips, keeping the rhythm going. His thumbs brushed into her pubic hair making her thighs tingle. Lara had never felt her body react like that before. All her senses were overwhelmed, her body not her own. She took a deep breath, Carn's testosterone smell making her almost giddy. She could not focus, her body shuddering. She felt Carn's thighs shudder, both of them reaching orgasm at the same moment. Lara closed her eyes as the euphoria flowed over her. No man had ever made her come like that before. Lara fell forward, Carn wrapping her in his firm arms, her body like jelly. Both of them still breathing heavily. Neither of them moved or separated, still feeling their bodies throb with delight.

They lay in each other's arms, their naked limbs entangled, as Carn dozed. Lara studied his attractive features; glad he had come over to the table. It would probably be years before they crossed paths again, yet it still felt good, the sex having been amazing. Taul had been an amazing and wonderful lover, but this, this was more. Her body tingled just thinking about the sex they had had. She smirked. The second time had been even more amazing than the first. She traced her fingers over the scar on his shoulder. She had had a few lovers over the years, most fleeting like this would be. But none, except this one, made her body react the way it had. She kissed him gently, never having thought that a chance encounter in the stable all those years ago would have ended up like this.

Sensing Carn was fully asleep, she slid out from under his limbs and quietly pulled on her clothes. She gazed back at his sleeping form and smiled; she would not forget this night in a hurry. She quietly left the room, knowing it was for the best to head back to hers.

Judging from Derwyn's behaviour, he seemed to be struggling with her just flirting with a man. Lara just realised, as she walked quietly to her room, that her brother had not been in Yarl whenever she met with Taul, so he had never seen that side of her. She would have to be careful from now on, as Derwyn would just get more protective the older he got. And being a male lycan, his protective nature would be strong, even more with her being his alpha. She was the leader of the pack, but from what she had read, the male family members felt a duty to protect a female alpha at all costs. Add in the fact that young lycans had to deal with their hormones while keeping their aggressive side in check. It would be a while before her brother would not overreact every time she spoke to an alpha type male.

CHAPTER 25

CARN slowly woke feeling content, a smile curled across his face, thinking of the night before. Yet when he rolled over, the other side of the bed was cold and empty. He sighed rolling back, staring at the ceiling. He had expected it, but there was still a slight pang of sadness that Lara was not there. He rubbed his stubbled chin with his fingers. As soon as he had seen her last night, he had been instantly drawn to her. Not many women had that effect on him. He sat up, his mind wandering back to the sex, it had been *amazing*. He had never been with a woman with so much stamina. He smiled remembering every inch of Lara's athletic body. Carn had not expected such an encounter at an inn in Spor. The place had always been dull, but would now be etched in his memory for life. Rubbing his eyes, he took a deep breath and climbed out of bed, he needed to get moving. He smirked; he could still smell her fragrance of lavender. He had not smelt that fragrance in years. He had not expected anything more than a fleeting moment, but it would be a while before he forgot Lara. He thought of the sex again, and quickly took a deep breath, he had to focus. His body began to portray where his mind was wandering. His thighs and groin tingled and he forced himself to think of something else. Grabbing his clothes, which were still scattered across the floor, he slowly got dressed. His mind wandered back to the night before as he tucked in his shirt, and he stared out the window, trying to focus again. He was acting like a giddy teenager. He went over to the bowl of cold water, threw some on his face and combed his fingers through his dark hair. That cooled him down a little and forced him to stop dreaming about the night before.

With a faint smile on his face, he went down into the quiet inn with his belongings. The innkeeper gave him a sly look. Carn smiled at him and ordered breakfast. Taking a seat, he glanced around, there were only a couple of travellers eating and no sign of Lara or her brother. He sighed as the barmaid brought him his food and gave him a broad smile. Carn smiled back, which made her blush a little. He watched her head back to the kitchen; he could always charm the ladies, but none drew him as Lara had.

It seemed Derwyn was very overprotective, yet he had seen brothers like that before. It usually ended up with them having a brawl, usually with him winning. But it looked like Derwyn could hold his own, and Carn was not sure who would win. Yet he did not think it would come to that, knowing his luck he would not cross paths with them again. Good from the point of view of the brother, but a shame not to have another night with Lara. Yet he would not forget that night in a hurry.

Once he had eaten, Carn was on the road again, his wolf trotting just ahead of his horse. The Sword thought about the new contract he would be picking up in Kerlish. Whenever he ran into Kraven, the old Sword would try to get him to take a hunter contract and he would always turn it down. The old man never got the hint that Carn just was not interested. Yes, some of the non-humans caused issues and needed to be dealt with, but others just wanted a quiet life like everyone else. He sighed remembering his father taking the hunter jobs, and some had been very unethical. Due to that, Carn had vowed never to go near them. Kraven always offered them as they were more lucrative, especially for the old Sword. To be honest, his father had been good at them too, the best on Kraven's books. Yet, after some time, even his father decided to stop, but the old Sword would still always try to sway them. Carn had to give Kraven credit, he knew what his contract Swords were good at, and would always try to give them the jobs with the largest payout. Which on most occasions were the hunter contracts, but that was mainly so Kraven could ensure his purse was filled more than his Swords. Carn smiled, he was good at his job, but would never take a hunter contract, it just did not sit well with him. He would keep to what he preferred, and that was bounty and security contracts, which gave him some flexibility and still paid very well.

Carn heard a commotion ahead; he slowed his horse as his wolf started growling. There had been rumours of opportunist robbers lately, and it sounded like some poor soul was their next victim. Carn sighed, he just could not go on by, he had to help. As he got closer, he saw one of the robbers slit the merchant's throat, the poor man did not stand a chance. Carn jumped from his horse, drawing his longsword, time to give the robbers a taste of his steel. The group of men turned to see Carn and two of the six walked towards him ready to fight. Carn smiled, taking a firm grip of the hilt. He had to admit he did like a good sword fight, even with those odds.

Lara was getting ready when Derwyn knocked on her door. Letting him in, she smiled. "You seem eager to go."

"Well, I thought we wanted an early start."

Lara pursed her lips. "We do, but it isn't a race."

He asked, "What about that glory hunter?"

"Well, I don't think he'll catch up with us. He doesn't even know where we're going."

"True. But still, I'd like to be on the move, if we can." He paused studying her suspiciously as Lara pulled on her boots. "Did anything happen with that Sword?"

Lara eyed him, her features innocent. "You mean Carn?" She shrugged. "We chatted."

She headed towards the door, as her brother narrowed his eyes and pursed his lips. He would know there had been more than just that, with picking up Carn's scent on her. She could tell from the expression he was giving her that he had, but was not pursuing it. She smirked, grabbing her stuff as they left the room. She did not lie to her brother, the two of them did talk.

As they walked to the main part of the inn, Lara was not sure if she liked the idea of her brother being so overprotective, it made it feel like she could not relax. She glanced at him. She also had to stop seeing him as a little boy, and would have to have a talk to him about situations like that in the future. It was nice that he wanted to protect her, but she knew what she wanted, and would not get hurt in the process. Also, to make him know that he had options, too. He seemed a little embarrassed by the serving girl last night. But unknown to him, she had seen him gawking at girls back at Yarl, and witnessed him turn awkward when they flirted with him. But not all could have been too awkward as she had picked up the scent of a girl on him every now and then. Nothing as intimate as her and Carn, but he had definitely kissed a girl or two.

When they sat down for breakfast, they were the only guests remaining, the innkeeper gave Lara a knowing look but did not say anything, having seen it all before. Once Derwyn had eaten, they paid for the board and went to get their horses from the stable. They were soon on their way to Kerlish.

As they rode down the main road, from Spor, Derwyn said, turning towards his sister. "So, you just *talked*?"

Lara realised that her flirting with Carn had bothered Derwyn and something had been brewing since they left the inn. "Aye, we *talked*."

"Really?" he responded coldly. "I can smell him all over you!"

Lara sighed, reining her horse to be even with his. "What happened between me and Carn is *my* business."

Derwyn glared at her; his face full of disapproval. "We are trying to get away from a hunter and you are, well, more than talking with a Sword for hire!"

Lara took a deep breath. "*Listen*, Derwyn. I am eleven years your senior. Though these days it doesn't look like it. I know what I am doing. Now *leave it.*"

Derwyn still seemed annoyed. Lara pulled her horse close to his and said sternly, "*Leave it, Derwyn.*"

He eyed her, then heeled the sides of his horse making him trot further ahead. Lara was tempted to go after him and have a full-blown argument but paused. It was not the place and it was best to leave him be, knowing her brother would come to his senses.

They had been travelling for a while, neither talking. With their heightened hearing, they could hear a sword fight in the far distance. Lara's hearing was even more sensitive, so she knew how many were involved, but could only imagine what they would run into. She stared at her brother's back. If they avoided the fight, it would add an extra day to the journey, and not what they wanted, especially with the mood Derwyn was in. It would be best to stick with the planned route. She wondered what the situation was ahead and knew they would need to continue with caution. If they needed to defend themselves, it would be prudent to use their swords, as it would not be wise to turn in broad daylight. As they took the bend in the road where there was a dip, the clash of swords was getting closer and they were certain it was on the main route. Lara gazed at her brother. Maybe a good fight would get rid of his frustration; it would definitely help her.

As they rounded the corner, Lara picked up the scents of a group of men and then Carn's. Lara sighed. She had expected to not cross paths with him for years, if ever, yet, she was going to run into him again within hours. Not ideal with how Derwyn was feeling, but Lara was more than open to seeing him so soon. When they got closer, they slowed as Carn came into view. He was fighting four robbers, and a wolf, which had to be his, was dealing with a fifth. There was a cart to one side that was probably a merchants, and horses, the robbers and Carn's.

Lara was about to dismount, saying, "We should help."

Derwyn pursed his lips. "Looks like he's managing it well."

Lara glanced back, she had to agree. Carn was surprisingly good with the sword. "Well true. He's a good swordsman."

He snorted. "I suppose."

She turned to her brother. "You *really* don't like him, do you?"

Derwyn shrugged. "Well, he seems alright, but not particularly."

Lara stared at him. "Look, as I said earlier, I can handle myself and it is not your concern."

Derwyn eyed her then glanced back at the fight when there was a loud clash of swords. "I know. But I feel that I must be there for you. I also think you could do better."

Lara raised an eyebrow. "Really?"

Derwyn answered, "He's a Sword. And a bit cocky, if you ask me."

Lara pursed her lips. "True. But I'm not after anything serious. Remember, I won't age."

"I still feel I should look out for you."

Lara smiled. The ride had calmed her brother and he was starting to see things a little more from her point of view, but her attention was pulled to the fight.

Carn yelled, "*A little help*?"

Lara went for her sword, almost surprised he had asked. "Oh, aye."

One of the robbers turned to see the two and smirked when he saw Lara dismount and head towards them. Derwyn jumped from his horse to join her and the two drew their swords. Within moments they were in the fight. The large man who had seen them first, was surprised at how strong Lara was, seeing as she had been dwarfed by his size. Lara and Derwyn held back their non-human abilities, not wanting to make it too apparent with Carn fighting alongside them. But they were quite skilled with the sword. The oversized thug did not last long, Lara made sure he was killed swiftly. With the odds evened out, the outlaws had soon been dealt with.

Carn gasped, sheathing his sword, and thanked the two. His eyes lingered on Lara a little longer as he commented, "So, our paths cross again."

Lara smiled at him, sheathing her sword, and acting a little out of breath to look as normal as possible. "That seems to be the case." She examined the bodies, and noticed the wolf had run off towards the trees. Lara wondered if it had sensed what she and her brother were. She then focused on the dead merchant. "Shame we couldn't help him."

Carn nodded. "I came across them right as they were killing him. I couldn't go by without doing something."

Derwyn sighed. "We should ensure he isn't left like this."

Lara responded, "And dead bodies out at night will draw things that are far worse."

Carn agreed, "Aye, we don't want to be around when those things come out."

Lara glanced at him, sensing he may have come across ghouls before. They pulled the bodies as far from the road as they could and buried them and the merchant. When they went to the merchant's cart, Lara picked up a scent. She glanced at the others, noticing Derwyn had caught the scent too.

She whispered, "Did you hear something?"

Carn shook his head. Lara placed a finger to her lips and slowly pulled back the tarpaulin covering the merchants' wears, to see a twelve-year-old boy's tear ridden face. He looked at them, scared, and Lara said softly, "It's alright. We won't hurt you."

He peered over the edge of the cart. "Where's papa? Did they kill him?"

Lara slowly nodded. "We weren't in time to save him."

He replied, "Papa told me to stay quiet."

Carn studied him and smiled softly. "You are a brave boy. We can help you back to Spor."

The lad shook his head. "Nay, my papa told me what to do. I have taken the cart between villages when he needs to get produce from elsewhere."

Carn smiled. "Your papa taught you well." He looked across at the tree line and pointed. "We buried your papa up there so the ghouls won't get to him."

The boy nodded. "Thank ya." He looked at the robbers' horses. "What about them? Can I have 'em? I think I could get some coin for them."

Lara smiled and they tethered the horses to his cart. The lad nodded thanks and rode off, back the way they had come. It seemed that even though initially scared, the lad was old enough to take care of himself and make a pretty penny in the process.

They then continued to Kerlish, Carn riding with them. The Sword's horse fell in step beside Lara's, and he leaned towards her wanting his conversation to be private from Derwyn, who rode slightly ahead.

"I was a little disheartened when you weren't there when I woke."

Lara smiled, turned towards him, and whispered even though her brother had heard every word Carn had said. "We both had early starts."

He smiled and raised an eyebrow, his saddle creaking from him still leaning towards her. "I didn't get a chance to say how *amazing* it was."

Lara focused on his eyes. "That it was."

Derwyn slowed his horse, and Carn reined his away from Lara, moving slightly ahead. Her brother glared at Carn as he rode by him and then leaned towards his sister, his saddle creaking.

He whispered, "I *knew it*. My nose is never wrong."

Lara smiled and shrugged. She was not about to explain her actions to her brother, he would just have to get used to it. He stared at her, then at Carn ahead, and shook his head in disbelief. He gave her a concerned look, keeping his voice low so Carn would not hear, "Just hope you know what you're doing."

Lara studied her brother, also keeping her voice low, "It's just a harmless fling. Don't worry about it."

He eyed Carn. "Does *he* know that?"

"He's a Sword, he's just after something casual as well." She leaned closer to her brother, squeezing his arm. "Don't worry. It's nice that you are looking out for me, but I'm a big girl and can take care of myself."

Derwyn replied, "Well it's hard not to be concerned, Lara. It's been you and me for years and for most of them, you have protected me. It's only right that I return that favour."

Lara smiled, studying her brother with affection. "We will always look out for each other." She winked at her brother. "And when you meet a girl, I'll be there, if you need me."

He grunted. "I don't think so."

Lara's smile grew wider. "Aww, come on, a handsome fellow like you? You'll have girls all over you."

Derwyn's cheeks flushed slightly, seeming awkward again, like he had the night before. He then nodded his head towards Carn. "So, is he riding with us?"

Lara glanced at her brother. The conversation about girls had made him uncomfortable and it was for the best not to push it.

"There's nay harm in him being with us."

Derwyn gazed at her, getting his composure back. "What about hunting?"

Lara smiled. "I can be pretty quiet. I can do it when he's asleep."

"You sure? He may be a light sleeper?"

Lara smirked, raising an eyebrow. "Well, I know that he's not."

Derwyn screwed up his face. "Please. I don't want to know, alright. But him being with us could still be an issue."

Lara sighed. "When we make camp, I will have a word with him. Figure him out, see if there could be any issues or not."

Derwyn responded, "Still think we should go our separate ways."

"True, but if he's heading to Kerlish too, we aren't going to stop crossing paths with him. And after coming across those robbers, having an extra sword would be in all our best interest," she told her brother. "Look, I admit that I will need to hunt in the next day or two, but that is *my* problem. So *I* will deal with it."

Her brother raised an eyebrow. "But if there *is* an issue, *we* need to deal with it, fast."

Lara agreed. If Carn reacted adversely, then it was for her to deal with, but she was also proud her brother would stand with her in a fight. She just hoped there would not be one.

CHAPTER 26

As the sun went down and with there being very little shelter on the route, they rode towards the bank of the large River Ker that wound its way near the main route towards Kerlish. They found a small clearing within a copse of bushes, which gave them a little bit of shelter from the cool breeze blowing across the open land. While Derwyn went to find dry wood for a fire from the nearby bushes, Lara helped Carn with the horses. As they unsaddled and brushed them down, the horses munched on the shrubs they had been tethered to. A brown wolf trotted over, stopping by Carn and nuzzling his hand when it reached his side. He turned and gave the animal a fuss.

Lara said, "You have trained her well."

He responded, smiling. "My papa and I always had trained wolves. They are useful with our work." He scratched behind her ear making the wolf nuzzle him more. "But I leave her to be free to roam, and she always runs off for a while after I've needed her." Then he frowned. "How did you know she's a she? Most I meet, say he."

Lara pursed her lips, having picked up the animals' pheromones. "A lucky guess."

She smiled, studying the wolf, her eyes never wavering as she gazed into its eyes. It seemed the wolf had not run off due to her and Derwyn, but she wanted to make sure it did not react to them now, especially her. The last time she had met one of Carn's family wolves, she had to show her dominance more prominently, but over the years she had learned how to ensure a wolf would not react to her vampire side and expose her. It was all about eye contact. She knelt, and the wolf trotted over to her. Lara focused on the wolf's eyes, neither gaze faltering. Lara had found that with her vampire side, she was able to soothe people with her gaze, and the same effect worked with animals. That was how vampires got their victims, but for her, it was to stop animals from reacting to her scent. She stroked the wolf, which licked her hand.

Carn smiled. "Kindred spirit . . ."

He trailed off, staring at Lara, recognition in his blue eyes. He had finally placed where he had seen her before. She tensed ready to deal with him, if need be, wondering if she should use her soothing gaze on him. Yet he did not go for his sword, he just frowned, as he remembered where they had first met.

"Wait. Aren't you the girl from the stables?" He paused studying her. "But that was about ten winters ago, you haven't aged a day."

Lara slowly got to her feet; her hands open, arms slightly out, carefully avoiding to make any sudden moves. Her eyes glanced towards his hands, making sure they were relaxed, steady. He seemed to be more in shock than anything else. She was ready to soothe him with her gaze, if need be, but hoped she could sort the situation without doing anything to him. She said softly, not wanting to sound as tense as she suddenly felt. "I need you to stay calm. What I'm about to tell you may be difficult for you to take in."

Carn frowned, studying Lara; he had not heard what she had just said. His mind had gone back to that morning, ten winters before, in the stables when the girl that now faced him had smiled, making his day. He had only been a teenager, and so overwhelmed that they had spoken. He had not forgotten about her for months afterwards, wondering if he would cross paths with her again. But he had expected an older woman. She had been a faded memory, even with those unforgettable eyes. But now he had realised who she was, her face from all those years ago was as clear as day. It seemed only a few days had passed, not years.

He said, "You look *exactly* the same. By Rosh, how is that possible?"

Carn saw movement. Derwyn rushed over, undoing his shirt, his features stern. Carn tensed, if the brother tried anything he would defend himself. His fingers twitched to go for the dagger on his belt, but Lara put up her hand turning to her brother and snapped, "Derwyn *nay*! I'll deal with this."

Her brother froze, seeming on edge, but did not go any further. Carn glared at him, glancing between the two siblings. All three were on edge. If either of them made a sudden move, his daggers would find their mark.

Lara turned to Carn, putting up her hands in a calming gesture. "Aye, we did meet all those years ago and aye, I haven't aged. I need to know this will not be an *issue*."

Carn shook his head, studying her concerned features. It was a lot to take in. It seemed she did not want any problems, but with how tense Derwyn seemed to be, Carn was not sure if he could trust him yet. He looked at Lara. It appeared she wanted to talk. Her brother, if that was who he really was, looked like he was ready to tear Carn's head off.

"Depends." He scowled at Derwyn, whose tension in the situation was visible. Carn's hand twitched, ready to go to his dagger, as he said sternly, "Is your brother, if that's who he is, going to back down?"

Lara glared at her brother and then turned back to Carn. "He won't do *anything*." She studied Carn intently. "We don't want any trouble, and what I am about to tell you, not many know."

Carn's mind was going through all the magical creatures he knew. He remembered the night before; she had been warm to the touch so that ruled out vampire and demon. He asked, still trying to figure out how she had not aged, "Are you some sort of witch or something?"

Lara shook her head. "Nay." She swallowed, suddenly looking nervous like she was about to tell him something she had not told anyone before. "Derwyn and I are from a family of lycans."

Carn regarded them, then he frowned. "So, you're werewolves, but I thought you aged like us?"

Derwyn gave a look of disgust. He stated, his voice tense, as well as his stance, "We are *lycans, not* werewolves. There is a *difference.* And we do age like humans. Lara's different."

Carn turned his full attention to Lara, studying her green eyes. His stomach twisted, feeling sick. What had he made love to last night? "Different?" He turned back to Derwyn, still feeling confused. "I thought werewolves and lycans were the same?"

Derwyn glared at him. "Werewolves are forced to transform with the lunar cycle! We *don't.*"

Carn frowned at them both, realising he was not as well read on demonology as he had once thought. Even his father had not been, as he had passed down most of his knowledge to Carn. Then again, it did not surprise him that his father lacked some knowledge. "So, you can change whenever?"

Lara answered, "Aye, and we take wolf form, not humanoid wolf form."

Carn slowly nodded while studying Lara, taking in the fresh knowledge and feeling foolish to have thought that two different species would be the same. Yet his stomach was still tense, wondering what Lara truly was.

"So how different are you from your brother?"

Lara's eyes never left Carn's. She took a deep breath. "I'm a hybrid. The only one."

"Hybrid of what?" Frowned Carn, his attention fully on her.

"Lycan and . . . vampire."

Carn stepped back; he felt the blood drain from his face. His stomach contracting in knots.

How could I have let a vampire get so close to me? His hand instinctively went to his neck, fearful that she had fed off him while he slept. Finding nothing, his hand slowly moved towards the back of his head, closer to his sword.

His features wrinkled in disgust. "*Vampire!*" *If she hadn't fed off me last eve, was that her plan for this eve?*

Lara put up her hands, her muscles tense. Her features flashed in panic for a moment, she did not want the conversation to suddenly go sideways. Her eyes were pleading with his. "But I *don't* feed. The vampire part of me is fully suppressed. My wolf side keeps it in check. But because of the vampire side, I'm faster, stronger and . . . don't age."

Carn felt a little shocked and focused on Lara's eyes, seeing the genuine concern there. His hand was still paused halfway up in reaching for his sword on his back. Slowly taking all the new information in. He really did not want to find out that Lara was the enemy, and from her features, he could tell she was desperate for everything to turn out all right. He had to admit, his sixth sense was telling him that it was fine, and Lara was not about to feed off him or Derwyn about to eat him. He thought about other non-humans, and how many wanted to have a peaceful life. It seemed these two were just the same.

"Oh."

Lara gazed at him, realising she had been hoping that Carn would accept what she really was. "So, you see, I am the girl you smiled at in that inn all those years ago. I have aged, but, just not physically."

Carn studied her, smiling slightly, his body beginning to relax as his hand returned to his side. He raised an eyebrow, a glint of amusement in his eyes. "So you could be older than me?"

Lara smiled, feeling the tension melting. "Maybe. How old are you?"

"Twenty-six."

"So, nay . . . well, aye." Lara shook her head, it was confusing. "So, I was twenty-one when I was turned, and I'm twenty-nine now. I just look like I am still twenty-one."

Carn gazed at the two siblings and took a deep breath, his shoulders relaxing. "By Rosh, that *is* a lot to take in."

Lara watched him carefully. "What we need to know is, are you alright with this? *Nay one* knows our secret, and we want to keep it that way."

Carn nodded quickly, moving his hand to his sides, keeping them both open to show he was not about to do anything. "Aye, I am. And don't worry, I won't say a word."

Derwyn relaxed, glancing at Lara, and then he started to set up the fire.

Lara turned back to Carn. "Thank you."

Carn smiled. "Look, my mind may still be running in circles but don't worry, your secret is safe with me. Just don't bite me."

Lara gave him a sideways glance. "I won't. Well, maybe a little." Carn seemed concerned then Lara added, smirking. "Only joking. Our bite is harmless to humans." She paused, feeling relief flowing over her. "I just need to be sure that you won't ever tell anyone."

"I understand." Then Carn asked, as they moved to the fire that Derwyn had managed to get going, "So why Kerlish?"

Lara sat beside him, then Derwyn sat next to her. Pulling food from the pack, he passed Lara a bottle. Then he scowled at Carn, his features still tense, as the Sword got some of his food out. Lara took a swig of the alcohol in the bottle, noticing there was still tension with her brother and then turned to Carn.

She said, "We need to move on for a while."

Carn gazed at her, offering her some of his food, and she declined. "Anything I could help with?"

Derwyn shook his head, giving Carn a stern look. "We don't need help from outsiders."

Lara glanced at her brother, then turned back to Carn and said, "We'll be alright, but thank you."

Carn inquired, gazing at her intently. "Has anyone found out what you are?"

"Nay," responded Lara. "We keep a low profile."

"Then why move now?"

Derwyn leaned forward. "You're pretty interested in our private business."

Carn turned to Derwyn, not letting the teenager intimidate him. "If we're travelling together, I need to ensure trouble isn't following you."

Derwyn turned to Lara. "I told you we were better off on our own."

Lara glanced at her brother. It seemed they had been on their own for so long that he was unable to trust any outsider. Lara turned to Carn, as he took out some oil and leather, then carefully pulled his sword free from the scabbard and placed it on his lap so he could clean it. Her wolf instincts were telling her that they could trust this Sword, but seemed it would take more to get Derwyn to feel the same.

"Forgive my brother. It has been just the two of us for a long time. Since you met us the first time, actually."

Carn said, eyeing Derwyn, pausing from wiping his blade, with the oiled leather. "Listen kid, I'm not a threat. I know you don't like me as I am a Sword, but I would never kill non-humans unless they were harming others. And I wouldn't harm either of you, and would do my utmost to help and protect you."

Derwyn responded, "Well, we don't need protecting."

Lara gazed at her brother. "Derwyn, we can trust him. I just know we can."

Her brother looked at her, pursing his lips, and glanced at Carn, as the Sword continued to clean his blade. "Still don't trust him."

Carn stopped what he was doing and took hold of the pendant around his neck. "On Rosh. Let me prove it to you over the next few days."

Derwyn shrugged. "But we don't follow your god for warriors. I will see by your actions."

Lara turned to Carn. "Forgive my brother, he will turn around."

He smiled while studying her. "If I have to show your brother that I can be trusted, *I will.*"

Lara peered up at the sky, the light fading fast, her brother asked, "Do you need to hunt this eve?"

"I do." Lara turned to Carn, and then Derwyn. "Will you both behave while I'm gone?"

Derwyn smirked. "As long as he does."

Carn raised his eyebrow, then glanced at Lara. "Hunt?"

"My sister has to hunt every four or five days. Keeps her bloodlust down."

Carn frowned at Lara a little concerned. "I thought you said you had it under control?"

Lara smiled, getting to her feet as she started to undress. "I do. This just ensures I don't suddenly weaken." She raised an eyebrow. "Especially with a human accompanying us."

Derwyn smirked. "Just remember that we could both overpower you, but my sister would be able to do it before you even realised it had happened."

Carn held his hands up. "Hey, don't worry. I won't try anything, I will be . . ."

He trailed off when Lara stood before him, naked.

She said, "What you are about to see now isn't as painful as it looks."

Her joints started to pop as she fell onto all fours, her body contorted when her joints snapped backwards and elongated as she transformed. Moments later, she stood before him in wolf form. Her wolf was over twice the size of a normal wolf, and she towered over the two in their seated position. The Sword gazed at her in awe.

He slowly outstretched his hand. Lara bent her head towards him, letting him stroke her fur. He whispered, "You're amazing."

She grunted, sniffing his hand, her green wolf eyes focused on him. Then she ran, leaving the camp behind.

Carn turned to Derwyn. "Your sister is magnificent."

Derwyn grunted and scowled at him. "Aye, she is. So just keep your distance."

Carn stared at him but said nothing, wiping the blade of his sword almost absentmindedly. The men remained tense, both of them continued cleaning their swords in silence the entire time Lara was gone.

CHAPTER 27

THE following morning was more relaxed after the night events, but there was still some tension as Derwyn was not fully convinced about Carn. The teenager rolled up his sleeping blanket and bedroll, glancing over at the man suspiciously. His sister liked the Sword, and she trusted him enough to tell Carn about who they were. Which, if it had been his choice, Derwyn would have said nothing. It certainly had not helped when Carn figured out that he had seen his sister years before, but then again, that situation would not have arisen if they had gone their separate ways as Derwyn had wanted. He sighed as he walked over to the horses, and readied the saddle for his. What was done, was done, but he would keep a close eye on Carn. He glanced across at Lara, as she rolled up her blanket, smiling at Carn and asking if he slept well. It had shocked Derwyn how forward she had been with the Sword that first night, seeing his sister in a new light. He sighed again, checking the fastenings on his saddle. She was a lot older than he was and he should have expected it. But for years his sister had been a motherly figure, it had been just the two of them and for a good chunk of that time, she had been his protector. He glanced back over, seeing them having a flirtatious exchange, it was something he would have to get used to. He had wished for her to be more like a sister and friend to him than a mother, and they seemed to be venturing that way more these last few days. It should not have shocked him so much, but he would always look out for her, especially since he had the strength of his lycan. He felt like it was his duty, for him to protect her after the years she had protected him. He had to admit though, there did seem to be chemistry between the two. Maybe she had found her mate. He would honour her wishes, but would still make sure she did not get hurt.

With the camp packed away, they rode back to the main road and continued their journey to Kerlish. As they rode along the main route, Lara, and he side by side, with Derwyn a little bit behind them, Carn said, "Last night, you never really said why you were moving on."

Derwyn opened his mouth to tell him it was none of his business when Lara answered, "I crossed paths with a hunter."

"Hunters." Carn's features filled with disgust. "They give Swords a bad name."

Derwyn raised his eyebrow. "Really?"

Carn answered, "They'll kill anything."

"Thought all Swords did, for the right price," Derwyn said with a slight bitterness.

Carn chuckled. "True. But those hunters have even fewer morals and will kill non-humans without a second thought."

Lara sighed. "Well, I gave the hunter a bloody nose. But it was in our best interest to leave, and quickly."

Carn pulled a face. "Understandable, even I avoid them. I came across one who took umbrage at me for having a trained wolf. How they deal with the larger cities that have a mix of humans and non-humans, I don't know. But I doubt you will cross paths with him in Kerlish."

Lara responded, steering her horse around a pothole. "Well, when we get to Kerlish, I want to see if I can find out why he was at Yarl. If he were on a contract, most would come from a big city."

"Well, the Venomous Woods is known for demon activity. So may have just been a passing whim."

"True, that's also why we chose it. So, we could have privacy."

"Good place to disappear," stated Carn, his eyes lingering on Lara a little longer than Derwyn liked.

"Until a hunter starts nosing around," responded Lara. "It could just be a coincidence considering the activity that's there, but part of me wants to know for sure."

Carn studied her intently, keeping his spirited horse in check. "Do you think you will find anything out?"

She shrugged, "Possibly. Kerlish is a big city, I can at least try."

Derwyn said, studying the two from where he rode behind them. "I still think it's a mistake to start asking questions."

Carn responded, glancing back at Derwyn. "I have to agree with your brother. It could cause you more issues."

Lara sighed, glancing between the two men. "True, but my wolf senses are telling me he wasn't there just to hunt the odd demon."

"I thought nay one knew of you," stated Carn, a quizzical look on his handsome features.

Lara eyed him and sighed. "Apart from a lycan family at Crowling. Years ago, I tried to see if they would take on Derwyn when he was older." She glanced back towards her brother. "But they made it *very* clear that they didn't want anything to do with me and wanted to take Derwyn there and then."

"So, you think they hired him?" Carn inquired, raising a perfect eyebrow.

Lara shook her head. "I don't know, it was years ago. But something was off."

Derwyn responded, "Packs can be very territorial and I think they felt threatened by Lara. She is superior to them."

She replied, a little sheepishly, glancing back at her brother. "I don't think they liked the fact I wouldn't bow down to their alpha."

Carn focused on her, pulling his horse back towards the road when it tried to venture off. "Then let me help you find out. I have some contacts at Kerlish who would know if there were any contracts out for non-humans. I have business in the city as I must negotiate a new one, and I can ask the right questions."

Derwyn replied, surprised that Carn was willing to help them. "Thank you."

Carn gave a nod to Derwyn, and raised an eyebrow at Lara who smiled and said, "I told you Derwyn would come round."

"Not fully yet," Derwyn responded. He was beginning to warm to the older man. He turned to Lara as his horse trotted up beside her and added under his breath, "I still think you can do better."

Lara smirked and rolled her eyes. Derwyn smiled and surveyed ahead. He was not about to admit that he was beginning to like the Sword, and his attitude. If he could get past the fact of how friendly Carn was with his sister, Derwyn could be friends with him. But even though he was beginning to like Carn, it would take a bit longer to get him to stop worrying about his sister, and not be so overprotective. His horse was getting a little flighty, wanting to go faster than the leisurely walk they were doing. He glanced back at the two as he passed them. He would give them a bit of privacy, and told them he would scout ahead. The route was deserted, but if they were going to be travelling with Carn for a while, Derwyn knew it was best not to become an unwanted third party.

CHAPTER 28

THEY had ridden along the main route for five days, when they could finally see the tall red stone walls of the city of Kerlish slowly coming into view. It was a very impressive sight to behold. On the top of the walls, equally spaced apart, were watchtowers with red and gold banners fluttering in the breeze. Compared to the rest of the city, the imposing walls seemed new. Yet after standing for hundreds of years, there were few places on the walls that, if you inspected them closely, needed repair. But with it being a peaceful land the walls were never needed other than to look stately.

Kerlish was well known for its spices and silks. Traders and merchants came from far and wide to sell, and of course, buy so they could trade the products further afield. Though the city was inland, it was built next to the large River Ker, which was wide and deep enough to take seafaring ships. Ensuring its docking fees were low, the city had become a busy trading port. It was hard to believe that it had once been a small market town, but over the centuries, it had expanded to become a maze of narrow, winding streets filled with shops, taverns, inns, and whore-houses. With it being so large and popular for its trade, the city had become a mixture of humans and non-humans. Most of the non-humans were able to hide in plain sight with the use of shielding spells, or it just being in their nature. Not many of the human inhabitants would know they could be neighbours with witches, werewolves, lycan and other creatures who were able to resemble normal folk. In such large cities, usually there was a known section called the non-human quarter. It was occupied by those who could not hide in plain sight: dwarves, elves and others.

The three stopped on the outskirts. Carn dismounted and gave his wolf a fuss, who had been trotting by his horse as they had been riding.

He peered up at Lara. "She hates cities, so I won't see her again till I leave."

Lara smiled softly and watched the wolf trot off away from Kerlish. She wondered where she would go with the wolf not being part of a pack. Lara turned to Carn as he also watched the wolf leave. He then remounted his horse and they continued.

The three rode slowly through the main gates, Carn a little further ahead, knowing the city well. Lara gazed up at the guards on duty in the watchtowers on either side, observing everyone entering and leaving the city. They all seemed relaxed, yet a city like this would have some skirmishes most days. She peered ahead at the main route through Kerlish. It was busy with people coming and going and several stalls had been set up along the way to pick up passing trade. The aromas of fresh bread, hot food, leather goods, perfumes and spices invaded Lara's senses like a hammer. She took in everything she could, realising how long it had been since they ventured into a city. She glanced across at Derwyn, he seemed a little overwhelmed by the bombardment of senses. With the new lycan abilities he possessed it would take him a while to train himself to focus his senses. It was one thing having them when in a small town, but in such a large city, he would have to learn to control it quickly. She wondered what he thought of being in a city once more, after leaving Naverac behind.

Lara's thoughts were broken when Carn made a low whistle to get her attention. She turned, and Carn pointed ahead, telling them that there was a small square where, he advised, one of the better inns was located that did not overcharge. Both Lara and Derwyn nodded, the three weaving their horses through the busy street to the small, open square. The square had a couple of streets and side alleys branching off it and there was a fountain in the centre with shops and the large inn lining the sides. They took the alley next to the inn and located the stables at the rear of the building. Leaving the horses with one of the stable hands, they removed their bags and belongings and entered the inn, The Wise Bard, by the side entrance. Inside was abuzz with music and conversation, and barmaids weaving in and out of rows of tables serving food and drinks. Lara had to concentrate hard to stop her senses from being overloaded, she had not been in an inn that busy since Naverac. She glanced over at her brother, seeing his features overwhelmed again, but he seemed to be getting them under control.

Carn reached the main counter first and greeted the innkeeper. "Good eve, Teth. Do you have rooms?"

The large man answered, studying the three. "Aye I do, you can have three of my best on the top floor."

Carn smiled, glancing at Derwyn and Lara, indicating they were exceptionally good rooms. Once the innkeeper had passed over the keys, Derwyn turned to find a table, ready for food and drink. Lara ordered the food and asked Teth what drinks he had on offer, after Carn ordered ale for himself and Derwyn. When the innkeeper gave her options for spirits, she asked for something strong and he offered her a drink called Volc, which had come from the north. Teth remarked it was the strongest drink they had, telling her it was made from root vegetables, and gave a small amount to try. Lara sipped the clear spirit which burned its way down her throat and was amazed at how good it made her feel, more than the strong wines she had been having for years. It seemed she had found a new drink that would satisfy her vampire side with ease.

The table Derwyn had found was near the back gave the three a view of the inn but also afforded some privacy. Lara placed down her drink and sat next to her brother. Carn sat opposite them, having brought over the ales. Lara informed them the food was on its way.

Carn surveyed the busy inn. "In the morn, I can give you a bit of a tour and also find out about the hunter for you."

Lara smiled. "A tour would be good, the last large city we visited was Naverac."

Carn scratched his stubbled chin. "That's a bit smaller than here, but would have the same issues that every large city has."

"I remember there were certain areas that it was best not to enter alone."

Carn agreed, "The same here." He told her. "I have been here a few times, and know those areas."

Lara noticed Derwyn's attention was fully on the occupants of the inn. Then realised it was actually only one, the serving maid stopped doing her rounds and headed their way. But it was not the food that was of interest. She smirked, glancing at her brother and then back at the girl when she stopped at their table. The blonde girl smiled warmly at Derwyn and then placed three bowls of sausages and potatoes in front of each of them, and a plate of bread in the centre of the table. Derwyn smiled and thanked her, the girl's eyes lingering on him a little longer giving him a smile before heading back to the kitchen.

Lara leaned toward him. "She looks nice."

Derwyn eyes were following the girl, then turned his attention to his food. "She seemed alright."

Lara smiled knowing he thought more than that. She whispered, "Why don't you talk to her when the inn quietens down?"

Derwyn shrugged and turned his attention to his food and started eating ravenously. Lara took a sip of her drink and turned her attention to Carn as he ate his meal.

He indicated to hers. "Not hungry?"

Lara smiled. "Can't eat normal food these days, and to be honest, my hunting usually sustains me. Anyway, I got in the habit of ordering food for both of us, but it would then always end up with Derwyn as he has a large appetite."

Carn glanced at her brother seeing he had almost finished his bowl already. "By Rosh, you eat fast."

The younger man studied him. "With being what we are, we have a very healthy appetite."

Carn raised an eyebrow. "I can see, nay wonder Lara always orders two."

Derwyn smiled as he took Lara's bowl to eat the contents of that one too. "To be honest, I could eat all three, well if you hadn't eaten it."

Lara laughed. "Better eat food fast with my brother around, as he will take it when you aren't looking."

They continued to talk for a while and as the inn quietened down Derwyn went to talk to the barmaid, like Lara knew he would, leaving her alone with Carn. Lara regarded Carn's features as he asked, raising an eyebrow. "So, as last time was pretty amazing; I was wondering . . ."

Lara focused on his blue eyes. "Well, would be a shame not to."

Lara looked around for her brother to find him engrossed in a conversation with the barmaid. She turned back to Carn, finishing her drink. "Your room or mine?"

His fingers laced into hers, studying her. "Don't mind as long as you stay till morn."

"Of course." Lara smiled. She was enjoying Carn's company and was not about to disappear in the night like the last time.

Derwyn left his sister and Carn talking and walked over to the blonde barmaid as she strolled back to the kitchen. He smiled at her, focusing on her pretty features. "Good eve, I'm Derwyn."

She grinned, her grey eyes lingering on his hazel. "Iowyn." She glanced across at the table where he had been sitting. "Carn is one of papa's regulars, but I don't remember seeing you or your female companion before."

Derwyn responded, glad he had walked over. "That's my sister, Lara. We haven't been to Kerlish before."

"So, are you Swords too?"

He shook his head. "Nay, we are just travelling south, and joined up with Carn after coming across some robbers on the road."

Iowyn gasped, placing her hand on his arm. Derwyn's skin tingled. She gazed up at him. "I hope you weren't hurt."

He smiled. "Nay, the robbers didn't fare as well." He placed his hand on hers and focused on her eyes. "I was hoping you could tell me more about Kerlish."

Iowyn lost herself in his gaze, but was quickly snapped from it when someone called her name from the kitchen. "I have my duties."

Derwyn sighed, glancing down a little disappointed. "Oh."

She smiled, squeezing his arm. "But I will be free soon. If you are happy to wait a little longer, I can talk then." She glanced past him. "It seems Carn and your sister have left."

Derwyn looked back and nodded, turning back to Iowyn. "They are very close." He focused on her features. "I would like to get to know more about you if I can."

She curled her hand into his. "I would like that." She leant forward on tiptoes and kissed him on the cheek. Her eyes focused on his. "I would like to get to know you very well."

He smiled. Iowyn was a little more forward than he had thought, but was not disappointed. "I'd like that."

She smiled broadly. "Go back to your table and I will join you soon. Then we can talk and if we like each other then, well . . ."

She raised her eyebrow and gazed up at him. Derwyn smiled broadly. "I'd like that."

Iowyn lingered on his features a little longer, sucking her bottom lip and smiling. "Good."

CHAPTER 29

L ARA opened her eyes; the morning sun was streaming in from the window and warming her naked back. She rolled over to see Carn dozing, the front of his naked, lean body only barely covered by the sheet. She rested her head on her hand and gazed at his attractive features from where she lay, dark stubble making his features more rugged. She focused on his profile and his full lips. Lara was finding herself being more attracted to him, there was some connection there and even Laycain had been ensuring their paths kept crossing. She thought of the night before and her skin tingled, the sex had been more tender, like lovers. She realised he was the first mortal that she wanted to get closer to and fully know her secrets. Taul had been nothing but a companion for sex and had never truly known her. Even though she felt she could talk to Taul, she never felt that she could have told him what she was. Yet with Carn, as he knew everything about her, she felt an actual connection. She had even felt that her wolf self was calm and tranquil around him. Her sensible side was telling her she should end it now, but Lara was finding Carn's company pleasant, and a few weeks would not hurt. Or at least until he took on a new contract, then it would make sense to end it then. She sensed his breathing change as he woke. He slowly smiled, causing dimples on his cheeks and opened his eyes, turning his head and focusing on her.

"Good morn."

She studied his blue eyes and smiled. "Good morn."

He leaned towards her and kissed her on the lips. "Feels nice waking up with you."

Lara took in his scent and snuggled up to him, not thinking about the future just yet. "So, will you show me the sights?"

He stroked her hair and smiled, kissing her gently on the crown of her head. "Where to begin, there's just so much, but I have a route in mind."

She pulled away from him a little, and regarded him. "How many times have you been here?"

He traced his hand along her back, Lara feeling the calluses from where he had used a sword for so long. "I've lost count. I grew up on a farm just outside of Kerlish. When my mama died, my papa took me with him when he had contracts. But we would always come back here when he needed more work."

Lara focused on his eyes. "Sorry about your mama."

Carn sighed. "I don't remember her that well, I was pretty young."

She asked, "Did your papa pick his contracts as you do?"

Carn glanced down, a shadow of guilt on his features. "Unfortunately, not, especially when I was younger. But when he started training me, he did start to choose more wisely." He brushed a stray hair off her cheek. "So, as it's just you and your brother, I'm guessing your parents died?"

Lara nodded slowly, her fingers tracing his bicep. "Aye, my mama died when Derwyn was only a babe. My papa died on the night I was turned. Vampires attacked the house killing my papa. I defended the house well, killing one. But the other was too fast, and being inexperienced in fighting vampires . . . in the struggle . . ." She paused, remembering the night. "I was killed, but of course due to what happened in the fight, I had already been turned before I died."

Carn focused on her eyes. "If you hadn't told me or if we had not met all those years ago, I would never have known. I have always thought I would be able to know a non-human when I saw one, but after meeting you and your brother it seems it would actually be hard to tell."

"It is. My brother and I have the advantage, yet my senses are even more heightened than my brother's. So, I can tell a non-human distinctively, even from a distance. But among humans, we are hard to find. You would need a talisman to be able to fully detect us."

He responded, "Aye my papa has one."

"Has one? Is he still alive?"

Carn pursed his lips. "He's south somewhere. Once I was old enough to venture off on my own, we parted ways. Last time I saw him was over four winters past."

"So does he still work?"

"He'll take his last breath working. He was already a Sword, well before meeting my mama. He tried to become a farmer, but his blood was always a Sword. What about your parents?"

"We lived on the outskirts of Lake Wood, but my papa wanted to ensure I knew everything about non-humans." She glanced across to her sword leaning against the wall. "That was my mama's. I found it when I was leaving. It's silver, so I think my parents knew how to defend themselves if needed."

"Always good too, as any danger can appear when you least expect it."

Lara gazed at him. "Well, I haven't fought many non-humans, Derwyn and I kept to ourselves. Yet I made sure we are both able to defend ourselves if needs be, in human or wolf form."

Carn studied her, lost in her eyes. "I could tell. You both are a lot stronger than you seem."

Lara smiled. "True, and in our wolf forms we are unstoppable."

"I'll make sure not to get on your wrong side." He glanced towards the window, the morning sun pouring into the room. "We better get up."

Lara untangled her naked limbs from his. "When do you have to see about your new contract?"

"Any time. I'd sooner show you some of the city before I have to." He propped himself up on his elbow and gazed at her as she climbed off the bed. "I think you'll like what Kerlish has to offer."

She gave him a backward glance, and a sly smile, her eyes lingering on his naked torso. "Oh, I do, so far."

CHAPTER 30

WHEN Lara and Carn came down for breakfast, she saw Derwyn talking to the barmaid near the entrance to the kitchen and there seemed to be that afterglow about them. She smiled, glad her brother had, even if fleeting, met someone.

Carn observed Derwyn as they sat down at one of the tables near a window, raising an eyebrow. "Seems that developed."

Lara smiled again, glancing over at the two. "More than I had thought."

Carn chuckled. "Well, the way they are behaving together, I'd say he ventured further than a few kisses." He raised his eyebrow at Lara with a mischievous grin and got up to order food.

She watched him go over to the main counter and order, a soft smile on her face. Then she gazed over at her brother, watching him talking to the girl. Lara wondered if she had been his first, yet she could not ask him. A sly smile touched her lips. She could certainly tease him some. Lara's thoughts were broken when she noticed Derwyn glancing her way. He said something to the girl and then strolled over.

Lara smiled at him, raising an eyebrow. "So?"

His skin flushed, and he looked a little bashful as he sat down opposite his sister. "There's nothing to say."

Lara focused on him, leaning forward, picking up the girl's scent on her brother. It was stronger than most of the others she had picked up before. They had definitely done more than just kiss. "Really? That's not what my nose is telling me."

"Alright." He glared at her. "I can't get away with anything can I with that nose of yours."

Lara chuckled, shaking her head. "Nay, you can't."

Her brother regarded her, realising that she would have picked up the scent of the other girls. "Did you?"

Lara smirked. "Aye. So, you like this girl more than Calisa?"

"How?"

Lara tapped her nose. Derwyn shook his head in disbelief, deciding not to mention his crush on Isla and glanced up as Carn came back to join them. The young man added. "Well, Iowyn is genuinely nice. But we may not be here forever."

Lara regarded her brother, glad he had started to have a life for himself. The barmaid, Iowyn, came over with porridge and fruit, she smiled at Derwyn and nodded a good morning to Lara and Carn.

Lara stared at her and asked, "Do you like my brother?"

The girl blushed slightly and glimpsed at Derwyn, who whispered, "Lara!"

She glanced at her brother, raising an eyebrow, and then turned back to the girl. "Sorry Iowyn, I'm just curious."

Iowyn smiled, glancing at Derwyn, her eyes lingering on his features, her lips curling seductively. "Your brother is very nice."

Lara studied the girl and then said, "Well, just don't hurt him."

Iowyn's eyes widened, she became a little awkward as shook her head. "Nay, never."

Lara smiled and turned back to her brother who looked embarrassed. "Don't be concerned, I'm happy for you." She regarded them both. "But be careful."

The girl nodded and rushed back to the kitchen when her name was called. Derwyn asked her sister, "Did you have to embarrass me?"

Lara laughed. "Of course! That's what sisters do." She leant forward. "Think of it this way; I could have embarrassed you *far* more."

Carn chuckled, taking a sip of his juice then sampled the porridge. Derwyn stared at him but did not say a word. He then turned to Lara raising an eyebrow. Lara knew that look. But her brother realised after his activities the night before, he could not say anything about hers.

Once Carn and Derwyn had eaten, Lara went with the Sword to explore the city. Derwyn wanted to look round on his own. Lara did not stop him, the more independent he was, the better. They had relied on each other for years and since he had turned eighteen, he needed to spread his wings. At some point, for whatever reason, they would part ways. The experience would be good for them both. It felt good to see him starting to enjoy life, what the future held for them both she was not sure, but this was the first step.

Lara loved exploring the city with Carn. The striking man happily showed her the best inns, blacksmiths, swordsmiths and where to go for extra clothing or anything else she or her brother would need. They entered the main market square which was teeming with traders and stalls overflowing with merchandise. The dais in the centre of the square was occupied by a man and woman busking. Their singing was drowned out by the market traders' shouts about their products and the odd bellow of livestock that was for sale to the south of the market. Being so busy, Carn gently took her hand, so they did not get separated. He absentmindedly brushed his thumb repeatedly across the back of her hand as they walked, making her skin tingle with delight. To Lara's surprise she liked him holding her, she did not need to be protected, but it still felt nice to know someone cared.

As they wandered around, Lara picked up a lycan scent. She paused studying the crowd, it was hard to fully pinpoint, but the scent would have been easy to track. Carn glanced back at her puzzled, she smiled, it was not his concern for the moment. She would venture on her own around the city later once he had gone to deal with his contract. If there was a lycan pack about, she would sooner find them on her own, and also, if she could, warn Derwyn.

As they continued to wander around the market, she thought about her father's book. There had been mention of packs over the land but there had never been a mention of specific cities, then again it seemed to only really focus on the family at Crowling. She recalled that the alpha there mentioned packs in the northern cities. It would make sense for a pack to be in the city; it was massive and a good place to disappear in plain sight. Once she was sure, she would add it to the book.

Are they protectors of the city? And if so, do they already know that we are here? I'll find out soon enough, especially if they don't like outsiders.

Carn stopped at a food stall and picked up fruit, passing an apple to Lara, she smiled as she took it. He was doing it out of habit, even though she had told him already that she could no longer eat normal food. She continued smiling, it was easier to just take it and play along. It did make her think about when she would need to hunt, but she should be fine for another day or two. Then she would have to venture out of the city, not as stealthily as when at Naverac, but she would have to ensure she did not run into any trouble because of it. Lara looked around; she would like to explore more on her own, so she could find some good routes out for when she did need to, but for the moment, she was enjoying the tour. As they left the market square Carn paused at a flower stall and spoke to the vendor. He then turned to her smiling, holding a small bunch of Lavender.

"As you like the scent, I thought you may like some."

Lara took the flowers a little confused. "Thank you, but what do you mean?"

Carn gazed at her. "The scent you wear. It's faint, but it is lavender, right?"

Lara felt a little sick, but smiled, studying him. *How could he know that scent? I didn't think humans could pick it up, being so faint, but maybe they could? Or was it that with him being a tracker, his sense of smell is more acute?* Whatever the reason she was taken a little off guard. She realised he was staring at her, waiting for a response. She smiled. "Aye, it is. Thank you."

Carn kissed her and took her hand. "Come on, more to see yet."

As they left the main square behind, Lara held the flowers, still a little shocked by the gesture and that he could smell the lavender. Yet the more she thought about it, the more it made sense that he may have picked up some sort of scent from her, and wondered if she should explain or leave it. Lara did not want the kind gesture to be lost when she explained that that scent meant she was a vampire. She focused on his back as he led the way across the city. She decided it was best to say nothing and just savour the kind gesture. She glanced down at the small bunch and sniffed them. No man had ever given her flowers before, and found herself falling more for the handsome Sword. Something she had thought she would never do.

Having walked around a few streets, Carn ventured into the non-human quarter on the east side of the city. There were still humans around, but compared to dwarves and elves and other non-humans who could not cloak their appearance, they were very outnumbered. Yet as they wandered around, Lara picked up the scents of other creatures; some having spells cast so they could venture about without being noticed, others kept out of sight until darkness fell. She even picked up a couple of vampires, as there would be some in a city. She glanced at Carn, wondering if he could pick up the scent. Then she remembered he had said that hers was only faint, and concluded that it was only from being so intimate with each other. Surveying the busy streets, Lara suspected it would probably be far worse at night, especially down some of the side alleys. Those would be teeming with several dangerous types of creatures. Ones who would have more freedom to do what they wanted hidden by the cloak of darkness, and probably not just keeping to that part of Kerlish. She looked around, during the day, everyone seemed to go about their business, no one bothered each other at all. Yet it would be wise not to venture into the quarter alone after dark.

By mid-afternoon, they had walked back to the central part of Kerlish. Carn slowed and stopped outside a tall building with white columns. A formidable man stood outside the large wooden doorway.

He turned to Lara. "This is where I need to go. Will you be alright finding your way back?"

Lara studied him. "Don't worry. I want to explore a little more. Will I see you later?"

Carn focused on her green eyes. "Most definitely."

He kissed her passionately and headed up to the door talking to the large man, who after a few moments let him enter. Lara peered up at the building and wondered what went on in there.

Turning on her heel, she glanced back, in time to see the door closing. She smiled then headed back towards the market; it was time to see if she could track down the lycan. Without Carn, she could move more briskly through the crowds. The lycan scent was faint but enough for her to track, and it was not heading to the east where most non-humans lived. It seemed that lycan, or pack, was hiding very much in plain sight.

CHAPTER 31

LEAVING the crowds behind, Lara made her way through the quieter streets, heading to the south end of Kerlish. As she walked, it was still only the one scent, stronger and easier to find with most around this part of the city being human. She also noticed the streets were cleaner and the properties larger, it seemed that it was the more affluent part of Kerlish. She slowed, picking up a second scent, one she knew far too well; Derwyn's. *Had he picked up the lycan scent too?* It would not surprise her as he had gone off to venture around the city on his own. She could hear voices ahead, down a side alley. Lara slowed again, recognising her brother's voice. It seemed that whoever he was talking to, was not just a passing conversation about the weather.

Reaching the alleyway Lara could hear her brother and someone asking too many questions. There was also a third scent, being upwind she had not sensed it earlier. Moving slowly, she made her way to the corner of the alleyway to see Derwyn facing two large men. They did not seem happy that her brother was there.

She walked up to them and smiled. "Can I help you, gentlemen?"

The two men turned and glared at her, one said gruffly, "Nay your concern, girl."

Derwyn smiled as Lara stood by him. She regarded the men, not letting the two intimidate her. "I beg to differ."

The tallest of the two turned to her and paused as he took in her scent, he glared at her with disgust. "What the feck are you?"

Lara smiled. "Well for starters, I'm his sister,"

The two men studied them. The first man said, "I doubt that. He's a lycan, but you're something different."

Lara said, cocking her head to one side, "True. One of a kind."

Derwyn smiled. "In more ways than one."

Lara asked, studying the men coldly, "Can I ask why you are being so unwelcoming?"

The tallest stated, "We don't like lone wolves here. They can cause trouble."

Derwyn sighed, glancing at Lara. "I told them that we are just passing through and won't cause any problems."

Lara nodded. "True, we won't. Also, a wolf not part of a pack doesn't mean they will be trouble."

The larger man stepped toward Lara. "Well from what we have experienced of lone wolves, they always do."

"Really?" responded Lara, raising an eyebrow. "I think you're thinking of werewolves, more than lycans. If you leave us be, we won't cause any problems." She stepped towards the larger man, letting her features change slightly, showing part of her wolf self. "But if you decide not to leave us be, then there could be a situation. And I don't think you want that, do you?"

The two paused, still glaring at her, the one who had not spoken yet said, "What the feck are you?"

"Someone you don't want to mess with." She let her features return to normal and smiled. "So, gentlemen, stop harassing my brother. We won't cause any trouble while we're here, as long as you leave us alone."

The two men stepped back, the taller one shook his head. "Just stay away from this side of the city and suggest you leave here as soon as your business is complete."

Lara pursed her lips. "That's fine by us. Good day."

Derwyn turned to leave, and Lara followed when she heard the larger of the two men mutter, "Whatever she is, a lone wolf is the least of our problems. We need to figure out where those vampires are."

Lara paused. She had picked up the scent of vampires earlier. She turned back towards them. "Vampires?"

The larger man snarled, "That's none of your concern."

Lara shrugged. "Fair enough. But I think I know where they might be."

They gawked at her, the larger man studying her with interest. "Really?"

She focused on the two. "Well, I have a better sense of smell than any lycan."

Derwyn turned back and nodded. "That's very true."

The larger man glared at the two of them, suspicion in his eyes. "What are you proposing?"

"Well, you say you will leave us alone, but part of me thinks you may still prefer us to leave before we have finished our business here. So, I am proposing that we help you and you leave us alone for how long we need to stay here, may it be days or even months."

The larger man pursed his lips. "So, you say you could track 'em?"

Lara smiled. "Oh, aye. I can pick up scents that are months old, not just days. Even ones cloaked by a spell."

The shorter of the two whispered, "We need to talk to Ivan."

The taller one nodded and turned back to Lara. "We will consider your proposal; can you meet us at the main market square after nightfall?"

Lara regarded them for a moment. "Agreed." The man gave a quick nod and the two lycans turned, heading away from them.

Derwyn studied his sister. "You know that could be a trap."

Lara smiled, glancing back to where the lycans had gone. "Oh, I know. Before we return to the inn, I want to ensure that we know the square well. Maybe leave our scent in a few places, confuse them."

Derwyn agreed. "Sounds like a good plan. Keep it on our terms more."

"Agreed. Also, in helping them, if it does give us more time in the city, then I think it's worth the risk. Come on, let's head back."

Brother and sister walked back towards the inn they were staying at, Lara asking, as they headed along the main road. "So, you like this, Iowyn?"

Derwyn frowned. "We aren't going to talk about that pack?"

Lara smiled, nudging him. "Aye, but I am more curious about this girl you are interested in."

Derwyn sighed, folding his arms across his chest as they walked. "I like her, but we may not be staying here for long." He focused on the lavender in her hand, raising an eyebrow. "And what's that about?"

Lara glanced down, realising she had forgotten she was even holding them. "Oh, them. Just something Carn gave me."

Derwyn smirked. "So, you are on to flowers now."

Lara stopped and glared at the back of his head. "Stop trying to change the subject. I was asking about Iowyn."

Derwyn shrugged as he turned to face her. "And like I said, it may not last as we will be moving on."

Lara folded her arms and gazed at her brother with affection. "So? Listen, I want you to be able to have as normal a life as you can." She glanced down, kicking the cobblestones at her feet. "I'm not going to age; you know that, right. So, I don't want you having to move every few years with me because people may get suspicious."

Derwyn sighed, studying his sister, placing a loving hand on her shoulder. "But I don't want you to be alone."

Lara laughed bitterly, glaring back up at him. "But I will be, Derwyn. I am going to live for many years, and I mean *many* years. I want you to know that if you do find somewhere where you feel you want to make a life, you can." She studied him intently. "It's not like when I do leave, you would never see me again."

Derwyn seemed deflated. "I know. I also understand the fact that I will age, and you won't. But I feel that I should be with you nay matter what."

Lara smiled softly and hugged her brother. "I love you, Derwyn and know you feel you should stay with me." She pulled back to study his hazel eyes. "But I'm telling you that I am not expecting you to, but I will not force you to stay in one place either. I just want you to know that if you decide to make a life. *Make it.* Don't think you can't because of me."

Derwyn sighed and asked, "So, what are you expecting with Carn?"

Lara shrugged, glancing down at the lavender. "Nothing. We are enjoying our time together, but when the time comes, we will part. Yet I'm not going to become celibate just because I won't age."

Derwyn smiled and gazed at his sister for a few moments then said, "With Iowyn; I like her, but I am not expecting it to be anything serious. It's a fling."

Lara smiled and gently squeezed his lean arm. "Then enjoy the time together. Just remember Derwyn, papa never dictated who I should see. But he did want me to marry into a lycan family, and I am not going to force that on you. All you must do, if you do find someone, you must be honest with her. I don't know what will happen if you do become serious with a human or even a non-human. But I have not read anything about half breeds." She paused glancing at him. "Look, I'm not expecting you to be thinking about having a family yet, but when you do find someone you are serious about, that will be a factor, especially if they aren't like us."

Derwyn took a deep breath, seeming a little sullen. "I know, and that is the last thing on my mind. But I will always think about that factor *if* I meet that someone."

Lara smiled and sighed, surveying their surroundings. "By Laycain, I wasn't expecting to be having that talk with you in a deserted street."

Derwyn pulled a face. "Does it matter where and when?"

Lara sighed, giving him another hug. "Not really." She glanced around. "Let's take a look at that main market and then head back, you must be hungry."

Derwyn smirked. "When am I not."

The two laughed and made their way through the city.

CHAPTER 32

ARN gave Lara a passionate kiss and reluctantly left her as he walked up the steps to the impressive building that was owned by Kraven. He had enjoyed taking her for a tour around the city and wanted to continue, but the contract had to be dealt with. He glanced back at Lara and then turned to the large man standing at the entrance.

Carn said, "Good day Horace, is Kraven in?"

Horace grunted, and Carn smiled, the large man was never much of a talker. Horace opened the oak door and let Carn enter. Before he stepped over the threshold, he glanced back to see Lara was already walking away, he turned back and stepped inside. The hallway was large, the walls covered in various swords and daggers of different designs from practical to some so ornate that they would be useless in battle. He glanced up at the animals Kraven had hunted over the years, the heads having been stuffed and arranged in aggressive poses. Carn had never understood the purpose, unless it had been Kraven's way to show off and intimidate all who entered. Carn sighed, the old Sword did not even need to try, he was a large and imposing man anyway. He remembered coming here as a teenager with his father, and Kraven had scared him half to death. More than the corridor ever did.

Carn peered ahead to see the door open. The old Sword was not in any confidential meeting, so it would be all right to enter.

He walked into the spacious study where Kraven sat behind an imposing desk, which still seemed small compared to his size.

The large man looked up and boomed. "Carn! How are you, my boy!"

Carn smiled, standing opposite him. It was always wise never to sit till he gave the word. "I'm good, Kraven."

The bearded man nodded, gesturing to the armchair before him. "Sit my boy."

Carn did, and regarded the old Sword. It was hard to age him with his scarred features. One ran deep across his face, barely missing his right eye, that he appeared to be winking. It was astonishing that he even survived the injury. It was only the greying of his beard that gave any indication that he was advanced in years. Carn remembered asking Kraven how he had got the large scar and he had chuckled reminiscing on how he had fought a werewolf in his youth and won. The young Sword wondered if Kraven knew there were, more than likely, lycan and werewolves in Kerlish, right under his nose. The old Sword always had a strong dislike of non-humans, which had been a bonding point with Carn's father. He and his father had never seen eye to eye, for he had always been more open-minded. Carn knew it was wise to keep his feelings to himself, as it would affect his contracts and maybe even his life.

Kraven studied him then glanced down at the paperwork on his desk, shuffling through the pile till he found the one he wanted. "Seems the client was very pleased with your work."

Carn smiled. "Well, I like to make sure I do a good job."

"You are one of my best Swords, Carn." He raised an eyebrow. "As good, if not better, than your papa."

Carn smirked, but he hated being compared to his father, which was one reason he wanted to branch out on his own. "So, what's the new contract?"

Kraven smiled as he got to his feet and went over to a shelf filled with rolls of paper, each one some form of contract. He started rummaging as he said, "Ah, it's one well suited. You will need to head for Palasses. There's a landowner there who is having trouble, some thugs causing issues and he needs them dealt with."

Carn asked, as he watched the large man rummaging through the papers, "Does he need protection?"

"Nay," he responded, concentrating on finding the relevant piece of paperwork. "He has his men, but they aren't skilled trackers. It will take a week, maybe two, to sort and tie off any loose ends. Ahh, here it is." Kraven paused and grabbed another contract before turning from the shelves. "So, I also have this one." He held up another roll of paper. "It's good pay, not your usual work. It's a bounty. And I suggest that you start being a little more flexible in these trying times."

Carn raised an eyebrow, wondering if it had something to do with Lara. "Oh, I'm intrigued."

Kraven smiled, walking back to his desk and placing both contracts down as he sat. "I think this is perfect for you. I know how good you are at tracking and the reward is high."

Carn leant forward, knowing that meant more coin to line Kraven's pockets. "Tell me more."

Kraven pointed to his scar. "Now, you know me and non-humans, lad. It seems there is a dangerous, rogue werewolf lass out there. I wouldn't normally take contracts like this, especially as it is from a non-human, but the pay was hard to dismiss. Think that's down to them being an influential family." He leant forward. "I also wouldn't just give this to anyone either. I can trust you to do a good job and I think, with our history, and me knowing your papa for so long, this would be a good one for you."

Carn smiled, and nodded, half tempted to correct Kraven on calling her a werewolf, but the old Sword would not care. The fact the contract stated "werewolf" meant even that family was keeping Lara's true nature a secret. Carn still felt ashamed of his own ignorance, that he had not known their was a difference. "It does sound very tempting."

Kraven chuckled. "Good lad." He leant back, unrolling the contract. "It seems this werewolf lass has rubbed some big alpha, called Stonelance, the wrong way in Crowling. Even killed innocents. They would deal with it themselves, but they aren't sure where she went. They thought she headed north. But, from what I heard, some stupid hunter alarmed her, so she's on the move again. Now they ain't sure, she may be even moving south."

"Hunter?" Carn raised an eyebrow, remembering what Lara had told him.

"Aye. From what I heard, the werewolf has dealt with him. Seemed he stumbled across her, and let her slip through his fingers. But he's of nay concern. He wasn't one of mine, he was from Adnama, so I don't care. More coin for us." Kraven smiled, showing crooked teeth.

Carn asked carefully, "So, is it just her? I need to know what I am dealing with here."

Kraven examined the contract. "There's a brother, but he's to be left unharmed. But, if necessary, he can be dealt with too. Yet they don't know if the brother split ways or not."

Carn pursed his lips, already thinking of ways to ensure Lara was never found. "Why aren't the werewolves dealing with it? From what I've heard, they keep to themselves and like to sort out their issues privately."

Kraven shrugged. "Nay sure. I think they may have their people out there, but they all know to keep clear of the big cities."

Carn raised an eyebrow, wondering when Kraven had been made to believe that. "You sure about that?"

Kraven leant forward. "Best to keep clear of non-human politics, lad. I do, and if any cross my path I deal with 'em!"

Carn asked, "Have you offered this to anyone else?"

Kraven laughed, leaning back in his chair. "As I said lad, just you. You are my best tracker on the books, well apart from your papa. But I think he's a bit old for this job, it needs young blood. If you don't want it, I can pass it to Vondric, but he's a bit of a loose Sword these days."

Carn nodded. Vondric was not the most reliable, and had caused several issues over the years that Kraven had to clear up. Carn focused on the older man; he was not going to give such an unreliable Sword such a lucrative contract. It was just a ruse to ensure Carn took it. The young man leant forward taking both the contracts.

Carn asked, "What's the time scale?"

"Well, the one in Palasses is as soon as you get there. The other, well, nay rush, but they want it sorted. I think you head for Palasses, but keep those ears open for anything on the other one as they do think she may have headed south. If you get delayed, send me a message and I can pull the Palasses contract or give him something to compensate. The amount on the other one will balance it out."

"Anything else?"

Kraven shook his head. "Nay, just my usual advice. Now, I have a meeting with some cocky sod. He thinks he can tell me what to do, but I'll put him in his place. So off with you, and keep up the good work."

Carn gave a quick nod as he got to his feet. He headed out of Kraven's study then greeted Horace as he left. He would have a word with Lara when he got back to the inn and let her see the contract. If what Kraven had told him was true, he could ensure Lara was left alone. He could send false leads and fulfil the contract in their eyes, and then she would hopefully be left alone. He was surprised that Kraven seemed to be willfully ignorant about where the non-humans were living. The quarter to the north was obvious, and Carn could not believe Kraven was oblivious to that. But then again, having known Kraven for years, he did tend to have his head in the sand over some issues. Yet Carn knew if that quarter caused Kraven's business to suffer, he would soon have a change of attitude.

CHAPTER 33

LARA sat at the back of the quiet inn, having something to drink. From where she was situated, she could quietly watch the customers scattered around the inn. Some seemed pretty content, but there were also ones moaning about things; from the taxes going up in the city, to issues at their farms. Lara focused on her drink, it seemed very few were worrying about non-humans. Then one conversation caught her attention, it seemed people had been going missing, usually vagrants or prostitutes, but it had been noticed by some. The pack were concerned about vampires and she wondered if they had something to do with the missing people. That would fall under their duty in protecting the city. But if the situation escalated, it could cause all non-humans, even the ones hiding in plain sight, problems. She wondered if there were vigilante groups like the ones she encountered at Naverac. Some would take matters into their own hands if the situation did escalate. She would find out more tonight when they met up with the lycans to see what the issue was.

Lara glanced up at the door when someone entered. She wanted to discuss the meeting with Carn once he returned, as his help would be useful. Even if just to watch their backs. Her wolf self was on edge as it felt that it would be a trap. She had to make sure they were well prepared.

She took a sip of her drink and leaned back in her seat, thinking about her brother and the conversation they had had earlier that day. She had not expected to have it in the middle of the street, but since they had discussed it, she wanted her brother to think more on what he wished to do. They had relied on each other for so long and she wanted to make sure he had a life he would not regret. Derwyn was in the kitchen helping Iowyn, having told the innkeeper he had experience working at an inn in Naverac. The man was happy for the extra help, and it also gave Derwyn an excuse to get to know Iowyn more. Lara could tell he liked the girl, but could not determine if he wanted to progress with it, or keep it casual? All she knew was he was happy and that was what mattered. When it came time to move on, she would ask him to be honest as to what he wanted. If he wished to continue travelling with her, so be it, but she did not want him throwing a chance at life away. It may not work out with Iowyn anyway, with her being human, but he may want to stay in the city longer if there was something there.

Lara sighed. For the first time, the reality that she would be in this world for an exceptionally long time hit her hard. Yet she wondered what she would see. One thing she was not about to waste, with all the time in the world on her hands, was the chance to explore. There were a lot of lands overseas, and she wondered what they would be like. She thought about Fashor, the vampire who had been alive, from what he had said, for centuries and wondered if they would cross paths again. If she kept crossing paths with Carn, it could be the same with a vampire who happened to be a good few hundred years old.

Carn returned late afternoon, and seemed serious when he walked over to where she still sat in the inn. He took the chair opposite her as she asked, "You aren't looking pleased with the fact you have just picked up a new contract."

He sighed, greeting the barmaid with a smile and asking for ale. "I need a drink and I think you will too."

Lara raised an eyebrow, and nodded to the barmaid when asked if she wanted another drink. "That bad?"

He leant forward. "Well, let's just say that I think a lycan family in Crowling aren't too happy that you're roaming free."

Lara regarded him, leaning forward. "What did you find out?"

Carn took a breath but said nothing as the barmaid placed a mug of ale in front of him and refilled Lara's. Once the girl had gone, Carn leant forward, placing a rolled-up contract on the table. "It seems there's a very high bounty contract out on you. Look."

"On me?"

She took the paper and unrolled it to read the contents. It was the Stonelances who had made it. Lara wondered if they had done it soon after she had left Crowling. She pursed her lips in concentration, she did not think the alpha would have done it, but was unsure of the other family members. The son was not too happy after meeting her.

Had he taken over in the last few years and decided to see if I was still out there? Or had it been out for years, but had not garnered much interest so they upped the bounty, as that figure is substantial. Could that be why the hunter was at Yarl?

Carn replied, "Luckily, it's not too widely known, only available to hunters and highly trained Swords as you are classed as extremely dangerous. If it was not for the high bounty, I think that if Kraven had taken it, this would have been sitting on his shelf for years."

Lara leant back taking a sip of her strong drink, placing the roll of paper on the table in front of them. "I see. They seemed to have elaborated quite a bit with the story of innocents being killed, as I have not harmed anyone. Not sure why they have said I am a werewolf." She paused glancing at Carn. "But then again, most, like Kraven, don't know the difference. I did warn them not to mess with me. It seems that to ensure the contract is fulfilled, they are making me out to be very dangerous." She smirked. "Which I am, but would never harm just anyone. I hope you didn't raise too much suspicion asking about it?"

Carn replied, taking a sip of his ale. "I didn't get a chance to ask. I got offered it."

"Really?" Lara raised an eyebrow.

Carn boasted, "I am pretty good at my job."

"Did you accept it?"

"I was surprised Kraven took it, as he's pretty anti-non-human. But, his greed ignored that the contract was from a lycan. So, when he offered it to me, I took it."

Lara stiffened, glaring at him. "I see."

Carn took her hand gently in his. "Nay, you don't understand. If I didn't take it, he was going to offer it to this notorious Sword. So, it was better if I took it and then never found you."

Lara relaxed slightly. "But the pay-out would be good for you."

Carn shrugged. "True, but I would never betray someone I cared about."

Lara lost herself in his eyes. "You . . . you care about me?"

Carn breathed, squeezing her hand. "Of course, I do. You are amazing, I've thought so from the first moment I saw you in that stable all those years ago. I would never betray you or your brother."

Lara smiled, never really thinking about how Carn felt towards her till that very moment, and then realised even with her concerns, it did not scare her. "So, what now? And how come the hunter was near Yarl?"

Carn responded, "The contract went to the two main agents in the north, mine and one at Adnama. It seems the Adnama one gave the contract to his best Sword, the hunter you ran into. From what mine told me; nay one knows where you are, all that was known is you had headed north. The description of you, as you have read, is vague, but it is stated that you will be with your brother. Kraven thinks he came across you by accident. I do know that when the lycans found out he lost you, he didn't see another day. But they don't know where you are now, only that you may have headed south."

Lara leant back. "I see. But if you do the same, they'll kill you too. Does anyone else know about this?"

Carn replied, smiling, "Don't worry, I have a plan. As for others knowing, from what I have been told, nay. But that doesn't mean that the family you ran into hasn't got their people out there. It seems they *really* don't like you."

Lara pursed her lips. "I knew there would be prejudice, but not to this extreme."

Carn took a sip of his ale. "I'm going to sit on the contract for a while, then when the time comes, I'll give false information. I also have another one for a job in the south. I don't have to leave for a few days, but I'd like you to come with me."

Lara gazed at him. "Really?"

Carn smiled, kissing her hand. "Why not? Look, I enjoy your company. Nay. I actually *really* enjoy your company and I think we could work well together. But if you want to go your separate way, I understand, and I can throw them off track for you with the contract." He focused on her eyes. "I know that our situation will never be happy ever after, but listen, I haven't felt like this about someone in a long time and . . . well, I think you are just *amazing*." His fingers laced into hers. "You have managed to overcome what has happened to you. You raised your brother, and made a life for yourself. Most would have given up, but you . . . you haven't."

Lara lost herself in his eyes. It had been a hard few years, but they had made it. She gazed at Carn realising she felt the same way about him, she just could not help it. At some point, they would have to go their separate ways, but the fact he was so willing to help with the contract, she could not just walk away. Then her senses picked up a familiar scent. "I'll talk to Derwyn to see what he wants to do."

Carn nodded. "Understood."

Lara smiled and added. "And thank you for taking the contract on, even if you don't get the reward."

Carn pursed his lips. "The reward is good, but I wouldn't trade it for what I have with you. Your friendship means more to me than coin."

Derwyn strolled over, then sat beside Lara and asked, "Have you told him yet?"

Carn regarded them both. "Told me what?"

Lara responded, "We have a meeting this eve with the pack here in the city. They seem to have a vampire problem. I said I would help, if in turn, they let us be. Which may not be an issue if we decide to leave soon."

"Leave?" asked Derwyn.

Lara nodded. "Carn has found out there is a bounty on my head." She grabbed the contract to read it again and pursed her lips. "It mentions you too, Derwyn, but not as a concern."

Carn said, "As you know, you're the main target, but if Derwyn interferes, it's to the discretion of the Sword as to what to do."

Derwyn's eyes shifted between both of them, then he grabbed the contract from his sister. He glanced up at the two before reading it and inquired, "Who set the contract?"

Lara responded, "The Stonelances. Seems they really don't like me. Not sure how long the contract has been out. Maybe a change in leadership has caused this now, I don't know. But it seems there is sudden interest. Carn has taken the contract on –"

Derwyn interrupted, glaring at Carn, "I thought we could trust you?"

Lara calmly continued, "But only to throw them off our trail and to stop anyone else from taking it."

Derwyn glanced at them both. "Oh."

Carn responded, "You can fully trust me. I'm not going to carry out the contract, just sit on it and give false information if they ask." He paused. "I asked Lara if you both wanted to come with me when I start my other contract in the south."

Lara gazed at her brother. "Listen, I haven't agreed to anything yet, and Carn isn't forcing us, it's just a suggestion. I think we need to discuss what you want to do, and I will honour whatever you decide." She studied the two. "But I'm still going to meet this pack this eve. On the morrow we can discuss what we plan to do next."

Carn leant forward. "So, what's this meeting this eve?"

Lara replied, "It seems there is a vampire problem, and the lycans are unable to find them. Of course, I came across a vampire scent in the non-human quarter, faint, but there are some there. Lycans can pick scents up pretty easily, but it was far too faint for them to notice it. I think the vampires have a witch helping them stay hidden."

"So, you're offering to help so they'll leave you be?" Lara nodded as Carn added, "What if this pack knows about the contract?"

Lara shrugged. "They could, depending on how independent the pack is, some like to keep to themselves. I know the Stonelances at Crowling had connections to the packs to the north. But how close they are, I don't know. But I also think it could be a trap as they know I'm not fully a lycan, so they will have their suspicions."

Carn pursed his lips. "Do you want me to be there?"

Lara glanced at Derwyn. "We can pretty much take care of ourselves, but say you keep out of sight to cover our backs. Have you fought non-humans before, specifically vampires? They are very fast."

Carn smiled. "Well nay, but I am pretty handy if you do need backup."

Derwyn smirked. "I would feel better knowing we had backup, if needed. Even if he couldn't keep up."

Carn glared at him. "Hey!"

Derwyn grinned. Lara glanced between the two and shook her head. "Behave, both of you. I know you're pretty handy with that sword, so you'll be a good asset to have, Carn." He nodded and smiled as Lara continued, "Best you keep out of sight though. Somewhere with other humans so your scent is masked. Do you know of a place where you'll be able to see the whole of the square?"

Carn responded, "Aye, there's an inn there, and I know the owner. It's also popular. I could get a good position."

"Perfect."

He smiled and the three went over a plan.

CHAPTER 34

L ARA and Derwyn had been standing at the centre of the main market square, for what seemed like hours, next to a small stone dais that was used for public speaking, as well as bards, and the odd humiliation of a criminal. It appeared the pack was making them wait, yet Lara was not going to let down her guard. Even though they were standing out in the open, they did not have to worry about archers, humans would have shot them down by now, but lycans were hands on fighters. If the alpha was involved, he would want to face her, just to find out what she was. She wondered if they were being watched, to see if they would give up. See if she and Derwyn would let their guard down, walk back to the inn and then get cornered. But that was the last thing Lara was going to do, and eventually the alpha's curiosity would get the better of him.

In the early hours, the city seemed silent, the light from the crescent moon in the clear sky and a few lanterns that were lit on the corner of buildings around the area gave an eerie feel to the square. Yet to their wolf eyes all was as clear as day. Lara inspected the square towards the small inn where Carn was watching, hoping he was able to see enough in the poor light. She had told him if he saw anything to whisper to her. He was far enough away for wolf ears not to hear him, but for her advanced hearing, she could.

Finally, she heard him whisper, "*Four from the south, heading your way.*"

It seemed the lycans had done waiting. Carn as a lookout was working for them. South was upwind, she and Derwyn would not pick up their scent, and the pack would think that would be to their advantage. She watched the south to see two coming into the square.

Lara whispered to Derwyn, "There should be four."

Derwyn nodded. "Glad we have that lookout. They are probably heading round the side."

"Agreed."

The two men walked towards them, one was from the encounter earlier, the other Lara intuitively knew had to be the alpha, he had that air of cockiness about him. She smiled as the two came closer, and stated, "I expected more of you."

The alpha smiled coldly. "I'm Ivan, my friend here says you know where the vampires could be hiding."

Lara returned his smile, and heard Carn suddenly whisper, "*Two more to the east.*"

She had already picked up the scents, they were faint but for her sensitive nose, she could smell them.

She smirked at the alpha. "Well Ivan, straight to the point I see, definitely an alpha."

He sneered, studying her with disgust on his features. "Seems Von was right, you are *something* different."

Derwyn glared at him. "So did your colleague also tell you the deal?"

"He did." Ivan nodded, his dark features cold and stern.

Lara stepped forward, not being intimidated by the alpha. "So, what now? Are you going to play along with the deal or change it all?"

He smirked. "You are untrained wolves that's for sure. You have nay respect for the pack."

Derwyn glared at him. "Oh, we know the rules of the pack. We just don't grovel to someone who isn't our alpha."

Ivan chuckled. "Very well, but you are in *my* city."

"*Your* city?" Lara raised an eyebrow.

He glared at her. "Aye. And wolves in *my* city follow *my* rules."

Lara glared into his eyes steadily. "Well, happy to disappoint." She glanced at the man standing next to him. "So, I'm presuming the deal's off?"

He glanced down from her accusing eyes, and Lara turned back to Ivan. "So why show up?"

He regarded her intently. "I want to know what you are, and you could still be a useful solution to our problem."

Lara smiled coldly. "I see. But I don't think I'll be willing to help you now. I feel there is yet another reason?" Lara almost knew what he was going to say before he uttered the words.

He sneered. "It seems there is a contract out for you."

Lara gasped, seeming astonished. "Really?" She sensed Derwyn tense, but he did not react, leaving it to Lara.

Ivan stepped forward, towering over her. "So, what are you?"

Lara locked her eyes on his. "What do you think I am?"

He took a deep breath, his eyes focused on hers. "There is a scent of a wolf, but something else, almost vampire."

She smiled. "I prefer to say a hint of lavender. Well, what does the contract say?"

He responded with disgust in his voice. "That you are something that needs to be put down. A hybrid."

Derwyn clenched his fists, starting to look tense and more obvious to the other two. "So, what now?" he snarled.

Ivan pursed his lips. "Well let's see, you take us to the vampires as you said. Then we deal with you. As for your companions, I'm not sure yet."

Lara went to question him when she saw a dazed Carn being dragged out of the inn by two burly men, she cursed, "Feck."

While talking to Ivan, she had not even heard the scuffle.

Ivan smiled. "Like I said this is *my* city. Did you think you could have some human help you out? I know everything that happens here."

Lara glared at him, raising an eyebrow. "Well apart from knowing where the vampires are, I'm thinking you don't control the non-human quarter."

Ivan smirked with disdain and Carn was held firmly when he reached the group. He glanced at Lara sheepishly, blood trickling down his forehead.

"Sorry, these bastards are strong!"

Lara gazed at him and shrugged. "True."

She surveyed the situation, trying to figure out how to get out of it with the least damage possible. With possibly six lycans, she and Derwyn could manage it, but not Carn. He would be downed before he could draw his sword, especially in his dazed state. She had to outsmart Ivan and the pack, and the vampires, along with whatever else was in the non-human quarter, could just be the distraction they needed. She would have to go along with it for now.

Ivan turned to Carn. "Kraven said he gave some Sword for hire the contract; I have a suspicion it was you?"

Carn smirked. "By Rosh, you must be the *cocky sod* he was talking about. You have your sword in many blacksmiths' fires, don't you. Who don't you own in this city?"

Lara snarled, "Vampires for starters." She glared at the alpha. "And that's what's stopping you from having control of the non-human quarter. You can't find them and eradicate them or at least control them. If you could, you would then have control of the entire city."

Ivan sneered. "Clever girl, and you are going to find them for me." He stepped closer, glaring down at her. "I know they have a witch cloaking them, we can't get a scent anywhere, but it seems you can."

Lara smiled, not letting her gaze waver. "Aye, I do have an overly sensitive nose and you smell like a *werewolf's ball sack*." Ivan sneered, Lara smirked. "So why should I help you now?"

With lightning speed one of his thugs clamped his hand tightly around Carn's neck and started choking him.

Ivan responded, "A little whisper tells me you have a soft spot for this human. I think you wouldn't want anything bad to happen to him, would you?"

Lara's lip curled in anger, but Ivan was right, she could not let anything happen to Carn. She focused on the Sword as he struggled to breathe, his features turning red.

Lara snapped, glaring at Ivan. "Alright! Let him go."

Ivan laughed, nodding to his man who released his grip. Lara cursed under her breath and glared at the alpha. "I'll find your fecking vampires."

He smiled coldly. "Good girl."

Lara glared at him and thought, *Then I'll rip your fecking throat out!*

She inquired instead, "Shall we get on with it?"

Ivan gestured his arm toward the north of the city. "Lead the way."

Lara headed through the quiet city towards the non-human quarter, Derwyn at her side. Carn a few feet behind them being held firmly by one of the pack members, another to the side of him. Ivan, and his three other men walked behind.

This was not how she had expected the night to go. She had thought that they would have some advantage, but with the tables turned, Lara had to think fast and try to figure out how to get out of the situation, with no casualties on her side.

Her brother whispered, "Hope you have a plan."

Lara glanced at him. "I'm working on it."

Ivan stated, having heard them. "Don't try anything foolish, as your human here will be dead in seconds."

Carn snapped, struggling to break free. "At least let's make it a fair fight!"

Ivan laughed. "Oh, I know how good a Sword you are. Kraven told me you are one of his best, but are you quick enough against a lycan?"

Carn snarled, pulling against the iron grip of the lycan holding him. "Happy to find out!"

Ivan chuckled again. "Maybe we will see how you deal with vampires."

Lara glared at the alpha and growled, "This has nothing to do with him, let him go."

"And lose my bargaining coin? Nay way. I know you are close to him and can smell him all over you. Also, the innkeeper was very generous with his information, especially when it came to his daughter, Iowyn."

Derwyn tensed then snarled, "Leave her out of it!"

Ivan smiled. "Again, I don't think so until this is done. Then I will give you a choice, die with your sister or join my pack, but know that you try anything, and poor Iowyn will die along with this human." He sighed studying them both. "Seems you must be siblings, both having a weakness for humans. My men will keep Iowyn and her papa company at the inn until this is all done with."

Lara glared at him realising once she had dealt with these, she would need to deal with his men at the inn too. She was thinking fast, Lara could use the ancient law to become alpha by killing Ivan, but was unsure if his men would abide by it. She had heard of a time when it had not worked, and the pack members sought revenge for the death of their alpha. But it was an option she could not dismiss as she had to get them out of this situation and keep Carn and Iowyn safe in the process. Lara still had one advantage; they had no idea what she was capable of. She just hoped it was enough.

When they reached the non-human quarter, she was hit with all the scents. Lara focused on narrowing it down to the vampires. Seemed some were out and about, their scents ventured around the streets, some fading as they headed into other areas of the city. She was amazed they had not come across any on the way, but then again, they had kept to the main streets. The alleyways would have been a different story. She looked around, getting her bearings then focused on a night demon on one of the roofs studying them. When she stared up at it, it grinned and then ran off across the rooftops. That was not about to be a helpful distraction. She took a deep breath and surveyed the streets, trying to remember which way they had been walking when she got the scent before. Lara picked up a stronger scent heading to the north of the quarter, a few vampires were heading that way. It seemed they were going somewhere before dawn.

She turned to Ivan. "That way."

He gestured in the direction she pointed. "Well, lead the way."

She glared back at him with distaste and started walking, knowing she would enjoy ripping his throat out. What she needed to do was try and provoke those vampires heading back to their shelter. Or maybe with it being such a large city, it could even be a coven. She thought that was what Fashor had told her all those years before. She kept focused on the scent ahead. The vampires were not far away. As she took a deep breath something made her stop, one of the scents was familiar, it was not Fashor, it was . . . Lara swallowed. *It couldn't be, could it?*

Ivan snapped. "Keep moving."

Lara glanced back at him, and continued, she could not afford to be distracted, but she could not ignore that scent. It seemed that bitch, Levana, was just moments away. After all these years, she was about to meet the vampire who sired her again. But this time, if she had to face her, she was not going to let her get the upper hand. She had slipped through her fingers in Naverac, and she would not let it happen again. Lara glanced at Derwyn, she wanted to tell him, but she could not. She would have to deal with the wolves and hoped she could kill that vampire at the same time. She closed her eyes for a moment, she could not get side-tracked, she had to keep focused and not let revenge take hold.

Ahead of them was a row of houses, the third one along she could sense the vampire scents fading as they reached the threshold and that had to be the one protected by a shielding spell.

She turned to Derwyn. "Do you smell vampire?"

He shook his head. "A few dwarfs, and demons, but nay vampires."

Lara indicated to the house, ahead of them. "They're in there. I can smell them." She glared back at Ivan. "That's where the vampires are hiding. From what I can pick up, there are a few in there."

Ivan and his men all took deep breaths not picking up anything.

Von stated, "Can't smell 'em."

Ivan looked at Lara, then at Carn. "You better not be lying to us *girl.*"

Lara sneered at him. "I'm not. I have shown you where they are, now let my brother and Carn go."

Ivan smiled and gave a quick nod to his man holding Carn. "Oh nay. I think I want to double-check and, to be honest, I don't want any loose ends."

His men moved with lycan speed to the house, one kicked down the door then the other threw Carn in.

Lara snarled, "You bastard."

She turned and moved at lightning speed, faster than the lycan. Yet Carn was already falling inside, as Lara passed the threshold she exposed her claws, and the lycan's throat was sliced before he even realised it. Lara glanced back at the dead lycan still standing, she hoped Derwyn moved fast as in the next few seconds, Ivan would realise she had just killed one of his men right in front of him.

CHAPTER 35

CARN had been so focused on the street outside watching for any more lycans. He had not heard the two sneaking up behind him until it was too late. He went for one of his daggers and sliced it upwards, nicking his assailant's arm. The large man barely noticed as he lifted Carn and threw him across the room. His body hit the brick wall hard with a painful crunch, winding him. Carn landed with a thud, dazed he quickly shook his head. Considering these men were large, one definitely bigger than him, they had been as quiet as mice. As he tried to focus, he reached for another dagger. The two men were on him again, one grabbed his hair and slammed his head against the wall. After three hits, Carn blacked out for a few moments. As he came too, he felt himself being pulled up. He opened his eyes and all he could see were stars. Blood filled his mouth as he inhaled deeply, struggling to focus. He tried to break free, but the two men had iron grips and were extremely strong. They dragged him from the room and down through the inn, the innkeeper looked on guiltily. Carn knew he had ratted him out, but from the fear in the man's eyes, Carn could not blame him. The Sword cursed; it was such a silly mistake. He should have been more aware and not relied so much upon the fact that he had been hidden, especially against lycans. He sighed, they were fast and strong, but he had not expected to have been downed so quickly.

When they reached Lara and the others, he eyed her sheepishly. He did not like that he had let her down, and that the situation was no longer in their favour. Yet when he focused on her eyes, he could see she was already considering a way out. Carn had to make sure to be ready, that is if he could get free of the thugs. After some threats, Carn almost lost consciousness from the larger man clamping his hand over his throat. Then they started to make their way through the city. Carn noticed Lara and her brother whispering, he could not quite hear what they were saying, but it seemed Ivan had. He looked at his captors, he had regained most of his senses and was walking, no longer being dragged by the man who was still holding him. Cautiously, he eyed the lycans a few feet ahead; they were just thugs, but three times as strong as him. He noticed one had his daggers and wondered if he would ever get them back, one having been his father's. If it had been more of a fair fight, he would have given them a good beating. He had not expected such large men to be so quiet. Carn had not even heard them enter the room at the inn. He could feel blood drying on his forehead, and a couple of throbbing bumps swelling on his head. He took a deep breath, his ribs and neck protested, and the taste of blood lingered in his mouth. Carn felt bruised and battered, but luckily, it did not feel like anything was broken. Maybe just his pride.

They had come to a stop; Carn regarded the buildings ahead.

Lara said, indicating to the house in front of them. "They are in there. I can smell them." She glared back at Ivan. "That's where the vampires are hiding. From what I can pick up, there are a few in there."

Carn turned to Ivan and his men as they all took deep breaths as Von stated, "Can't smell 'em."

Ivan turned to Lara. "You better not be lying to us *girl*."

She sneered at him, Carn seeing the disgust in her eyes for the lycan. "I'm not. I have shown you where they are, now let my brother and Carn go."

Ivan smiled and gave a quick nod to his man holding Carn, the Sword felt their grip tightening. He took a breath knowing something was about to happen.

"Oh nay, I think I want to double-check and, to be honest, I don't want any loose ends."

Carn felt his sword being placed in his scabbard on his back. Then suddenly, the man lifted him off the ground like he weighed nothing, and moved with lycan speed to the house. One kicked down the door, and the other then threw him in, like a rag doll. Carn landed with a thud and slid across the polished floor of a large hallway, sliding to a stop at the foot of the stairs. A large group of men and women all around him.

Carn looked up and smiled. "Sorry to barge in."

Instantly, they all reacted showing their fangs and ready to pounce. Carn put up his hands, trying not to seem like a threat, and understood why he had been given his sword back. At least Ivan, or one of his men, wanted him to have a fair fight. Then suddenly, Lara appeared beside him, having run into the building at lightning speed. She pulled her sword free, studying the vampires slowly surrounding them. Carn slowly got to his feet keeping alert. Lara glanced at Carn. "Try and keep up."

Lara jumped straight up, flipping in the air, and landing a few feet away. But with that fast movement, four vampires fell to the floor, headless and turned to dust.

Carn's eyes widened, and gasped. "*Keep up?*"

Lara shrugged and spun around killing two more vampires. Carn pulled his sword free, his eyes focused on the vampires moving towards him and took a breath. "Here goes nothing."

Lara knew Carn would not be as fast as her, but he was still a good swordsman. Lara picked up her brother's scent, seeing him running in with his sword drawn. She had no idea what the situation was outside, but for now, they had to deal with this one. She glanced back to see Carn fighting two vampires well and would be able to handle himself. Turning, she again picked up the familiar scent. She peered up to see Levana on the upper landing, seeing her face again brought back that night vividly. Her mid-section twinged a little from that fateful night in Naverac. She jumped upwards effortlessly onto the large landing.

Levana glared at her and snarled, "You *again!*"

Lara smiled coldly. "Missed me?"

The vampire sneered. "Why won't you just die!"

"I'm like a bad smell, you can't get rid of me."

The vampire glared at her. "I'm going to eat your heart right in front of you!"

Lara took a firm hold of her sword, noting that Levana was not armed. "Well, let's see, shall we."

The vampire ran at her in a rage, but with Lara fully knowing her extra abilities, Levana seemed slow. Lara spun, bringing her sword round and slicing it into her arm. The vampire screamed in anger, flipping round to continue to fight. Lara swung her sword again, the vampire used her claw-like nails to parry her blade. Levana lunged, but Lara flipped out of the way. She would not let the vampire get to her mid-section like she had the last time. Levana glared at her, but before she could attack again two more vampires ran at Lara, separating the two. The female vampire took the opportunity to run. Lara could not get to Levana as more vampires ran towards her. Lara cursed, Levana had got away again. She quickly turned her attention to the vampires attacking her. Lara killed two, but they were skilled fighters, and she wondered if they were cleansers. Lara did not have time to find out, she still had Ivan and his men to deal with. She turned back to the fight below, Carn was still warding off vampires, dust scattered at his feet as Derwyn dealt with the others.

She jumped off, landing next to Carn, and snapped, "Time to go."

Lara killed two more vampires pushing Carn towards the door, she needed to end this fast and the sun would be up by now. She looked up at the blacked-out window above the hallway. She then glanced back to see the cleansers coming her way. Lara had to act fast, she grabbed one of the vampires next to her and with her super strength, threw it at the window. The body shattered the glass, and burned to ash instantly as the sun touched it. The other vampires screamed when the sunlight filled the room. Panic took over, all ran from the light, forcing the cleansers back. The ones who did not have talismans vapourised in the sunlight, the rest ran for cover. She was surprised how few had protection from the sun. The three rushed to the main entrance, the remaining vampires were too busy trying to save their coven to give chase.

Lara asked, "Where's Ivan?"

Derwyn quickly answered, "Outside. He was mad that you killed one of his. He then pushed me in. I heard him say to kill anything that came out."

Lara stopped at the doorway picking up lycan scents. She turned to the two men, all of them covered in vampire blood and dust.

She heard Ivan shout, "YOU ARE DEAD HALF BREED!!"

Lara kept her attention on the two men. "Derwyn, you need to get to the inn fast, and stop his men holding Iowyn and her papa. You're faster than Carn would be."

Derwyn nodded, studying his sister. "What are you going to do?"

"Deal with Ivan."

Derwyn glanced at Carn; the older man smiled. "I'm her back up."

The teenager raised an eyebrow. "Really?"

Carn shrugged, Derwyn turned to his sister, ready to run. Lara ran out, her sword drawn, taking out two of the men before they could even react. Derwyn ran out heading away from the fight and towards the inn. Carn ran out last with his sword drawn, a war cry bellowed from his lungs. His sword clashed with one of the lycans, after fighting vampires he was more used to the super speed and held his ground well. Lara knew he would be all right and concentrated on the others. Soon only Ivan remained.

He glared at her. "So what? You may be a lot faster, but that doesn't mean you can beat an alpha."

Lara glared at him. "Let's find out." She glanced at Carn and ordered, "*Inn!*" He seemed reluctant to leave her, but Lara snapped, "*Now!*"

Carn nodded and ran off, grabbing his daggers from the fallen thug who had them. Ivan watched him go and turned back to Lara. "I'm looking forward to claiming the bounty on your head."

Lara gave him a black look and cracked her neck. "So, what will it be?"

"You seem pretty fast in human form, let's see how you do wolf to wolf."

Lara smiled. From what she had read, and from what her father told her, alphas were strong, but even more so in their wolf form. Lara surveyed the street which was empty, except for the bodies of Ivan's men. All the non-humans knew it was best to keep out of sight. Even the vampires who had protection from the sun were staying inside and not venturing out for revenge.

She turned as Ivan ripped off his shirt, she snarled, "Your overconfidence will be your downfall."

He smirked and started changing. Lara quickly unbuckled her belt and ripped off her shirt and started to change, her trousers ripping in the process. Her large grey wolf stood her ground facing the larger brown wolf. Being an alpha, he was bigger than her, but she would still be able to outdo him in speed and strength. He ran at her and she jumped to the side. Lara landed smoothly on her paws and dug her teeth deep into his neck as he passed. He pulled free and snarled, running at her and biting down on her leg. Lara yelped and pulled free and ran around him in a blur then clamped her jaw around his neck once more. She bit deep, not letting go, mauling him as much as she could. He was heavier than her, but she was still stronger. He managed to break free again and grabbed her neck with his jaw, biting down hard. His teeth dug deep into her skin and muscle. He then threw her across the road. Her body hit the wall of the vampire's house with a deafening crunch. She got back up shaking her fur, she had to be quicker. Her wounded leg throbbed. Ivan was staggering, he had lost a lot of blood from the last attack. She needed to act now. Yet she felt a little weak too, she could feel blood trickling from her wounded neck. She assessed her leg, it would not take her full weight, but she could still be quick. She ran at him as fast as her leg would let her. Her claws slashed across his back, her teeth ripped the flesh on his neck. He yelped and staggered back. She stood facing him, growling, her wolf features full of rage, and she pounced, tearing his throat open. Ivan staggered and fell to the ground. His wolf body convulsed and changed back to its human form. The neck wound exposed his throat, the ravaged flesh pouring with blood. Lara limped slightly from her wounded leg as she moved over to him, and watched as his life drained away. She then slowly turned back to her human form, slumping to the ground from exhaustion.

Lara was bleeding badly and one rib was probably broken, but she needed to get to the inn. Forcing herself to stand, she cried out in pain. Staggering over to one of the lycan's bodies, she winced as she removed the man's shirt. She put it on, with him being a larger man it was like a short dress on her. She then grabbed her sword, belt and boots, biting back the pain at some movements. Then mustering the rest of her strength, she hobbled as quickly as she could through the non-human quarter and the city.

CHAPTER 36

W HEN Lara arrived at the inn, all was quiet. The fight was already over, Ivan's men were dead on the floor. The proprietor, his family and staff sat huddled in a corner, whimpering and scared, a couple of them slightly wounded. Derwyn was comforting Iowyn and her father, both seeming to be in shock.

Carn sat to one side cradling a wounded arm and dropping her belongings at her feet, Lara slumped down next to him. Her wounds were healing slowly, but still, she was exhausted.

Carn studied her; her bare legs were spotted with blood and dirt, and a new wound that must have been inflicted by Ivan. "You alright?"

She nodded, her ribs burning in pain. She stared at his arm, the smell of the blood oozing from his wound was intoxicating. It made her begin to crave it, and she licked her lips. She forced herself to turn away.

Carn leant towards her. "Lara?"

She clenched her fist, focusing on the floor, trying to calm her senses down. "Just . . . give me a moment."

She could feel her fangs extending, she had not had the urge to feed in years but her reaction had to do with all the events and her wounds. She took a few deep breaths.

Carn got up and moved to crouch in front of her. "Lara?" concern in his voice.

She put up a hand and pushed him back. When she glanced at him, her eyes were slowly changing as a blood tinted mist spread over them. Red and purple veins feathered out from her eyes, across her face and forehead. Her face had contorted to accommodate her fangs. Carn's face paled as he was confronted by her vampire side for the first time.

Suddenly Derwyn ran over, grabbing Lara by the shoulders, and pulling her away from Carn. He snapped at the older man, "*You're fecking bleeding!* Keep back. Let her regain control." He turned back to his sister. "Lara, focus on my voice. Take a deep breath."

Lara glared at him; her features altered, her fangs extended, and the feather-like red veins had spread to cover her face from her fully red eyes. Her voice was deeper and more menacing as she said, "I *need* blood."

Derwyn squeezed her shoulders, studying her intently. "Nay, *you* don't. You're weak, but don't let the vampire side take hold."

Lara looked across the inn when she heard Iowyn scream. The young woman had headed over to help, then saw Lara's vampire features. Derwyn, still holding his sister's shoulders, glanced back at the barmaid. "She won't harm you; she just needs to regain control."

Derwyn turned to Carn when he said, "Let her have some of my blood if it will help her."

Lara took a deep breath, shaking her head. "*Nay!*" she gasped glaring at Derwyn. Her hands gripped his arms tightly. Her nails grew like claws. "I need to hunt…. now."

He shook his head. "But it is daylight now, you will be seen."

Lara clenched her fists, the vampire side was subsiding, she could feel the fangs receding as she regained some control. She glared at the innkeeper. "Give me some of that Volc, *now*."

Teth nodded, seeming scared, and shakily passed her the demijohn of the clear liquid. She grabbed it and Lara gulped some down, knowing it would ease the craving. After a few moments, she was finally back in control. She turned to Carn and then Iowyn and Teth, she hated anyone seeing that side of her and could see the fear in the latter two's eyes. Lara turned back to Carn; she could smell the blood oozing from his wound, but at least now with the strong alcohol she was finally in control of the craving. She needed to hunt, her wounds were deep and she needed to heal, but Derwyn was right; not in full daylight. She watched as Derwyn passed Carn some cloths to clean up his wound.

Lara slowly moved and sat next to the Sword and studied him. "Sorry you had to see that." Her eyes focused on the wound, the blood still drawing her.

Carn focused on her. "Are you sure you're alright?"

She shook her head. "Nay." She gazed into his blue eyes. "But I *can* control it."

"Look, if blood will help you heal . . ."

Lara studied him and smiled softly. "Nay I daren't. If I weaken just for a moment, I may lose control. I can't let that side of me win, *ever*."

Carn nodded then turned his attention to his arm, cleaning it up and bandaging it. Once covered over, Lara was able to pull her eyes away from it. She looked across to see Derwyn talking to Iowyn who kept glancing across at her with fear in her eyes. Lara sighed, it seemed it was time to leave. Teth would want her gone as soon as possible, and she could not blame him. She glanced at Carn after what had happened, could she let him be in danger like that again? Lara would need to have a good talk with him, it seemed she would never be able to have a quiet life. She leant back on the chair; she was still weak, the wounds taking their time to heal. Lara closed her eyes, knowing rest would help, letting the sense of feelings from her wolf self flow over her. That always helped calm her and her vampire side.

The inn remained closed for the day, Derwyn and Carn helped to clear up the mess leaving Lara to rest for a while and heal. Once she had got into some of her own clothes, she ventured out to the barn and found some rats. The blood from them helped her heal and helped get her vampire side fully back under control. When Lara came down later to help, the innkeeper and his daughter kept glancing at her nervously. Derwyn had explained, but there was still fear in their eyes. To Lara's relief, Carn seemed all right with it all, but she would have to talk to him and decide what they did next.

Carn wanted them to go with him, and it was very tempting to take the offer to accompany him to the contract in the south as they could leave Kerlish behind with a solid plan. But Lara wondered if it would be safe for him. She nearly fed on him after that fight, and she worried if she would be able to stop herself if it happened again.

By late afternoon, the three knew it was in everyone's best interest that they left Kerlish. Derwyn seemed a little forlorn as he mounted his horse, having decided not to pursue Iowyn any further and feeling too guilty that he had put her in danger. Teth gave them a generous food pack and wished them luck on their journey. Derwyn focused on Iowyn who stood by her father looking sad, he nodded a farewell to her and then egged his horse onwards, heading south out of the city. Lara and Carn said good day to the innkeeper and followed suit on their horses. Lara regarded the city as they took the main road out, wondering if any of the wolf pack remained. If they did, what would they do without an alpha. The contract on her was still out there, if any of the surviving wolves knew that she was involved, she had to be careful. Carn was still going to give out false information when he could and Lara hoped that, at least for a while, they would be off her trail.

By not leaving the city till late in the day they would not be able to cover much distance, but they would be able to find a good camping stop, one where Lara could go and hunt. Even though she was healed, she still felt weak. Carn told them they were heading to a small port town named Crystal Neck where they could either take the ferry across the Crystal River, or they could ride along the banks to Channel End and a bridge, called The Enchanted Bridge which would take them over the river and continue south to Palasses. All agreed they did not fancy any trouble, and they chose to travel cross country, avoiding the small port and camping off the beaten track. Brother and sister agreed that when they got to the large coastal city, they would decide their next move.

They set up camp in a clearing near some brush and as they were settling the horses, Lara studied her brother. He had been quiet since they left the city and knew what would make him feel like himself again.

"Why don't you come hunting with me? We haven't done so in weeks, and the run would do you some good."

Derwyn glanced at Carn who agreed and then turned to his sister. "It would be good to have a run."

She gave a soft smile seeing the sadness in his eyes. He had liked Iowyn and it was a pity it had ended the way it had.

She turned to Carn. "Will you be alright while we go hunting?"

He smiled at her, his eyes glinting. "I'll be fine." He raised his eyebrow as Lara began to strip, his eyes lingering a little longer on her breasts. Lara smiled at him mischievously before transforming into her wolf form.

Lara trotted up to Carn and felt his fingers raking into her thick fur. She could still feel the calluses on his hand even in her wolf form, and her skin tingled at his touch. She rubbed her head against his arm and studied him. Their gaze was broken when Derwyn growled behind her. She turned and grunted, glancing back at Carn, she then trotted off and followed her brother as he ran off hunting.

When they found their kills, the wolves ate a couple of rabbits each. Then they both laid down on a high point looking across the plains and seeing the campfire Carn had set up in the distance. Lara gazed at her brother in his wolf form, wondering what lay ahead for them. Licking his paw, he looked up at her and grunted. She sniffed the air, time to run back.

The two wolves trotted up to the campfire to see Carn's wolf dozing at his side. The Sword gazed at the two large beasts then turned away as they changed back. Lara pulled on her clothes and sat, Carn's hand gently brushing her thigh as she sat beside him.

He asked as Derwyn joined them, "Do you both feel better now?"

Derwyn nodded, and Lara stated, "It always helps. It seems to clear our minds and just be free."

Derwyn agreed, placing wood on the fire. "It just makes you realise what's important."

Carn said, glancing at Lara and then at his wolf, "I haven't seen her since we arrived at Kerlish. Yet she always knows when I am travelling again."

Lara leant over and stroked the wolf's fur, not waking her. "Wolves have a sixth sense."

Carn smiled, focusing on Lara's eyes as she sat back up again. "Very true."

Derwyn sighed, getting to his feet. "I'm going to get some sleep."

Lara eyed him, knowing her brother was letting them have some privacy. Lara turned back to Carn, studying his eyes. "So, we never really talked about what happened."

Carn gazed at her. "What is there to say? It was good to fight by your side, and would do it again in a heartbeat."

Lara smiled. "The same with you, but that's not what I was talking about."

Carn contemplated her, raising an eyebrow. "Oh, at the inn, afterwards."

"Aye." Nodded Lara, glancing away from his eyes. "You saw my other side, not many have seen that."

"It was still you, and you kept it well in check."

Lara studied him. "You offered me your blood."

"And?" stated Carn. "I would offer it again if I knew it would help you."

Lara leaned closer to him, taking his hand in hers. "But the risks are too high. I may have been unable to stop, and you would have died."

Carn smiled, raising her hand and kissing it. "I know you would have stopped." He sighed, studying her eyes. "Look, like I said before, I *care* for you. I know this isn't something that will last forever, but while I am in your company, I am happy, warts and all."

Lara smiled softly. "I have to agree I feel the same, but there will be a time when we will have to part."

Carn focused on her green eyes. "I know. But till then, let's just enjoy every moment."

Lara found herself lost in his gaze. She was going to enjoy their time together, but when they reached Palasses it would be time to part ways. She cared for Carn, but she could not continue to put him in more danger, even with him being a good Sword. He was helping with the contract, but what would be best for her, and Derwyn, was to disappear. And that meant getting onto a ship and leaving Moonstar for a while. Carn was not going to like it, and that was why she would not tell him

235

anything until all had been arranged in the city. Till then, she was going to make every moment count.

They continued in the morning and travelled along the main route by the river which was so wide and deep it was used by seafaring ships. They travelled toward Channel End, taking the road up into the mountains that the river cut through. Near the peak was The Enchanted Bridge that crossed the gorge. When they reached the bridge, it was an impressive sight made from several large oak and maple trees with large metal rivets keeping the structure in place and strong against the elements. It had been a marvel to see, and many wondered how they had managed to build it over such a large deep gorge, but things like that would be easy to make with the help of a strong sorcerer. For centuries, it had survived the elements without needing any repairs. It had to be protected by magic to have lasted so long, and probably had visits from sorcerers to ensure the spell to protect it remained strong. Hence the origins of its name.

As they crossed the bridge, which was wide enough for a carriage and two horses, Lara peered over the side, watching as a ship in full sail passed beneath them. She wondered what was on the ship, and suspected when it left Kerlish its hold would be full of silks and spices.

Just past the bridge was a large, popular inn where the three hoped to get something to eat and a room for the night. They managed to find a table in the busy inn and had something to eat and drink but there were no rooms available that night. They reluctantly continued on and found a good place to camp, Lara taking the first watch.

Lara sat by the fire, studying the shrubland and the small woods they were camped next to. Placing some branches on the fire, she looked across at Carn sleeping, his wolf curled up by his feet. She smiled softly, enjoying the time she was spending with him. She knew that even though they would part ways soon, she would cross his path again someday. She stared upwards at the clear night sky, thinking about where she and Derwyn had been, and where they would travel to in the future. She sighed, it was unknown, but there would come a time when she would be travelling on her own, all that she knew would be too old or gone. Her thoughts were broken when the horses became restless, and Carn's wolf woke to sniff the air and growled softly.

Lara glanced at it. "You sense it too, don't you girl?"

The wolf grunted at her, and Lara sniffed the air too. Something was not right. She searched the small woodland they were camping by. Using her senses, she could make out something in the trees. She could see its blood coursing through its veins and from the scent, it seemed to be some sort of demon. She moved over to Carn and Derwyn, slowly shaking them awake.

Carn looked up at her. "What is it?"

Lara glanced up at the trees, then back at the two men. "There's something in there. Watching us."

Derwyn sniffed the air picking up the scent. "Smells like a demon."

Carn glanced towards the trees unable to see anything, he turned back at the two. "Glad I have you two around." His wolf growled softly towards the trees. "And her."

Lara said, "Not sure why it's just sitting there. Think it's not sure what I am."

Carn studied her. "You are unique."

She smiled, glancing at the two men. "I'm going to investigate. If it heads this way be ready, it may go for the horses."

The two nodded. Lara pulled her sword free and walked towards the trees. The creature was still staying up in the branches, but it was watching her. She peered up into the tree seeing it, it looked like it had wings. Lara tried to remember all the books she had read when she was younger. It was probably a Darlon, they were shy, but would drink blood from livestock or horses. The fact it was watching them made her wonder if it were getting desperate, that was when they would venture closer to humans. If it was hungry, Lara did not want it going for their horses. Lara jumped up into a nearby tree, landing on a branch close to the demon. It turned towards her, its wings unfurling to make a move. She jumped across, landing on the tree it had been perched in, just as it jumped into the air. Lara cursed, but knew where it was headed. She jumped down from the tree and ran towards the camp. The Darlon swooped down at the horses, making them skittish. Derwyn and Carn were trying to keep the demon back, Carn's wolf growling and barking at it. Lara ran over to join them. Then Lara jumped up in the air, slicing her sword across the demon. As she landed, so did the two halves of the Darlon. She did not want to kill it, but they could not afford to lose their horses either.

The two men placed hands over their noses as the smell from the demon's insides drifted towards them.

Carn glanced at Lara. "Impressive move."

She inspected the two halves. "We better drag this into the trees."

Derwyn asked, "What about ghouls?"

"They won't venture this way, but let's move from here by first light."

The two agreed and Derwyn and Lara pulled the remains into the woods while Carn made sure the horses had calmed down. Once they settled back at the camp, Lara remained on watch. After a while of not being able to get back to sleep, Carn came and sat by her glancing over at Derwyn, his sleep restless.

Carn sighed and studied Lara. "Do you think there will be any more of them out there?"

Lara shook her head. "Nay, they're all pretty much loners. It's rare to see one be so brazen. I didn't want to kill it, but had little choice."

Carn smiled, poking the embers of the fire with a twig. "You made the right call." He gestured towards Derwyn. "Seems your brother is warming to me."

Lara gazed at his features. "I knew he would."

Carn sighed, glancing up at the sky and then back at her. "When we get to Palasses what's the plan? I will have to carry out my contract, so I may be gone for several days. I was then, with your help, going to come up with a plan about yours."

Lara studied him. She was not ready to tell him of her full plans yet, she wanted to see all the options regarding ships when they got to Palasses. "I don't want to be constantly on the run. I'm going to sit with Derwyn and discuss options."

Carn nodded while studying her. "Listen, if it was me, you should try and get as far away from here as you can. I can sort out the contract, but there's still the issue of anyone from that pack coming across you."

She gazed at him and smiled softly. "I need to see what Derwyn wants to do. It has been me and him for years. But he's at an age now where he needs to make his own decision." She sighed studying Carn's blue eyes. "Part of me knows I need to make a wise choice, and that may be leaving here for good, but I am torn. This is my homeland and then there's you."

Carn kissed her gently, his hands combing into her brown hair, and gazed at her features lovingly. "We knew this wasn't going to last, in more ways than one. Whatever you decide, I will honour it."

Lara gave him another soft smile and kissed him, lost in his gaze. She wanted to ask him to join them, but wondered if it would be fair to ask that he give up his life here. There was still the contract to be dealt with, if it was not handled, she knew they would never be able to return. Their moment was broken when Derwyn sat up and cursed. Both glanced over and the young man looked a little sheepish, realising he had interrupted a tender moment.

He sighed, "Sorry, I just can't get to sleep."

Carn smiled. "Same here."

Lara squeezed Carn's hand, hoping they would be able to continue the conversation later, and looked up at the sky. "It's not long till dawn, shall we just get moving now?"

Carn agreed, "It will gain us some time. And to be honest, even without a wolf sense of smell, I can still smell that fecking demon."

Lara and Derwyn both wrinkled their noses and agreed. Stamping out the fire, they all got up and packed away the camp.

CHAPTER 37

T HEY travelled for seven days; the weather having been favourable for most of the journey. There had only been one day of constant rain, but they reached an inn a day later where they were able to dry out their clothes, get some hot food, a hot bath and a good night's sleep. They continued for a couple more days, then the night before they would reach the city of Palasses, Lara went hunting. She wanted to make sure she would not have any cravings while they were in the city.

As they rode along the main route, they could see the great city ahead of them. Just like what had happened at Kerlish, Carn's wolf had left them and ventured off towards the nearby forest. Palasses was a lot bigger than Kerlish, and surrounded by a large, ornate, sandstone wall. Green and blue banners fluttered in the sea breeze atop the watchtowers, which were dotted evenly around the top of the wall. The wall itself seemed almost new in comparison to Kerlish's, partly due to Palasses being a more affluent city. Yet because of its more impressive walls and size, it would have a fair share of seedy back alleys and inns. As she looked around, she picked up a lycan scent as well as dwarf and elf, all coming from the east where the non-human quarter had to be located. The city was large enough to have a pack, confirmed by the lycan scent, but she was unsure if they knew about the contract? It was not worth the risk of finding out. It would be best to keep a low profile and hope the city was big enough that they would be able to hide with ease.

That was yet another reason why it would probably be for the best to leave Moonstar for a while, something she had not been able to stop contemplating since Kerlish. They rode through the city, taking in the busy atmosphere with street stalls overflowing with produce. The siblings followed Carn who knew of a pleasant inn they could all stay at. He led them through a large square and headed to the north end, taking a side street.

The White Ox, even though popular, still had a couple of rooms available. Lara did not mind sharing with Carn, they had been sleeping together most nights anyway. With their horses settled in the stable next door, the three sat in the inn having sausages and potatoes. Lara, as usual, had a strong drink instead. The inn was busy and the conversations were in full flow. Lara leant back lost in thought, wondering how long before she would be leaving her homeland behind. She glanced at her companions, she had managed to suggest her plans to Derwyn, then gave him some space to consider the options. But she had not fully shared her thoughts with Carn, yet. They had spoken about her leaving, and he had agreed that it would be a good option, but since arriving in Palasses, Lara knew for certain that was what she was going to do. The conversation would be a hard one to have so she had to time it right. Yet Carn would understand, and it would be for the best for all of them. Maybe in a year or two, they would return. Moonstar was their home; and as much as the situation was not ideal, Lara knew in her heart, she would be here again.

Lara and Carn lay in each other's arms, Carn tracing his fingers across her naked stomach. She gazed up at him and asked, "So what's the contract you have here in the city?"

He studied her. "A business owner has an issue with some thugs. I need to track them down. I will be seeing him in the morn to get all the details."

Lara nodded. "What about the one out on me?"

Carn kissed her softly on the lips. "I will send a message to Kraven, in the next day or two informing him I saw you heading east and will pursue once this other contract is arranged."

Lara twisted around to study him more clearly. "I think I'm going to explore the city and talk to Derwyn about what we do next."

Carn smiled softly, hope in his eyes. "Welcome to stay with me."

Lara kissed him. "I know, but I must think about other packs and lycan families. I don't think any will except me but also need to think about what Derwyn wants to do. With that contract out on me, and even with your help, I'm still on edge."

Carn focused on her eyes. "I understand. I'm hoping my misinformation will make you feel less like you're constantly on the run. It seemed Derwyn liked Iowyn, a shame it got all messed up."

Lara sighed. "He did. I partly thought he might have wanted to make his own choices, but then, with what happened, everything changed."

Carn kissed her gently. "That pack seemed to have too much control and I had nay idea he was involved with Kraven."

"That didn't help matters. If I had known, I wouldn't have arranged to meet them."

Carn shrugged. "Even if you hadn't arranged to meet them. I think we would have come across them at some point anyway. He most likely had regular meetings with Kraven and knew of the contract shortly after it was received."

"Ivan knew we were at that inn, and if we hadn't arranged that meeting, he would have tried to take us out there. But by meeting them, we brought the fight to them." She told him. "Derwyn and I know this will be our life for a while, but it doesn't have to be for you."

Carn smiled, taking her hand in his. "Hey, my life isn't all quiet and dull, I'm used to this sort of thing, being a Sword, you rub some people the wrong way. Every time I go to a town or city, I will bump into someone who doesn't like me."

"But for me, the people who don't like me have teeth."

Carn chuckled. "Very true." He raised an eyebrow. "Are you still thinking about moving on?"

Lara glanced away from his eyes, feeling guilty. "I think it may be the best thing to do. At the moment, I'm getting too much attention and feel I need to disappear for a while. They'll lose interest and if you announce you dealt with me in a month or so, then all the parties involved will move on."

Carn responded, "They may want proof."

Lara studied him. "Remember the vampires at Kerlish."

He nodded. "There wasn't anything left once we killed them."

Lara gazed at him, sitting up a little. "So, I'm part vampire, I don't think there will be anything of me if you did kill me. As for Derwyn, well I could have parted ways with him, and he isn't the issue. The Stonelances aren't that bothered if he is dealt with or not, it's just me."

Carn said, brushing a stray hair off her shoulder, "Think that may work." He studied her eyes. "Where are you thinking of going?"

Lara kissed him softly. "Better you don't know."

He slowly nodded. "I agree." He sighed while studying her features. "I knew this day would come. And I think you had kind of made up your mind after we had killed that demon," He smiled softly. "But it still hurts."

Lara cupped his cheek in her hand, losing herself in his gaze. "I think this is for the best. But I will return . . . one day."

Carn placed a finger to her lips. Lara smiled as she felt his other hand roam down her stomach, his fingers combing into the hairs at her groin. She closed her eyes, her body zinged in anticipation. Carn kissed her and gazed into her eyes. "Enough talk, let's make the most of our remaining time together."

The following morning, Lara woke to find Carn had already gone, but he had forewarned her the night before that he would have an early start. Part of her wished he would have woken her, but when they had made love, she could tell he was hurting at the knowledge they would soon be parting ways, and he probably just needed some space. Going down to the main part of the inn, she did not see Derwyn, he was either still asleep or taking some time to consider all his options. She wanted him to think about what she had proposed fully, and if he decided to stay in Moonstar she would understand.

Lara left the inn, regardless of whatever Derwyn decided, she would still need to find a ship. She walked across the city taking in the atmosphere of the busy streets. The city had a different feel compared to Kerlish, it was more affluent and seemed to have more scholars. Add in a busy port for ships from across the ocean, meant there were more people with accents Lara did not recognise. She somehow felt that if there was a pack, they would not be as controlling. Which made her feel a little more relaxed.

As she reached the wharf, the sea air invaded her nostrils, the breeze cooling against her skin. The docks were very busy, and she soon found the harbour master barking orders from the doorway of his office, as some dock hands seemed to not be pulling their weight. Getting his attention, she managed to find out that a ship was due to arrive later that day that would be heading out to the open sea. It seemed it would dock for a few days, then would be heading to Barberium in the west by sailing around the coast to the north and then out to sea. That would be perfect as they could leave the land of Moonstar behind for a while and explore the world. She would miss the cocky Sword for hire, but it was still the best thing to do.

Once she had finished her business at the docks, knowing she would have to return later to see the captain of the ship that would be arriving, Lara wandered the city for a while giving her time to think about the decision she was making. She still wanted to make sure it was the right thing to do, and with the ship not arriving for a few hours, she had time to think it through. Yet, if she did not take this way out, she would always be looking over her shoulder and Derwyn would not be able to have a life. Leaving gave them a chance at freedom, although they would have to start all over again. Her one hope for Derwyn would be that he finds someone he could settle with, and have as normal a life as he could. If Derwyn decided not to go with her, it would be strange being on her own, but she would learn to live with it. Carn would manage to end the contract, but some people would still recognise her. If she vanished for a few years, whenever she did return, she would be a faded memory. Lara knew she would cross paths with Carn again, it just seemed to be destined.

After wandering the city for a few hours, Lara found herself in the non-human quarter. She needed to find a witch, one that would not ask too many questions. If she did go with the ship option and leave Moonstar behind, then she would be on one for some time, and that would require a talisman to keep her cravings at bay. Asking around, she found there was a witch in this part of the city who could help. Following the directions she was given, Lara stopped and scrutinised the small shop down a dark side alley. It looked dodgy, but Lara had little choice. It was a risk, as up to now they had kept a low profile, but most witches liked to keep to themselves and having so many different clients, they would not tell the lycans anything if there was a pack here. Taking a breath, Lara entered the shop, the air within was thick with herbs and incense. Every surface was cluttered with books, bottles, and jars full of different colours of liquid or objects. Lara glanced at a jar full of eyes and felt sure they were following her. She turned her attention to the middle-aged woman, her grey hair up in a tight bun, standing behind the jumbled counter.

"Can I 'elp ya, lass?"

Lara smiled. "Aye. I heard you can make a talisman to reduce cravings?"

The woman studied her, her grey eyes full of wisdom beyond her years. "I can lass. Depends on the craving?"

Lara responded, "Blood craving."

The witch pursed her lips. "Aye, I can 'elp ya. Why would ya need such a thing?"

Lara smiled softly. "I was told you would be discreet."

"Aye. I have many clients and I keep things secret. Even with one of a kind like ya." She paused while studying Lara. "Don't worry lass, nay one will know ya was 'ere."

Lara regarded the woman. It was hard to distinguish, but she could make out a few scents of demons, vampires, and werewolves that had been in her store. The herbs masked them well, but Lara could still make them out and knew her secret was safe.

The witch eyed her. "Ya still need to feed, but ya will last longer than ya normally do. It'll only last about ninety days."

Lara nodded. "Understood and will suffice."

The witch smiled and went into the back room. A few moments later, after Lara heard the witch casting spells, she returned with a small amulet. It was gold with a black stone within it.

As the witch passed it over, she stated, "Keep it on ya person at all times. That will be six gold."

Lara raised an eyebrow. "Six?"

"Aye. Four for the amulet, two for me silence."

Lara reluctantly paid. As she passed over the coins she added, "If anything alerts me to someone knowing I was here, you are dead."

The witch chuckled, placing her grubby fingers to her lips. "Don't worry lass. As ya can smell, I have many clients and all 'ave secrets. The coin is just a guarantee for both of us."

Lara gave a sharp nod, taking the amulet and quickly exited the shop. Lara wished she had not come, but on a ship she would need something, otherwise it could end in disaster.

She returned to the docks later that day after exploring more of the city. The ship had arrived and was being emptied of its cargo for the city and merchants that arrived from near and far. It did not take Lara long to find the captain.

The tall dark-haired man studied her, his face as dark and hard as leather. "So ya want passage?"

Lara nodded while studying him. "I will pay handsomely. It will be for me and maybe one other."

He pursed his lips, eyeing her up and down. "I don't want any trouble."

"And there will be none. I just want passage. Nay questions asked."

He raised an eyebrow. "Well, that will be extra, any cargo?"

She shook her head. "Nay, just the two of us and our belongings."

He pursed his lips, studying her for a few moments. "A hundred and ya have a deal."

Lara had expected more, but was not about to argue, and shook his hand to seal the deal. Lara gave him twenty coins to ensure that she had a cabin secured and then headed back across the city to the inn.

As Lara walked back across the city, she picked up a familiar scent and paused. She looked around and saw Levana weaving through the crowded street ahead of her. Lara sneered at seeing her and was not about to lose the opportunity. Lara kept at a safe distance and followed the female vampire. Lara wondered where she was heading as she would not be so bold to feed in the middle of the day. *Could there be a coven here?* The city was large enough to have one. *Or had Levana followed us and waiting for the opportunity to pounce?* Lara was not concerned about that, only that she had the opportunity to face her once again.

Levana took one of the side alleys to cut across the city to the non-human quarter. Lara picked up the pace knowing this would be the perfect location to face her. As she entered the side alley, she saw the vampire ahead and she pulled her sword free and shouted, "LEVANA!"

The vampire turned and smiled broadly. "So, we cross paths again *bitch*."

Lara glared at her, keeping a firm hold of her sword. "I doubt this is a coincidence."

The vampire smirked and strolled back toward her. "I found out from the remaining lycans at Kerlish that there's a bounty on you. So, I made a deal. I find you and take half the reward. I'll get my revenge for what you did at the coven and for Von."

Lara responded, concerned for Iowyn and Teth. "So how did you find me?"

"I knew you would be trying to avoid anyone with the contract and if it was me, I would be trying to leave Moonstar. So, as this is the closest city that had a port that took seafaring ships, I came here." She paused, cocking her head to one side. "And it seems I made a wise choice."

Lara glared at her with disdain. "Do you know that the lycans were behind that attack on the coven? The alpha wanted control over you."

"Well, he's nay longer in charge is he, you saw to that. Their new alpha wants you dead and I said I could do it before the cleansers came looking for you."

Lara cursed, the last thing she needed was cleansers looking for her as well. She kept her features neutral so Levana could not see how concerned she truly felt. With Levana talking to the lycans, she worried if they knew about Carn. She hoped not, as the plan of him dealing with the contract would be in jeopardy.

The vampire studied her. "So, shall we see if you last longer than you did the last time we met in an alleyway?"

Lara glared at her, gripping her sword. "You won't win this time Levana."

She laughed. "Oh I will. Once you are dust. I'll find those two men the pack said you were with and drink them dry!"

"Well, I will be glad to disappoint you."

Levana screamed in fury and ran at Lara. The hybrid parried the vampire's claw-like nails and spun around, the tip of her silver sword nicking Levana's shoulder. The vampire inhaled sharply when the silver burnt her skin, then she lunged at Lara, her claws barely missing Lara's chest. Lara jumped back and thrust her sword, slicing deeply across Levana's midsection. The vampire cried out and cradled her wounded stomach.

She glared at Lara. "You will pay for that."

The vampire ran at her in rage, her body already healing. Levana lunged at her again; Lara bent backwards, and the vampire's sharp nails sliced through nothing but air. The vampire hissed in frustration, then spun round and glared at her. Lara smirked; she was not as naïve compared to the time they had met in Naverac. This time she was not going to fail. Levana used her claws as if they were daggers. Lara parried with her sword again, every blow the vampire tried to land was blocked by her blade. Levana ran at Lara again, her features filled with the rage that consumed her. Lara used that to her advantage. Using her extraordinary speed, she spun round with her sword. Levana had stopped in her tracks. Lara frowned, wondering if she had struck her mark. Then a blood red line appeared across Levana's long neck. Her eyes widened and her mouth opened as her head slid to the side. Her body instantly disintegrated into dust.

Lara stood watching as the body vanished. The dust was caught by the wind and scattered down the alleyway. Lara took a deep breath and sheathed her sword, feeling a weight lifted from her shoulders. Turning on her heel, she left the alley behind and walked across the city to the inn.

She found Derwyn sitting at the back of the inn, lost in thought. She sat opposite him and smiled, stating, "Levana is dead."

He looked up at her. "When?"

"On my way back from the docks. It seems she made a deal with the remaining lycans."

Derwyn looked concerned. "Did . . ."

Lara studied him. "I believe they are unharmed. I don't believe she even knew who you or Carn were. The way she spoke she was only concerned about me and she would have boasted if Iowyn and Teth had been harmed."

Her brother nodded, seeming to be a little relieved. "Let's hope you are right."

Lara placed a hand on his. "I will ask Carn to check on them."

He smiled, took a deep breath, and asked, "So what about the ship?"

Lara leant back in her chair, informing him that the deal was set. And her brother agreed with her plans.

He sighed, his fingers fiddling with the handle of his tankard. "I'm coming with you. There's nothing to keep me here, and a new start will be good for both of us."

Lara smiled, placing a hand on his. "It will be hard, but better than living looking over our shoulders every day. Even when Carn buries the contract, I still feel there may be someone we cross paths with that would know what I am."

Derwyn gazed at her. "Have you told Carn?"

She nodded sadly. "Aye, and even though sad, he knows it's the right thing to do."

He looked down at the table as he clasped the tankard with both hands. "I have to admit, he's a good man. I'm glad he's going to sort out that contract on you."

Lara gave him a side eye. "You're going to miss him, aren't you."

Derwyn pulled a face. "I wouldn't take it that far."

Lara chuckled, feeling a little less sad, and started to talk about what they needed to do next. It would be best to split the duties between them, and she gave him tasks for the next day. One of which was to talk to the captain and find out anything else they may need for the voyage.

They had not yet been made aware of any packs within the city, but there would be at least one. And from what Lara had detected at the witches' shop, she concluded she and her brother would be low on their list. That was not something they could know for sure, and they hoped she was right, but as an extra precaution, they would keep a low profile. Especially if Levana was correct about the cleansers, which was something Lara was not going to tell Carn or Derwyn, unless she really had to.

CHAPTER 38

CARN woke early, he rolled over and regarded Lara as she slept. She was so beautiful. He ached, deep in his chest, remembering their conversation the night before. He knew the day was coming but it still hurt. He studied her features, tempted to wake her, his hand hovering over her shoulder, unsure. Carn sighed and slowly got out of bed; he would let her sleep as he needed some time to think. He was not going to try to make her change her mind, deep down he knew it was the right thing to do. He wondered if they would ever cross paths again. He hoped so.

Once dressed, he grabbed his sword and quietly left the room. He wandered down to the almost empty inn, where he ordered breakfast. Once he had eaten, Carn went out to the stables to get his horse. The contract owner had a townhouse to the north of the city, he could go on foot but it would be quicker on horseback. Carn needed to know exactly what his duties would entail. The man did not need protection, but it seemed, from the information, it was more just dealing with thugs. Carn needed to know if the thugs were organised or not. If there was a contract involved, it almost always meant it would not be the latter, hence why his tracking skills were needed. Carn had a feeling it would be something to do with goods going missing, which would have a major impact on the landowner's business. In his experience, they usually ended up being turf wars, but he needed more information before he made any assumptions. Carn took his time as he rode across Palasses, the city slowly coming to life in the early hours. At least it gave him time to think.

He would miss Lara greatly and it would be a while before he could move on. Part of him hoped they would cross paths again, as they had so far. All those years ago as a teenager, he had never expected that he would have come across her again, and yet they had. Anything was possible.

He pursed his lips as he started thinking of the best way to complete her contract. It was interesting, what she said about how vampires leave nothing behind when they were killed. Due to the fact she was one of a kind, no one knew for certain what would happen when she died. It was possible that she would die like a vampire, and he would not be able to give them proof, only his word. But as far as Kraven knew, Carn's word was his bond. The situation in Kerlish did not seem to have broken Kraven's trust. It seemed that Carn's involvement with Ivan and his pack had never been found out, and his reputation as a Sword for hire was still very much intact. It also helped that Ivan and his men were killed before anything could have been made known after that night.

Carn knew if he handled it right, the contract could be closed with ease. He just needed to get the timing spot on. With Lara and Derwyn leaving Palasses, that could explain why he did not have anything on Derwyn. Carn could easily state he left Moonstar, and that would be confirmed by witnesses if he asked the right questions. Then after a few months, he would say he came across Lara and had dealt with her. He sighed, glancing up at the blue sky. He was content with that plan and it would then let Derwyn and Lara start a new life.

He turned his attention ahead, and the current contract, glad that he had it. At least it would keep his mind busy once Lara had gone. If he focused on his job, the parting would be made a little easier. He sighed; he had not felt like this about a woman in years.

Nay thinking about it. Not ever.

Carn smiled softly, his mind wandering to them making love the night before. Lara would always have a special place in his heart. He would never forget her.

The meeting with the landowner went much longer than anticipated. The large man had insisted on knowing Carn's history with his previous contracts and was just very talkative, so it was early evening before he could leave. Carn had been right, the man did not need protection; he had his own men for that. The situation was thieves who were targeting and intercepting his transport of goods and supplies. That they seemed to disappear into the Dark Forest to the north of the city certainly did not help the issue. The forest was notorious and known to be used by thieves. The dense foliage of the trees made it hard to keep one's bearings, and many travellers who thought it would be a shortcut to the City of Daggers usually got lost if they did not stay on the only path through. Carn knew the area well and that the City of Daggers was used by any Sword or hunter that wanted to deal in the more dangerous contracts. He sighed, remembering his father would go there on occasion to make extra coin. Carn wondered if any of his father's acquaintances were still there. He shook his head, never understanding why the name suggested it was a city when it was more of a ramshackle collection of huts.

Carn realised why he was being hired for his skills; the Dark Forest was not the easiest to track anything in. It had been a few years since he had ventured to the centre, but he still knew the hidden routes. It would not be an easy job, but it was one he could complete. He would need to head north in the next few days to see if he could track them down. Yet, once he started tracking them, he would not be able to return to Palasses until it was done, but he was not going to miss Lara leaving. The landowner said he would not have another supply run for a good eight days. Carn had suggested that it would be best if a false supply run was sent out in about six days to use it as bait, and the landowner agreed to the idea. That gave Carn time to ensure he would be there before Lara left. He would never be able to forgive himself if he did not see her off. He could then head north to start tracking the thieves, and use the fake supply run to catch any he had missed.

It was late evening before Carn returned to the inn. When he entered, he immediately found Lara sitting on her own near the back, cradling a drink and seeming a little nervous. Carn strolled over to her and smiled but there was a pang of sadness in his gut, as he knew she was going to find passage on a ship that morning. From the look in her eyes, she had, and now she needed to tell him the dreaded news.

He sat opposite and studied her. "I'm guessing you found a ship?"

Lara sighed, "Aye. It's all been arranged. We set sail in a couple of days."

He smiled softly, taking her hand in his, feeling an ache in his heart. "Then we better make the most of these last few days."

She asked, "But your contract?"

"I'm not needed for a few days as he doesn't have another run ready. I just need to find the thieves and deal with them. They are camped north of here, in the Dark Forest. I need to track them down and have arranged a fake run in six days. I don't need to go anywhere for about three." He gazed at her features, he wanted to remember every bit of her. "So, till then, I am all yours."

Lara smiled; he loved that smile. He had told himself all along this would be something fleeting, with no attachments. Now, about to go their separate ways, he felt pain in his heart knowing he would miss her so much. He could see in her features that she felt the same.

She sighed again, "On Laycain, I am going to miss you."

Carn got to his feet and pulled her from behind the table, he kissed her passionately and whispered, "Come on."

She smiled as he took her hand, giving her a gentle tug and they went up to their room. When they entered, Carn locked the door and pulled Lara towards the bed, slowly undressing her. He wanted to make sure he remembered every moment. Slowly removing her clothes, he kissed her gently across her shoulders, taking in her scent. Never wanting to forget it. She gently took hold of his head and pulled his lips to hers. They stood pressed against each other and kissed passionately, savouring every touch.

He gazed at her then slowly kissed her breasts sucking on her nipples, making her gasp. He then ventured further pulling her trousers down as he kissed her stomach. Then his thumbs caressed her thighs as he kissed her loins making her moan in delight. He could taste her, that sweet taste he could never get enough of.

He gazed up at her. Lara's features flushed, her body aching for more. He stood, took her in his arms and laid her on the bed. Carn quickly stripped and straddled her, gazing at her lean body, savouring every inch. She leant upwards pulling him down to her, kissing him again. The skin of his thighs prickled as she moved her legs letting him have access, the head of his penis brushing against her groin making him grunt in delight. He pulled back gazing at her, moved his hips and entered her. Lara gasped as he thrust deeper, her back arched, wanting more. He grabbed her arms, holding them above her head, then he leaned down kissing her. Their loins moved in unison.

Carn bent his back kissing her shoulders. Lara pulled her arms free of his and curled them around his back. Her nails scratched his skin as he thrust again, going deeper, making both their bodies shudder. Her hands slid down his back to grip his firm buttocks, keeping their connection. She pushed her hips against his, still wanting more. Their bodies filled with euphoria as they both came, shuddering.

They lay tangled together, still connected as one. Both gasping as their loins continued throbbing. Lara gazed into Carn's blue eyes. Their love for each other was clear to see. Carn kissed her softly, wishing they could stay like that forever.

CHAPTER 39

ERWYN laid on his bed unable to sleep. When Lara told him that the passage had been arranged, it hit Derwyn that they were finally leaving Moonstar. But he had mixed feelings; excited about starting a new life, but sad that he was leaving everything he knew behind. It had not worked out with Iowyn, and he wondered, if he had not killed those men, or helped Lara in her vampire form, that things could have been different. He sighed, his eyes focused on a crack in the ceiling. When Lara told him of leaving, there was sadness in her eyes, and even though she kept convincing herself that she would not get attached, she had grown close to Carn. Derwyn smirked. Secretly, he would miss the Sword for hire too, which shocked him. He had never thought he would start to like him. But Carn made his sister happy, and he had kept his word.

Derwyn rolled over trying to get to sleep but his mind would not rest. It was going to be interesting reaching Barberium, and he wondered what it would be like. He would hopefully have time to venture to a book shop in town to learn more. He was curious to know if there would be lycans and werewolves, and if so, would the same rules apply over there.

But he felt that like here, non-humans would hide from the humans whenever they could. The prejudices between them would never end, no matter where they went. He just hoped they would be more welcoming towards his sister.

Derwyn had finally managed to fall asleep and at dawn, he was up and ready to sort out all the tasks his sister had given him. Lara had told him all he needed to know about the ship and captain, where to go and who to talk to. He came down to find the inn deserted and would probably not see Carn or Lara for a while. After having breakfast, he wandered across the city to the docks to get the final details from the captain.

The docks were busy even at this early hour. Trying not to get in the way as he dodged between the boxes of cargo, he looked around trying to find the ship Lara had described to him the night before. At the far end was a large, impressive ship. As Lara had said it was made from black ebony like the wood only found in the northern hemisphere. It was known to be light but strong, which meant the ship would be fast on the open water. The figurehead was that of a large raven and the ship's name was carved and painted on the side in a bright blue. Ignoring all the other ships large and small, Derwyn reached the far end of the docks where The Black Raven was moored. As he moved closer, it was even larger than he had first thought.

Stepping onto the gangplank he shouted, "Permission to board? I wish to talk to Captain Raven."

A ship hand came into view holding a mop. "Who's askin'?"

Derwyn stepped up further not wanting everyone on the dock to hear the conversation. "My sister came to see the captain yester morn about getting passage."

The young man nodded and ran off. Derwyn slowly made his way up to the ship while he waited but did not step aboard. After a few moments, a tall dark-haired man with tanned, leathery skin walked up to him. Just from his stance Derwyn knew he had to be the captain.

The man eyed him up and down. "Aye, I can see the resemblance. Come aboard lad."

Derwyn stepped onto the ship. "My sister asked me to talk to you about arrangements."

He pursed his lips. "Let's talk in the cabin."

Derwyn fell in step beside the large man, surveying the quiet deck with just a couple of crew scrubbing and tidying up. He did not say anything as they moved towards a door near the back of the deck. They entered a large cabin with a view out of the stern, towards the open sea. The captain leant against the large table in the centre which had several charts scattered across it.

He looked Derwyn up and down again and said, "So, me lad, what do ya want to know?"

Derwyn replied, "My sister didn't mention our horses and wanted to know what you suggested."

"Sell 'em."

Derwyn was a little taken aback by the captain's bluntness. "Understood, we did think as much."

The captain smiled and seemed to relax a little. "Sorry lad, didn't mean to be so blunt. I ain't used to guests, only used to talkin' to the crew." Derwyn nodded, and the captain continued. "I'd keep the tackle and saddles; I know a good stable at Gor that won't swindle ya."

Derwyn smiled. "Thank you."

The captain added, "I have a good cabin for ya both next to mine, it has two bunks. Hope ya don't mind sharing."

Derwyn responded, "Nay, that's fine with us. We don't want to cause too much disruption."

The captain laughed. "Ahh, with ya sister on board there will be." He leant forward. "Me lads may stare, but they're harmless."

Derwyn smiled. The captain had no clue that the crew were the ones who should be worried. "Understood. My sister said you were a fine captain, with a fine crew."

The man smiled proudly. "Aye, that we are. And as ya sister asked, this deal is between me and me men."

Derwyn said, "Thank you. When do you need us to be here?"

"Three days from now, we'll start loading at dawn and will leave on the tide, by mid morn." He paused studying him. "Be 'ere before we set sail, otherwise I'll be leavin' without ya, even with payment made. I have a ship to run, and the voyage is a long 'un."

Derwyn understood and nodded. "We will be."

The captain spat into his hand and took Derwyn's shaking it. "Deal lad, see ya then."

Derwyn followed the captain back to the gangplank and walked onto the docks. He had to admit, even with his bluntness, he liked the captain, he seemed a good man and he treated his crew well. Derwyn could see why his sister went with this Captain Raven. It was not just for the fact he had the only ship that was heading across the sea in less than a fortnight. They needed someone they could trust, a captain who would keep their presence on the ship to his crew only, not that they would ever know what they were.

With all the fine details sorted with the captain, Derwyn walked back across the city to let his sister know that everything with the captain had been dealt with. Unable to find her, and knowing she would want to have time alone with Carn, he spoke to the innkeeper about where they could sell the horses and was surprised when the man offered a good price for them. They went to the stable, but Carn's and Lara's horses were not there. The innkeeper was not too concerned, going by the condition of Derwyn's horse and seeing how well it was cared for. And because they were friends of Carn's, he gave Derwyn a good deal for his and Lara's steeds. The innkeeper stated that he would let them still use their horses until the day of their departure. If they had gone elsewhere, they may not have had that option. The innkeeper was satisfied with the agreement and promised to give them payment, minus their bed and board, on the evening before they left.

The young man stroked his horse's neck. "I'm gonna miss you girl."

The horse snorted and nuzzled his hand wanting a treat. He smiled, getting oats from the feed bucket, and let her eat from his hand. He patted the horse's neck again and left the stables. Derwyn wandered across the city until he found a bookstore. Enjoying a good search of the shelves, he finally found a few books on Barberium. The storekeeper was willing to let Derwyn sit in the corner and quietly read. The young lycan soon found himself lost in the books, staying at the store for hours.

Derwyn sat in the inn savouring an ale and enjoying a large plate of sausages and dumplings. He had read a couple of books on Barberium, one which he purchased, knowing Lara would find it interesting too. He was pleased to find out how similar it would be to Moonstar and he wondered if that place would become his home. His sister wanted him to have a normal life, as much as he could, but he was uncertain if he wanted to stop travelling with Lara. He took a sip of his ale, watching the serving girl weaving between the tables with ease. Being with Iowyn was an incredible feeling, and maybe he would find a nice girl out there. Maybe even one from a good lycan family. He smiled softly, that was something he really did want; a family. He sighed, thinking of Lara. He felt guilty that a family was something his sister would never have after him. But she seemed to love her life, and what it would give her. Knowing his sister, she would travel far and wide, and he was almost jealous that he would not live to see all that she would see. He glanced up towards the ceiling. He had not seen her all day, but he could not blame her and Carn for spending their time remaining together. He knew if the tables were turned, he would be doing the same. He leant back in his chair and smiled, looking forward to what lay ahead, whatever that would be.

CHAPTER 40

THE guest room at the inn was quiet, clothes lay scattered across the floor, and a tray of finished food and drinks was also on the floor near the bed. The morning sun filtered in through the window, warming their naked bodies. Carn studied Lara as she dozed on the bed. They had spent hours in the room, just savouring their last few days together, but he wanted to do something more, and had an idea that would hopefully make some lasting memories of their final days together. He knew of an area not far out of Palasses where they could have time together alone that was not within four walls. He kissed Lara's shoulder and sat up. Lara raised an eyebrow at the sudden movement.

Carn smiled. "Come on, I want to show you something."

Her eyes lingered on him as he climbed off the bed, and she stretched her naked body. "But it is so comfy here."

Carn gazed back at her, as he searched the floor for his clothes. "I know, but you will *love* this."

She propped herself up on an elbow. "What do you want to show me?"

He smiled. "Then it wouldn't be a surprise."

Lara reluctantly climbed from the bed. "Alright, let's go then, just as long as we end up back here later."

Carn kissed her passionately. "Oh, most definitely."

They both dressed, having to find pieces of clothing that had been thrown around in their haste to make love. Leaving the room behind, Carn took the tray back down to the innkeeper. They then went to the stables, saddled their horses, and they were soon riding slowly through the busy streets of the city towards the north gate. Carn led the way glancing back at Lara. It had been a wonderful time just being together, with no other distractions, and he had been thinking about taking her there since it was agreed to part ways. Even though Carn knew it was the right thing to do, it would still hurt.

Once beyond the city gate, Carn encouraged his horse into a gallop, leaving the main routes and heading across the country towards the woods, behind a large farm. He glanced towards the buildings, he had nearly trained there to join the Guardians of the Stone, but his father would not allow it. The guild was a cult in the man's eyes. Carn shook his head slightly, it was not meant to be; by the time he had left working with his father, and got himself established as a Sword, the opportunity had passed him by. He half wondered if he had pursued it what he would have been doing now. He glanced at Lara, and wondered if he would still have crossed paths with her again. Carn took a slow, deep breath, he would show Lara the clearing he had found, and perhaps make some memories there. He glanced to the side, Lara's horse keeping pace with his own.

She asked, almost shouting to be heard above the rush of air as they rode. "Where are we going again?"

Carn gave her a big grin. "You'll see."

She smiled and looked ahead, the horses slowing as they reached the woods. Carn took the lead through the trees knowing they were nearly there. He stopped his horse and dismounted, Lara following suit.

He smiled and grabbed her hand. "Come on."

He pulled her gently into the clearing, which was a perfect circle of trees. The area was open with lush green grass and a deep clear pool in the centre. He heard Lara gasp and turned to her.

He smiled. "I knew you would love it."

She looked around at the clearing, amazed at its simple beauty and smiled. "I can see why you wanted to bring me here now."

Carn kissed her passionately and started to strip. "Come on, let's take a dip."

She raised an eyebrow as she watched him remove his trousers and gave a sly smile before she started to pull off her clothes. Carn walked into the water; it was cool but welcoming. He swam slowly to the centre, and tread the water to turn and face Lara, watching her strip. She entered the water a few moments later and swam over to him.

She kissed him, as she floated in the water then asked, "How did you know about this place?"

Carn smiled, his hand brushing against her naked skin in the water. "Now that would be giving away all my secrets."

He curled his arms around her body, pulling her close, she stopped treading water letting him hold her. Lara studied his wet features and smiled a little, sadness reflecting in her eyes.

He brushed a strand of wet hair from her face and kissed her softly. "I know I'm going to miss you so much, but we knew this—"

She placed a finger against his full lips and smiled softly. "Let's not think about it just yet."

His hands slid up her naked back, paddling his legs to keep them both above the surface. "That sounds fine to me."

He kissed her pulling her body against his in the water, Lara curled her legs around his waist, and he entered her. They slowly began to sink as they kissed and made love. Carn pulled one of his arms free from her and gently moved them both through the water towards the shallow section but making sure their embrace was never broken. As soon as his feet touched the gravel floor of the pond, he placed his arm around her once more, not wanting the moment to end.

Lara traced her fingers across Carn's muscular chest, his firm skin drying in the sunlight. They were laying on the grass bank by the pool listening to a lone bird twittering in a tree nearby. Lara snuggled her head against his chest listening to his breathing as he dozed. His muscular arm curled around her, his fingers slowly making circles on her shoulder. Neither of them wanted the embrace to end. Lara was so pleased that Carn had shown her this place. It was so tranquil she could see why he wanted to bring her here, and it was a moment from many that she would never forget. Lara tried not to think too much about what was coming, but she would miss him more than she had realised. Lara smiled, they had crossed paths before, and knew it would not be the last time she saw this attractive man. She closed her eyes and focused on the moment, listening to Carn's breathing making her drift to sleep.

Lara woke with a gentle kiss on her lips and Carn gazing at her, smiling. "It's getting dark, we best head back."

She slowly sat up seeing the sun was going down and studied Carn. "This place is so peaceful."

He nodded, sitting up. "Aye, it's good to come here to get away from everything."

Lara gazed at him, seeing a shadow of sadness in his features. He had mentioned how he had a difficult childhood with his father, and that it had been hard being on the road with him when he was a teenager. Lara wondered if this was a place he had found when they had travelled, and if whenever he had been at Palasses, it had been a good place where he would go when he wanted to escape it all.

"I can see why."

He got to his feet and started to dress, turning back to Lara studying her naked body as she stood.

She smiled at him and pulled on her clothes. "Thank you for showing me this place. It will be a day I will not forget."

Carn gave her a passionate kiss, his gaze lost in her eyes. "Neither will I."

Once dressed, he took her hand and led her back to the horses and they rode back to Palasses, arriving at the inn after nightfall. They found Derwyn eating at a table near the back and the two sat with him. Lara asked about the tasks she had left him with. While they talked, Carn got back up and ordered food and drink.

Derwyn said as Carn came back to the table. "The innkeeper will buy the horses from us. He said we can use them till we leave and then he will give us payment."

Lara agreed with the arrangement. Carn nodded too, but was distracted by the food brought by the barmaid, not realising how ravenous he was.

Lara took a sip of her drink and focused on her brother. "And the ship and captain?"

Her brother smiled. "A good man and he will keep his word, but did warn us to ensure we are there on time, otherwise he'll leave without us."

Carn responded, swallowing a mouth full of potatoes. "Sounds like a typical captain." Lara glanced at him, raising an eyebrow, and he added, "He sounds good and trustworthy, but they also know the business, and can't afford to delay setting sail with cargo to deliver. He also must catch the tide, especially if the wind is right."

She nodded, understanding what he meant, then turned back to Derwyn. "Are you still willing to come with me? Carn said he could make sure you would be safe if you remained as that contract is only for me."

Her brother smiled. "I am, and I want to see what's out there." He took a sip of his ale. "Besides there's nothing to keep me here."

She smiled while studying her brother, happy that he was coming with her. She was prepared for him to say he wanted to part ways, but it did feel good that he was staying by her side in this. And with leaving Carn behind, she felt she needed someone with her, even though she would never admit it.

It was not long before Derwyn said his goodnights and headed to his room. Lara turned to Carn as he finished his ale and slid her fingers over to Carn's hand, her fingertips touching his. "So . . ."

He smiled while studying her, taking her hand in his as he put his ale down. "So, maybe a little nightcap?"

Lara raised an eyebrow. "I wouldn't say nay."

He kissed her, pulling her to her feet as he stood. "Come on then."

Leaving the bar area behind they went up to their room. Savouring the last of their time together.

On their final evening together they all met in the bar area of the inn, found a table near the back, and had food and drinks ordered.

Carn sighed and studied Derwyn, as he ate his meat pie and vegetables. "I'll miss you, kid."

He glanced up, focusing on the older man. Having not seen his sister or Carn for the last couple of days, he smiled. "I'm surprised to say it, but I might miss you too."

Carn laughed, giving Derwyn a friendly slap on the shoulder.

Lara smiled leaning forward towards her brother. "I knew you would like him in the end."

Derwyn turned to her, raising an eyebrow, smiling. "Now *liked* is a strong word," he leaned towards her. "I still think you could do better."

Carn looked shocked, Lara kicking Derwyn on the shin. The young lycan chuckled, putting up his hands in defence. "I was *joking.*"

The other two laughed, then Carn motioned to the barmaid for more drinks. The Sword leant forward, squeezing Derwyn's arm. "You take care of your sister for me."

Derwyn nodded, glancing at her. "I always will."

Lara gazed at the two men and smiled. Derwyn picked up his ale and said, "Let us toast."

"To what?" asked Carn.

Lara smiled while picking up her mug. "New beginnings."

They all nodded, their mugs tapping together.

Derwyn smiled at the two, and said to Carn, "So, what are your plans when we're gone?"

Carn took a big swig of his ale and stated, "I have a group of thugs to track which will take some time. But I have also sorted out my plan for your sister's bounty. Kraven will take my word, I know it, so I will state that I killed your sister but, like vampires, she dissolved to dust."

"And me?" asked Derwyn, studying the Sword.

"I was going to say you left for a new land via ship. As far as the contract stated I was only to deal with you if you interfered, which you can't do if you had gone your own way. With the fact these last few days you have been sorting out the arrangements for yourself and Lara's passage, it is easy to say that you arranged to leave and then had gone. You may have left with your sister but when I ask the right questions, all would have said you arranged it all alone."

Derwyn liked the plan. "That's good. You've thought it all through very well, thank you."

Carn replied, "Nay problem. I wanted to make sure that you both could have a new life with nay issues. I'm hoping this will do it."

Lara studied Carn, taking his hand in hers. "Thank you."

Carn focused on her eyes and smiled. Derwyn shifted in his seat feeling a little awkward. "Why don't you two have an early night? I'll sort out everything with the innkeeper."

The two glanced at him. Lara smiled and nodded, kissing Carn as they left the table. Derwyn watched them go, and knew, once on the ship, he would have to lift his sister's spirits. He felt sad; this was his sister's life from now on, unless she found happiness with someone like her, maybe even another vampire. He sighed, gazing at his ale. None of them knew what lay ahead, but he hoped they would all find happiness in whatever form it came to find them.

CHAPTER 41

SOON the morning arrived for the ship to depart. Derwyn had already taken their belongings down earlier and returned for anything he had not been able to carry down the first time, leaving the two to have their last moments together. Lara spent the night with Carn, and it was sad to be finally parting. The two walked hand in hand to the large docks. The docks were just as busy as before, but Lara was able to see her brother ahead of them waiting near The Black Raven. On seeing them approaching, Derwyn headed up onto the ship, while Carn and Lara stood on the dockside holding hands.

Carn sighed while studying her. "So," he drew out the word. "This is it."

Lara looked up at him, her fingers curling around his. "Aye. But have a feeling we'll cross paths again."

He smiled, kissing her passionately. "You can count on it."

Lara glanced up at the ship when they heard the captain barking orders. They would be setting sail soon. She turned back to Carn, reluctant to let him go. She hugged him as hard as she could, never wanting the moment to end.

He placed his forehead against hers gazing into her eyes. "Take care of yourself."

Lara smiled sadly taking in all his features not wanting to forget anything. "You take care, too. May Laycain watch over you," she whispered, her eyes lost in his. "I'm holding you to a drink in a few years."

"I'll be waiting." He gave her a side glance. "And maybe a bit more."

Lara chuckled, raising her eyebrow. "You can count on it."

She turned towards the gangplank and started to board. Carn was reluctant to let her go, they held hands for as long as they could till they had no choice but to part.

Carn smiled sadly at her and said, "You will always be here." He pointed to his heart.

Lara walked backwards up the gangplank onto the deck of the ship, not wanting to take her eyes off him as her vision blurred from the tears welling in her eyes.

She placed a hand on her heart. "You will be with me always."

Carn nodded, smiling. Lara had to step along so the crew could pull the gangplank up and moved to stand on the side. Carn peered up from the dock as the ship set sail, both wanting to see the other for as long as they possibly could. As the ship left the docks behind, Carn was lost in the crowd of dockhands and crates. Lara sighed, focusing on the city of Palasses and the hills beyond, wiping the tears from her cheeks. That was Moonstar, her birthplace.

She sighed as Derwyn came up beside her, placing a caring hand on her shoulder. "Feels strange leaving it all behind."

Lara agreed, "It does but it doesn't mean we won't return one day."

Derwyn said, "I know." He took a deep breath and regarded his sister. "I know it wasn't easy, but I think you'll see Carn again."

Lara smirked, trying to stop any more tears from falling. "You never know."

She sighed and studied her brother. She had to get used to leaving people behind, and some would be hard, like with Carn. "Well, let's think about pastures new, and what life will be for us."

Derwyn smiled. "Well, I don't think it will be dull, that's for sure."

Lara chuckled, her brother was right, it would be a new life but somehow, it would still be an adventure.

Carn stood on the docks until the ship was out of sight. The dock hands weaved past him to get supplies to their owners. Some were moaning and swearing that he was in the way. Yet Carn did not care, he was not about to stop watching that ship until it was out of sight. He took a deep breath, and surreptitiously wiped a stray tear from his cheek. Turning from the sea, he headed back into the city. He suddenly felt very alone, and he needed to get back to working. With his mind focused on the task at hand, he would not think about Lara too much. He clenched his fists trying to keep focused. He had not expected it to hurt so much. The pain in his chest was like a dagger twisting in his heart. He looked up at the sky and sighed, he had to think about the positives. Lara was safe, and their time together had been wonderful. They had crossed paths before; he knew they would again. He just had to be patient. Their time together had not been a lifetime, but it was intense, and she would always have a place in his heart.

Reaching the inn, Carn ordered ale. He would have one drink and then he would head north to track the thieves on the contract. As soon as he started tracking them, he would not have time to dwell on the past, and it would be good to have something to focus on. He leaned back in his chair savouring the ale and smiled softly to himself. Whatever happened from this day forward, he would always have fond memories of Lara. He would deal with this contract and then in a month he would confirm Lara's death. That would hopefully put an end to the pack tracking her, yet, part of him knew they would not just stop. But with the added boon that Lara was off on a ship, there was no chance of them ever finding out the truth, and by the time she did return, it would be a forgotten memory. Carn glanced down at his ale wondering when Lara would return as they had never really broached the subject. He had not even asked where the ship was heading, but then again, he did not want to know. For the moment, it was best for him to know as little as possible. He smiled remembering their toast the night before. This was a new beginning, and he needed to focus on what lay ahead not what was left behind.

AJ Ashton

LARA WILL RETURN
IN
OUTCAST NEW BEGINNINGS
BOOK 2

Lara Tarrenfall left Moonstar behind fifteen years ago, determined to build a new life for herself and her younger brother, Derwyn. In Barberium, they found more than survival; they found purpose.

Derwyn has risen to prominence within a pack and built a family of his own. Lara has carved her legend as a Sword for hire, feared and respected enough to name her own price.

But when a mysterious sorcerer offers her a contract unlike any other, Lara is drawn into a challenge that threatens everything she's fought to protect.

And then there's Carn, the man she once loved and had to leave behind. As destiny weaves its threads tighter, Lara must face the question she's avoided for years. Will she ever open her heart again... or is love another battle she can't afford to fight?

AUTHOR BIO

A J ASHTON was born in the 70's, in Derbyshire, UK. She still lives in the area, juggling a full-time job and being a mother.

From the age of seven, after seeing a rather famous sci-fi film, for the first time. Her creativeness to write was born. Inspired by a strong princess being rescued by a notorious smuggler. She wrote sci-fi, but her passion was soon drawn to fantasy. Where the world of Zentos was born.

Outcast Origins is the first book in the Tarrenfall Chronicles trilogy and the World of Zentos series. It will give you an insight into her fantasy world, with mystical creatures, magic, and Swords.

Sign up for A J Ashton's monthly newsletter at
www.ajashton.com

For more information about the world of Zentos, visit my website for maps and a bestiary, which will be continually updated.
www.ajashton.com